LOVE

is like

GLASS
SLIPPERS

Fragile • Rare • Crystal Clear

James J. Thompson, Jr.

Edited by Debbie Burke,
author of *Tasty Jazz Jams for Our Times*™, *Vols. 1-3*
and *Death by Saxophone*

PEANUT CITY PRESS
TELLING OUR STORIES

February 2024

CONTENTS

Foreword...9

From the Author..11

I: Short Stories... 15

Chapter One: "Ada Mary Louise" 17

Chapter Two: "A Declination of Independence" 28

Chapter Three: "The Red Bottom Shoe Mystery" 36

Chapter Four: "Falling Out of Love" 44

Chapter Five: "My Harlequin Romance" 54

Chapter Six: "Reincarnation of a Romance".........................66

Chapter Seven: "Eavesdropping on a Love Letter" 70

Chapter Eight: "Locker Girl 2: What's Her Name?" 82

Chapter Nine: "Carol, My Feline Love" 88

Chapter Ten: "First Promise Ring" 95

Chapter Eleven: "My Heart Transplant" 106

Chapter Twelve: "The Man Who Was Caught by a Butterfly" 108

Chapter Thirteen: "The Runaway" 110

Chapter Fourteen: "The Hands of Mr. Cleed Spurlock".....................113

Chapter Fifteen: "Little Pieces of Conversation" 118

Chapter Sixteen: "Mr. Agnes" 121

Chapter Seventeen: "Unmailed Love Letters to My DNA"................. 126

Chapter Eighteen: "The Scenic Route" 131

Chapter Nineteen: "The Wedge of Allegiance" 135

II: Poetry 48 Poems About Love (More or Less)............................141

Chapter Twenty 143
    "Love is Like Glass Slippers 2"................................. 143
    "Chameleon Love" 144
    "Umbilical Cord" 145
    "Black Gold" 146
    "Before Juneteenth"... 147
    "After Juneteenth".. 148
    "Love Lines to an Iceberg" (A Cold Love) 149
    "My Significant Other" 150
    "Life Partners" 152
    "Heroes and Lovers" 154
    "Today I Met a Girl".. 156
    "Premeditated Sex 2" 158
    "Hey Man, I Love You" 160
    "What is Brotherly Love?" 161
    "The Walls That Love Built"................................. 162
    "The Wisdom of Understanding" 163
    "Close Encounters with an Angel in Five Parts" 165
    "L. U. S. T. 170
    "Love Me Because I Love You" 171
    "Secret Secrets" 172
    "Scattered Reflections"...................................... 173
    "Talking to a Tree" 174
    "The Rose Inside of Us"..................................... 175
    "Dreams and Wishes".. 176
    "Perception" 177
    "Solo" 178
    "Please, Tune Me Back In".................................. 179
    "Forbidden Fruit" 180
    "The Golden Watch"... 181
    "A Peace of Time".. 182
    "Today I Saw the Wind"..................................... 183
    "Capturing The Day".. 184

"Free Spirits"..185

"With New Eyes"...187

"Space"...188

"Fireflies"...189

"Consequences" 190

"A Something-for-Nothing World" 191

"A Sense of Humor" 192

"The Psychology of Preaching" 193

"When I Have Fears"..194

"Things That Make Me Cry"..195

"Love Indigo"...196

"Wedding Day Duet"..197

"Jumpin' the Broom"..198

"Keeping a Hold on My Soul" 199

"Suns Set"...200

"Siamese Twins" 201

III: Essays 203

Chapter Twenty-One: "Buy Any Means Necessary".........205

Chapter Twenty-Two: "Peanuts, Twilight Zone,
and Sexual Healing"..207

Chapter Twenty-Three: "The Ghettosburg Address".........225

Chapter Twenty-Four: "Our 50th High
School Class Reunion" (1972-2022) 232

Chapter Twenty-Five: "The Supreme Court Jester"..........235

Chapter Twenty-Six: "Classy-fied" 237

Chapter Twenty-Seven: "Real Men Do Cry... Unless!" 239

Chapter Twenty-Eight: "Thoughtless Killers" 241

Bonus Writings..243

Chapter Twenty-Nine: "Sweet Potato Coffee" 245

Chapter Thirty: "Bill of Fights" 249

Chapter Thirty-One: "On Being Baptized" 261

Chapter Thirty-Two: "The Missing Corpse" 265

Chapter Thirty-Three: "Karma" 267

Chapter Thirty-Four: "Self Portrait" 276

Chapter Thirty-Five: "Vulnerable"...277

Chapter Thirty-Six: "Invulnerable" 279

Chapter Thirty-Seven: "The eNIGma" 281

Chapter Thirty-Eight: "Three Kilos" 283

Acknowledgments...293

About the Author..299

DEDICATION

This book is dedicated to those who have fallen in love—if only once ("Rare"); to those who have fallen out of love regularly ("Fragile"); and to those who have stayed in love forever ("Crystal Clear").

As to the question, "Why the name Peanut City Press?" there are three logical answers. First, my hometown where I was born, Dothan, Alabama, is known as "the Peanut Capital of the World." So, as a nod to Dothan, I selected a name for my publishing company that would honor my birthplace. Second, *Africans were the first people to introduce peanuts to North America; the peanut was regarded by many Africans as one of several plants possessing a soul.* And third, *peanuts are plentiful like people, and sometimes people are like peanuts: nutty with many stories to tell.*

Genesis 37:17 (King James Version)
"And the man said, 'They are departed hence; for I heard them say, 'Let us go to Dothan.' And Joseph went after his brethren, and found them in Dothan."

FOREWORD

Omnia vincit amor.
Love conquers all.

Virgil, the Roman poet, scratched this noble notion, this aspiration, onto a page of parchment in 47 B.C. In the two millennia since, we've seen a lot of evidence to the contrary, dramatic moments when love arrived late, when love lost out, when love was a no-show.

It hardly matters. Love still carries our dreams. Love still lays us down to sleep and gets us out of bed in the morning to face the world. Love may not conquer all, but it conquers enough.

James L. Thompson, Jr.'s new book is about the conquering kind of love. As his title tells it – **Love is Like Glass Slippers: Fragile. Rare. Crystal Clear.** There's a writer's faith here – a belief that this most precious of emotions ought to be held up to the light, twinkling, for all to see.

As a glass slipper refracts light and scatters colors, this charming new book holds that kind of love and many others up to a light. We behold a prism of words, sparkling here, dazzling there, radiance on top of radiance. The facets are poems and short stories and essays informed by the author's sixty-nine years of life and...here's that word again...love.

Friends know the *Glass Slippers* author as Shack. He inherited the nickname from his father, dubbed "Shacklebones" as a teen by friends teasing him for his gangly frame. Shack, the son, carries the nickname as a tribute, an act of love – a kind of love conquering even death, which took his father on Good Friday in 2012, three months shy of his ninetieth birthday. (Shack's mother, 101, still lives ably and comfortably in Dothan.)

Glass Slippers marks history, of a sort. It's the first imprint from a new publishing house, Peanut City Press.

The name comes from Shack's hometown, Dothan, Alabama, known as the Peanut Capital of the World – or Peanut City – because of the importance of that tasty legume to the local economy.

At one point, more than half the peanuts grown in the United States were tilled within a 100-mile radius of Dothan. The nut rose from common cattle feed to a billion-dollar staple of U.S. households largely thanks to the efforts of a Black scientist named Dr. George Washington Carver, who developed dozens of commercial uses for peanuts and turned it into a valuable cash crop.

Glass Slippers is Shack's fourth book (his first two are out of print now). He published his last book, *Just My Imagination (Running Away with Me)*, in February 2023. It's about love too, at heart – it's a sincere literary love letter to Dothan, particularly the economically challenged neighborhood known as the Baptist Bottom where the author grew up.

What does love like Shack's conquer?

It conquers a blank page. It conquers the voids left by historians who can't – or won't – tell and record the old stories that now risk oblivion as time marches on. When Shack puts his love in words and puts those words down on parchment in his books, they conquer forgetting and indifference … and even worse things.

We owe Shack Thompson. His writing sets out to conquer.

With love.
Charles McNair

Author of the following four literary works:

The Epicureans, 2023
Play It Again, Sam: The Notable Life of Sam Massell,
Atlanta's First Minority Mayor, 2020
Pickett's Charge, 2013
Land O' Goshen, 1994

FROM THE AUTHOR

"I Love You"

W hy is it so difficult and awkward at times to say these three little words? History has shown that these three words can cause stomach butterflies and racing hearts when said all at once to someone we care about regardless of gender or race.

I vividly recall the first time I eagerly said, "I love you" to a girlfriend I was dating. I paused for a minute and waited for an echoed response. The look on her face changed as she bowed her head and softly replied, "I am very fond of you, too."

The look on my face changed when I realized she didn't exactly feel the same way about me. My heart felt crushed to know she was only just fond of me. It was my first bout with unrequited puppy love, but it still hurt. I vowed after that to never say those three words together again to anyone else until the feeling was mutual. But how does one ever really know when that loving feeling is mutual?

Thousands or maybe millions of songs, poems, and books have all been written and named "I Love You" by people in all walks of life. Many of those nature shows on television have shown images of various mismatched animals being in love with each other, i.e., a cat and a bird, a dog and a deer, an elephant and an owl, a bear and a tiger.

Whom we fall in love with seems to be out of our control. There's nothing more heartwarming than to see a giant and a person of short stature holding hands walking down the street together. Mother Nature has a glorious sense of humor and seems to dictate when to tell Cupid to fling his arrows. Sometimes being shot in the heart with a love arrow is more threatening than being shot with a real bullet because of the slow death side effects when love goes wrong.

When love goes right, the sun shines all the time and every day is like a beautiful Saturday with balloons and roses. Even though the roses may carry enough thorns to one day burst the balloons, I would rather experience that loving feeling – no matter how short-lived.

When I was sixteen and in high school, I wrote my first book about love with my close friend and classmate Stanley J. Davis. The name of our so-called book was *The Diary of Love* and it only consisted of a fifty-page spiral leaf notebook with handwritten stories we invented to impress the girls. Needless to say, we didn't know a thing about love, but the young girls who read our notebook were convinced that we were authorities on the subject. As a matter of fact, our notebook became so popular among the girls that one day someone stole it and we never saw it again. That was the end of our joint literary collaboration on the subject of love.

As I got older, I thought I had become more sophisticated about love and knew how to tell right away. Love at first sight was in full swing, and it caused my heart to have many hits, misses, and sleepless nights. I found out that getting older didn't necessarily make me any wiser about love.

With *Love is Like Glass Slippers*, I am literally walking in the shoes of characters I have created to get inside their heads and hearts to narrate their stories about love; I also share some of my personal stories about love. I enjoy using distinct voices and finely conceived personas to spin yarns that feel authentic; each story gives the reader both a familiar point of view and one that reads like non-fiction.

Since my high school days, I have had the opportunity to experience the many different facets of love on many different levels. Like most people my age, I've gone through heart joys and heartbreaks to gain the wisdom I have acquired through time. I still think that love is the most amazing thing in the world, and I cannot live without it. I would not be able to produce a whole book on the subject if I did not know what I was talking about. Every day I am filled with love that I want to share with the world.

My experience with love as a son, a brother, a husband, a father, a lover, and a friend has been the cornerstone of my happiness.

Everything I know about how to love a woman was taught to me by a woman, including my mother. With every courtship I had, I learned something different from each female to help set me apart from the average man. I now believe in setting a really high bar when it comes to being in love and staying there.

After you have read my book, I hope you will have gained some valuable insight into the well-known truths that *love truly is a many-splendored thing, all is fair in love and war* and *love means never having to say you're sorry* – although there's nothing wrong with saying you're sorry if you really mean it. Because real love is *fragile, rare, and crystal clear like glass slippers.*

A very special *Thanks* to my book editor, the award-winning multi-book author Debbie Burke, my book formatter, the wonderful Richell B. @ Richell Designs, and the best book cover designer, GetCovers.com.

And last but not least, a huge THANK YOU for my good friend and Pulitzer-nominated author, Charles McNair, for encouraging me to write.

I

SHORT STORIES

Short story – A story with a fully developed theme but significantly shorter and less elaborate than a novel.

I have a knack for writing short stories and creating "mini-novels" or "mini-movies" with a myriad of interesting characters. I find it easier to create separate short stories versus one long novel. Maybe these short story exercises are just the prelude to the novel hidden within me.

Hopefully, I am able to extend my next creative manuscript into a full-fledged novel that will be the start of many more books. I still consider myself to be an aspiring writer who has yet to find his true stride. I truly wish that you enjoy the short and shorter stories in this new book. They all have been individually crafted with the central theme of LOVE in mind.

CHAPTER ONE

"ADA MARY LOUISE"

The very first time I fell head-over-heels in love was with an older woman; she was thirty-one and I acted like a newborn. The pleasant, motherly smell of her permeated my body and made me smile when I looked at her. Her kisses were the sweetest I had ever tasted because they were the kisses of life. I can still smell the Johnson's Baby Oil and powder she used on me before pinning my diapers.

We gazed into each other's brown eyes as she tickled my chin and cooed at me. I regularly sucked her breasts like a pacifier, and she nourished me with her love. I didn't know it then, but she would become the woman of my dreams and the love of my life; I would love her my whole life and for the rest of hers, too.

Every boy falls in love with his mother, and I'll always love mine. I am my mother's second child and her only son; we have a special bond like none other. As of this writing, my mother is 101 years young and she still has the sweetest kisses I have ever known. My mother shares her astrological sign of Gemini with me.

* * * *

My gorgeous mother was born in Houston County, Alabama, on Tuesday, June 6, 1922, in the Chinese Year of the Dog and given the name Ada Mary Louise. When she was born, she became part of the Greatest Generation, characterized by the date range of 1901-1924. People born during this time were patriotic and driven people who lived through the Great Depression and many of the men also served in World War II.

The 1920s is credited as the decade for the birth of the Jazz Age and also the decade when women were granted the legal right to vote, but the Women's Suffrage Movement had begun much earlier.

Growing up, my mother's closest family members and friends called her Ada Mae which she did not prefer. Her parents were Judge Dowell Daniels and Emma Jane Reynolds. My mother was the youngest of seven children born to them and she has outlived all her family members.

Her father was known to be a not-so-tall, cruel man; his first name Judge did not make him a real judge, but he tended to harshly judge everyone else by his own shortcomings.

Being born in 1871 probably made Judge Daniels a victim of the times when he fathered my mother in the 1920s. It was truly a man's world in the 1920s and reportedly my grandfather epitomized and proudly represented the caveman mentality that was prevalent then. Women were less than second-class citizens and that included his wife and female children. Fortunately for me, my grandfather died at seventy-nine in 1950, well before I was born in 1954.

Although the nineteenth amendment ratified in 1920 legally guaranteed American women the right to vote, it was decades after that when it felt comfortable and acceptable for women to actually cast their ballots. That comfort took much longer for Black women like my mother and grandmother, especially in the South.

Being very different from my grandfather, my grandmother was as good and gentle as a saint. I got to know my mother's mother very well. Emma Jane Reynolds was born on Monday, September 11, 1882. She had no way of knowing that her birth date would infamously coincide 119 years later with the tragic date when planes flew into the World Trade Center in New York in 2001. If she were still alive today, my grandmother would be 141 years old.

We all called her Granny, and she was my favorite grandmother. I lived with her when I was fourteen, up until her death on March 2, 1974. She was near ninety when she passed away and I was a sophomore in college. My grandmother was part Cherokee Indian, and she taught me much about being good and living a clean, Christian life. I miss Granny and dream about her often. I have no doubt that she's in heaven.

As she grew older, Ada Mary Louise dropped the name Ada altogether and preferred to be called Mary Louise. Many people today know her as Mrs. Mary Louise Thompson, and few would ever believe that her first name is actually Ada.

The beginning memories I have of my mother are all good. I cried constantly but not necessarily from hunger or discomfort; sometimes I just wanted to be near her every chance I could get. I was very selfish, spoiled, and proud of it.

I recall a time when I almost set our house on fire in an effort to gain my mother's attention. The *shotgun house* we rented had no central air or central heat. We used fireplaces for warmth and window fans for air conditioning. The fans only recirculated warm air in the hot summers.

It was fall or winter and my mother had just put a pile of wood on the fire in the fireplace. I was a curious two-year old in diapers watching her every movement. When she walked away, I grabbed a thin stick of kindling wood from the fireplace by the cool end and held it in my hands. When the stick suddenly caught ablaze, I panicked and dropped it near the bed. Soon, the bed sheets and quilt caught on fire and started to smoke and burn the bed.

I ran in to get my mother to show her the fire. My mother was able to quickly put it out before it burned down our little wooden shack. When she got the blaze under control, she looked at me and asked me what happened.

I looked sheepish and told her that our neighbor Mr. Ben Sheffield came in and set the bed on fire. My mother looked over at the door and noticed that the door was still latched on the inside, which meant that Mr. Sheffield would have had to re-latch the inside door before he left since I couldn't reach the door.

My mother knew I had lied and committed a deadly sin. Rather than punishing me, she taught me about the Ten Commandments in the Bible. As I grew older, I felt ashamed every time I saw Mr. Ben

Sheffield because he was a good, honest man who didn't deserve the lie that I had told. I chose him because he was the only neighbor I knew then. His son, Mr. Amos Sheffield, later became my favorite barber and friend.

Obviously, I had no idea what love and affection were, but I knew that I felt something incomprehensible toward my mother. My dreams of her were heavenly and the two of us walked on cotton candy clouds and played non-stop. The obvious love we had for each other was maternal, not sexual.

My mother was very protective of me and I of her. I felt that she would give her life to protect me. As I grew older, I vowed to protect her with my life at all costs. To this day, nothing is more important to me than the love, honor, and respect I have for my mother.

Although we were considered poor, I never had a clue about that. My mother was a good seamstress and she made much of the clothing that my sisters and I wore. I remember seeing her with the paper patterns she got from the store to use while she sewed me a new shirt and pants on her trusty foot-pedal Singer brand sewing machine. I can still envision the corduroy shirts and pants she made for me, and I was proud to wear them to school to show them off. We didn't have many store-bought clothes other than a pair of dungarees (blue jeans) and a pair of Top Dollar tennis shoes (sneakers).

Back then, almost everyone with little money shopped at the Top Dollar store in downtown Dothan; they were the Dollar Tree of that time but with a bigger inventory of things to wear.

Our downtown also had a few Five-and-Dime stores like Newberry's and Kress, which meant that everything inside cost between a nickel and a dime. It was unbelievable the things you could actually buy with a nickel and a dime. Many things were so cheap then because they were made in Japan, not China.

Right next door to the Top Dollar store was the Western Auto store, which was a sporting goods store that sold many toys and bicycles all the kids wanted. We would normally just window shop and look through the glass at the many shiny new girls' and boys' bicycles; Schwinn bicycles were very popular back then. Every Christmas I asked

Santa for a new bicycle, but he never left one for me under our skinny, artificial tree.

My mother always told me she was afraid I'd get hit by a car if I rode my bike into the streets, and that was her explanation for not getting one. I was the only sixteen-year-old boy in my neighborhood who didn't know how to ride a bicycle.

She was the one who would help me with my schoolwork and encourage me to do better. I believe my knack for creativity came from my mother. She would always read and sign my report cards for school and tell my father when I had a low grade in a class. My father was the disciplinarian who would punish me when I failed in one of my classes. I would have rather my mother discipline me than my father because he didn't believe in sparing the rod; his punishments motivated me not to fail any classes.

I loved my mother's cooking. Growing up, I never heard the term "soul food" because I thought everyone ate the way we did in the Baptist Bottom. My mother would routinely serve fresh butterbeans, corn, collard and turnip greens, lima beans, black-eyed peas, fried chicken, tomatoes and rice, beets, okra, squash, and salmon croquettes or fish patties. I never acquired a taste for the fish patties but had to eat them anyway.

* * * *

Being the only boy living with three sisters was not that much fun for me because I always felt that they got things before me and that I was an afterthought. So, when I turned fourteen, I asked my mom if I could go live with Granny who lived about a mile away on Houston Street, not far from the Baptist Bottom.

Without telling my father right away, my mother agreed to let me temporarily move to Granny's house just as an experiment. My dad didn't like it at first until he realized he had one less mouth to feed; Granny fed me and gave me my own separate room away from my sisters. I soon became the man of Granny's house and started to experience my independence and semi-privacy. I would sneak to talk to girls on her party line telephone, which was not private back then.

I had certain chores to do at Granny's like cutting the grass, taking out the trash, washing the dishes, and raking the leaves, but mostly I had it pretty easy. I stayed at Granny's house all the way until I finished college and never returned to live with my parents and sisters.

I remember seeing my mother dressed in her starched white uniform and white shoes she wore to work at Moody's and Flower's Hospitals as a nurse's aide. From 1945 to 1951, she worked at Moody's hospital where she started out just changing the bed linens in the hospital rooms. From 1951 to 1985, she moved over to Flowers Hospital and continued the same work. The early Flowers Hospital was a former home and had only twelve beds in 1951.

My mother's lack of formal education limited her from being a real nurse; however, she was later able to work as an assistant to Dr. Paul Flowers in the operating room where she often administered anesthesia to patients. This was a risky move by Dr. Flowers to allow her to put patients to sleep with anesthesia when she had no formal training. However, my mother learned fast and never had any issues whatsoever.

Her attention to details made her a trusted and loyal assistant to Dr. Flowers, and it also made some of the White nurses envious of her close working relationship with Dr. Flowers.

At the time, I didn't realize she was a pioneer in her field and that she was the first Black person in Dothan to work in such a trusted position. Some of the White nurses resented my mother for being able to work closely with Dr. Flowers without having the proper nursing credentials. She was subjected to daily mistreatment by some of the nurses.

My mother told me one story that involved a White nurse giving her a bag containing a stillborn baby. The nurse told my mother that Dr. Flowers had instructed her to bury the baby since the hospital was not equipped with incinerators at the time.

My mother told the nurse that she was not in the funeral business, and she would wait to ask Dr. Flowers himself if he instructed her to bury the baby. My mother was wary of the nurse and felt that it was a trap to get her fired. When Dr. Flowers arrived, my mother asked him if he had instructed her to bury the stillborn.

Dr. Flowers erupted and said, "No, Louise, I did not leave instructions for you to bury anything. I told the nurse to remind me to take the bag with me before I left yesterday."

Dr. Flowers fired the nurse on the spot and told the staff that if anyone else ever used his name to perpetrate lies like that, he would fire them, too. My mother went back to work and kept her job. She had defiantly illustrated that she was nobody's fool.

I didn't know anything about racism or sexism then and how it may have affected her on her job; I only saw her when she came home from work, and she always appeared to be happy. Years later, I learned that she did face constant racism and sexism at work, but she always put on a smile when she came home so as not to discourage us from doing our best in school.

Tragically, my mother faced an unimaginable horror two years after she retired from Flowers Hospital in 1985. My older sister, Anita, went into the hospital in early July in 1987 to get some tumors removed from her ovaries. She was a thirty-seven-year-old schoolteacher at the time and waited until school was out for the summer so she could have time to recuperate before going back to school the following term.

Anita was the first one of us to go to college. She attended the Historically Black College and University (HBCU) Alabama A&M University, in Huntsville, Alabama, and graduated with a degree in City Planning; she worked in city planning in Anniston, Alabama, before becoming a teacher.

My sister chose the other local hospital in town, not Flowers, for her surgery. By all reports, the surgery went well without a hitch; however, the anesthesiologist gave her too much anesthesia and none of the nurses checked on her to make sure she was okay and awake after surgery. Consequently, Anita never woke up and died in her sleep on July 7th. My mother had lost her oldest child due to a mishap in a hospital with anesthesia, something my mother had done time and again without any mishaps. We buried Anita on July 11, 1987, and I became my mother's oldest living child after Anita's death. On that day, a big piece of my mother died along with my sister.

My mother had to forfeit all of her dreams in life in favor of making sure her children could follow their own dreams. It seemed no sacrifice was too great for her when it came to our education. Being a very strong woman may explain why my mother has persevered through so many years to reach her current age of 101.

It boggles my mind to think of all the things she might have witnessed since her birth; she is like a walking history book and a living treasure.

She was born during the Roaring Twenties, which was also referred to as the Jazz Age. The invention of the TV occurred during the same decade. The end of the 1920s was known as the Great Depression (1929-1941), which consumed the 1930s and some of the 1940s as the longest depression in U.S. history. How my mother was able to successfully navigate her way through all these events and survive all these things as a poor Black woman in the South is a big mystery to me, but it speaks to her resilience.

The Nazi invasion, the Holocaust, and World War II dominated the 1940s; the Tuskegee Airmen Red Tails were born and were responsible for helping to desegregate the American military. The Tuskegee Airmen were said to have fought in two wars simultaneously: World War II overseas and racism when they returned home to the U.S.

Where my mother lives in Houston County, Alabama, is only 107 miles from Tuskegee, Alabama, also home of the horrific Tuskegee Experiment, which was a federal government syphilis study conducted in Tuskegee on 600 Black men between 1932 and 1972.

Many Black men died from this forty-year government-sanctioned study, and the highest payment they received for participation in this study was $15 to pay for their funeral expenses in the event of their death. These men were lied to by the White doctors and nurses who represented the federal government; there were never any White patients used in this syphilis experiment.

My mother survived the Atomic Age of the 1950s, which also heralded the Golden Age of Television (1948-1959), and the first color TV unveiled in 1951. The 1950s signaled economic growth and upward mobility for many people as a huge rebound from the long years of the Depression; it also saw the end of World War II. She married my father in 1950 and had four baby boomer children between 1950 and 1958.

The 1960s brought both the Vietnam War and the Civil Rights Movement. The Bay of Pigs and the Cuban Missile Crisis helped to usher in the now famous "generation gap" that characterized the 1960s. Although none of these things had a personal impact on my mother, it affected us all collectively as we tried to deal with this new mass identity crisis.

However, the death of President John F. Kennedy in 1963 and the death of his brother Bobby Kennedy and the Rev. Martin Luther King Jr., both in 1968, did have a profound personal impact on my mother and me. I remember my mother crying regarding all three deaths, and I developed a phobia of riding in convertible cars or on motorcycles. To this day, I have not and will not ride on a motorcycle, and I do not like convertibles.

The biggest event of the 1960s had to be July 21, 1969, when American astronaut Neil Armstrong walked on the moon as the first human ever to do so. He piloted the Apollo 11 space shuttle to reach the moon before any other country could plant their flag there.

The Watergate hearings dominated the 1970s, but there were some other milestones during this decade such as the fact that the American voting age was lowered to 18, and there was an upheaval in both politics and inflation. My mother made sure that I registered to vote when I turned eighteen. She was very proud of the fact that Shirley Chisholm was the first Black woman and Black person to run for the U.S. presidency in 1972. Chisholm's campaign motto was "Unbought and Unbossed" which encouraged Black women everywhere to stand up and be counted.

The '70s was my favorite decade because I discovered the sweet soul music sounds of groups like The Dells, The Delfonics, The Moments, The Dramatics, The Stylistics, and many other falsetto-led male groups. My mother watched me march off to college after high school in 1972; she once visited me on campus to see if I was actually going to class. Although I never saw my mother wear an afro hair style, I sure did in the '70s.

My mother was able to read about the falling of the Berlin Wall in the 1980s, and she witnessed the arrival of the AIDS epidemic when she was still working in the medical field. She approved of my still wearing an afro amidst all the big hair frenzy of the '80s. Chemically treated Jheri curls for Black men and Black women began to replace the afros in the 1980s.

Lest we not forget that Jesse Jackson became the second Black person to launch a presidential campaign in 1984. Jackson's unofficial campaign slogan was said to be "Run, Jesse, Run." The double meaning in that slogan was obvious to many as he ran for president, and also was running from assassination attempts from domestic terrorist groups like the Ku Klux Klan.

The 1990s saw the first internet browser being introduced in 1990; the popularity of hip-hop began; the Soviet Union fell; and the Cold War ended. As a country, we started to see a relative rise in peace and prosperity jump-started by low oil prices, innovation, free trade, and investment in new technologies like computers.

My mother was seventy-eight when the year 2000 rolled around. She lived through the war on terror, the Afghanistan War, and the attack on the World Trade Center. But most importantly to her, she was alive when Barack Obama became the first Black president in the history of the U.S. She understood the importance and gravity of that moment of Black pride and how far we had come as a country; she was very proud to claim President Obama as her president.

It has been these last twenty-three years since the year 2000 that seem to have given my mother some pause and major concerns. She has lamented the resurgence of racism and poverty, the increase in suicides in our country, and the violence throughout many of the streets in almost every state; she also is very upset about the increase in Black-on-Black crime throughout the state of Alabama and our entire country.

She fears we are still fighting some of the same battles like voting rights, education, and equal pay that she felt we had won years ago. She constantly prays for the world to find some measure of peace and regain its footing. My mother is still an optimist for the most part despite all the evidence to the contrary.

Today at 101, my mother has that same resiliency she's always had and she knows that she is blessed to still be alive and in her right mind. Her fingers and legs ache from arthritis, but she doesn't complain much. I feel blessed to still have my mother, too.

For many years, she made quilts by hand and sold them to friends and family. Anyone who was lucky enough to get one of her quilts received a masterful work of art and Black history at the same time.

I always thought I was more like my father, but after much more reflection, I have come to realize that I actually have more of my mother's spirit, spunk, and creativity. My mother is very smart and would have been a wonderful student in school had she not dropped out after being bullied and teased for not having any shoes to wear to school. Had all things been equal in her life, I am sure my mother could have been a registered nurse and ranked with the best of them regardless of skin color.

My mother has always been a good singer and a good dancer. When we attended her ninety-ninth birthday celebration, she got on the dancefloor and danced along with the young people. When someone shouted to her to "drop it like it's hot," she did. I was amazed to see my mother go down to the floor and come back up like she was a teenager. You haven't lived until you see a 99-year young woman *drop it like it's hot.*

I am very proud of my mother and all that she has accomplished in her long life. Without the love and the inspiration she has given me, I would not be able to share this writing with the world. I am acutely aware that it is still possible for my mother to outlive me; yet I wanted to honor her with her flowers while she is still young.

In closing, I would like to proudly tell the world that I AM IN LOVE WITH A 101-YEARS-YOUNG WOMAN named Mrs. Ada Mary Louise Thompson, and I always will be.

CHAPTER TWO

"A DECLINATION OF INDEPENDENCE"

When my father, James L. Thompson Sr., turned eighty-nine years old, we considered placing him in a nursing home. His health was deteriorating, and the rest of the family was too busy living our lives to stop and offer him around-the-clock care. He had a stroke at age seventy-eight and was not really the same man after that; he needed professional medical care that we could not offer. It seemed the most convenient thing for us to do was place him in a nearby convalescence facility. When he learned about our plans, he dreaded the idea and his body initiated a mental and physical revolution.

My father was very proud, independent and considered himself a man's man. He was born James L. Thompson in 1921, but his middle name of "L" did not stand for anything else.

The Great Depression in the U.S. occurred from 1929-1941, however, my father was born poor anyway. He quit school in the fourth grade to look for work to help feed his family. He was the oldest child, with two younger sisters named Ruby and Sarah. He was responsible, mature, and he avoided getting into trouble like the other boys his age. My father found odd jobs to keep him busy until he became an adult.

At age twenty-two in 1943, he joined the Army during World War II in order to make good on his independence. The Army required him to create a real middle name to replace the "L," so he selected Lewis as his middle name. He was looking to gain his independence.

His time in the military was mostly spent doing menial jobs such as working in a supply house separating uniforms and other clothing from equipment; he never saw any combat action. The highlight of his Army time was when he was briefly stationed in Marseilles, France; however, he did achieve the rank of Corporal before he was honorably discharged three years later. Like most Black men who went to war, he never spoke about his real military experiences and all the extra, overt wars he had to fight while in the U.S. military and when he came home in the 1940s.

In 2023, I wrote to the National Personnel Records Center for the military to try and obtain copies of my father's military records so I could learn more about his history; however, the military sent me a one-page declination letter to say that my father's records were most likely burned up in a fire on July 12, 1973, and they were not going to consider my request any further.

When my father came home from the war to Dothan, Alabama, and the Baptist Bottom where we lived, he married my mother, Mary Louise, and they began our family with the birth of my sister Anita in 1950. After that, my father went to work as a groundskeeper at the Dothan Country Club. Due to his lack of education, that was about the only job he could get at the time.

He spent his time driving tractors, mowing lawns, and occasionally serving as a caddy to make extra money. During this time, I was born in 1954. Two sisters, Emily and Patricia, followed me two years apart from each other.

My father moved on from work at the country club to spend the rest of his professional career working in construction for the large Slingluff Construction Company. The owner, Mr. Betts Slingluff Jr., really liked my dad and treated him like he was part of his extended family.

My father got me a job mowing the Slingluff family residential home lawn when I was a teenager, and I worked alongside my dad with the construction company when school was out. My big claim to construction fame was digging the hole for the coin fountain on the bottom level of the Northside Mall. It was hard work, but I wanted to follow in my dad's footsteps and do construction work when I got older.

His days working in construction were spent doing manual labor and hard work where he used his own hands to eke out a living for our family. He worked many long days and was usually exhausted when he came home; however, he still managed to operate his own café called Shack's Grill in the Baptist Bottom at night and on weekends.

While other boys could be seen playing catch with their fathers in the backyard or being taught how to drive by their dads, I was not afforded the same quality time with my dad. He worked all the time, and I came to understand that this was how we were able to eat food and wear clothes to go to school.

Although he was not book-educated, my father knew how the math behind money worked and how to write his name. He didn't believe in borrowing money from anyone, and he only trusted banks as far as he could throw one.

As a child, I never saw my father in a suit or attending church on Sunday. It wasn't until I was almost forty that my father started going to church on an irregular basis. He believed in partial tithing in church but wholly helping out friends at a time of a family death; he would often be the first to bring the mourning family a box of food, a case of soft drinks, and a strong hand to help out where needed.

From watching my father work hard at everything he did, I unwittingly copied his same work ethic and independent spirit when I started my professional work career. I wanted desperately to follow in his footsteps when it came to construction work and working with my hands, but I was not blessed with the same skills.

One of my high school counselors advised me to get a vocational trade because she didn't think I was smart enough to go to college. I was delighted to hear that, so I took a brick masonry class during my senior year of high school. At the end of the school year, my brick mason instructor suggested I should go to college because I was not skilled enough with my hands to make a living as a brick mason.

While my father only finished fourth grade, he paid for my college education so I could earn a master's degree in college. Even though I had a college degree, I learned that I would still never be as smart as my father. How he was able to master a successful, honest living and send his children to school to outperform him and my mother, I will never know.

Most people say I get my sense of humor from my father. He was a natural comedian without realizing how funny he actually was. When I was a teenager, I remember him asking me to take his car and go pick up some items he needed from the store to stock his café. I had a bad habit of innocently telling him I didn't know where someplace was or how to get there if I really didn't want to do the chore for him; we didn't have GPS then and I couldn't read a map.

Usually, my father would give up and go get the things himself and leave me to play with my friends. One day, he got fed up with my excuses. This particular time, he angrily blurted out, "You ain't never died either, but you know where hell is, don't you?" I quickly got the point and drove to pick up his items from the store.

My father acted like he was the unofficial mayor of the Baptist Bottom. People would come into his café and consult him about all kinds of things and gossip. I remember one time a man came into his cafe and told my dad that he just heard that someone they both knew had recently died. The man was seeking confirmation from my dad. My dad responded, "I know he's dead because I went over to Hawk's Funeral Home and interviewed the body yesterday."

My father didn't use our dial telephone because he probably couldn't understand how it worked; once I handed him the phone and he immediately started yelling into the receiver so the person on the other end could hear him. I was too afraid to tell him that he didn't have to speak that loud, so I let it go. He didn't wear wristwatches and I never saw him wearing a pair of eyeglasses.

He didn't believe in going to doctors, either. When he would complain about his aching back, he would send me to the store to buy some Doan's Pills for back pain relief and he would self-medicate. When he had a stroke at age seventy-eight, he was still working on a construction job site. We think he just didn't understand that he could retire and no longer had to go to work since he had been working for so long. The other reason was that most of his friends worked with him and he liked seeing them all.

The attending physician told us to get all of my father's affairs in order because he didn't have long to live. As it turned out, my father mostly recovered from his stroke with few symptoms, and he outlived his attending physician.

So, when the time came to discuss placing my father in a nursing home, he refused to participate in the discussions; he insisted that he did not want to lose his independence and be housed in a hospital with old strangers. My sisters and I tried to explain that it would be fine because we would be close by to visit him regularly. He quickly remarked, "The only time I see you all now is when you want some money. I'll probably never get any visits from you if I'm in there."

The biggest issue arose when my father learned that he would be required by the state to sell his house in order to help pay for his care. My parents were separated then, and they lived in different houses. In Alabama, it's legal to take all of the assets of a person going into a nursing facility to help pay for their perpetual care. That also meant he had to give up any bank assets and his monthly Social Security check. My father had worked too long and too hard to give up all that he had worked for since he was just a child; he did not want to be taken care of by Medicaid.

I later recalled that my father's mother— my grandmother— had spent her last years in a nursing home. My father had made the decision to place her there for the same reasons we were contemplating placing him in one. His mother had been diagnosed with diabetes and had both her legs amputated. As a young child, I remember our father taking us to visit her in the nursing home every Sunday; however, I never realized it was painful for him to see her like that. I was too young to consider what he must have been facing at that time. Now it became much clearer to me why he had such a dreadful fear of nursing homes.

Although he could not read that well, my father had a great mind for reasoning. He didn't factually know that Medicaid first began in 1965 under President Lyndon Johnson or that two-thirds of American nursing home residents care is paid by Medicare. He also didn't know that there was a personal needs allowance of $25 per month established with the original bill. That amount increased once to $30 per month in 1987 and had not received a cost-of-living increase since. What he did know was that he had more money than that in the bank and he was not going to be driven into poverty by giving all his money to the state. He sensed a loss of dignity and independence if he went into a nursing home, and that was not a game starter for him.

In order to reach a compromise, he reluctantly agreed to let us take him to the nursing home for a non-obligatory walk-through to see if he would like it. Due to his age, the facility required that he take the tour in a wheelchair. That was a big mistake, and that visit did not go well. When my father looked around and realized where he was, he fell into a deep depression and ceased to say anything throughout the visit. His new reality was that this place could be his home. It felt like a big hospital with elderly and sickly strangers, add to that the fact that he might be sharing a room with one of those old strangers.

The rooms looked bland and sterile. They were all painted and decorated the same with an austere appearance. One room had a small TV with an antenna, a bed, a chest of drawers, a folding table, and a calendar on the wall. Another "inmate's" room had a radio, a framed black-and-white family portrait, and a small green plant sitting in a window. The bed in each room was the center of attention with a small closet for a few clothes; residents were expected to spend most of their time in bed dreaming about yesterday and wishing for tomorrow. That must have felt like solitary confinement.

After the brief tour, we met with the facility manager, who explained some of the benefits of being placed at her facility. She touted things like meeting new people, daily games and discussions, morning devotionals, the beautifully landscaped property, etc.

Then she made the fatal mistake of telling my father that the state of Alabama would provide a monthly stipend of $30 to help pay for things like lotion, soap, toothpaste, etc. Looking at his face, I knew that was the end of the deal for him. Although my sisters and I explained we would stop by and bring him extra food and things, it was not the same as him buying things with his own money, on his own time, and with his own independence. It was during this time that I think my father lost his will to live.

Here was a man who had survived almost ninety years of independent living but was now being offered the prospect of losing all his money, his independence, and himself. We ended the visit and brought our father back to his own home that he had purchased with his own money. We felt that it was best to delay the nursing home option for a later time.

A few months went by, and I received a call that I should go visit my father sooner rather than later; I understood what that call may have meant. I immediately arrived at his home for what I called a wellness check, but in reality, it was to confirm my suspicions of pending doom.

When I laid eyes on him, I knew that something had changed. It was obvious he had not eaten very much, but I thought he still looked fairly strong. I sat with him for a few hours. When I got ready to leave, he reached out and grabbed my hand to shake it and almost broke it; he still had the strength of a man who had worked hard with his hands all his life.

At the time, I did not take his gesture as his saying goodbye to me. I thought that I would come back and sit with him again sometime. As I walked toward the door, I heard him softly say, "I love you, son." I was stunned because in all his years, my father had never uttered those words to me. I always felt his love, but he had never said it until then. I responded, "I love you too, Dad," and walked through the door.

The next day, my middle sister called me to say that our father had passed away early that morning. I wanted to cry but I couldn't. In my heart, I understood why he left, and I appreciated the way he chose to leave. He died the way he lived. His independent spirit would not be confined to a world that declined to let him be the man that he always had been. He died on Good Friday, April 6, 2012, three months shy of his ninetieth birthday.

Although my father was now gone, I knew that I would see him again alive fairly soon. After the funeral, we all went our separate ways to mourn. My mother went home with my sisters, and I went home to be with my wife and son. Strangely, I was still unable to cry; the tears refused to fall from my eyes, and I could not understand why.

I arose earlier than normal the next morning. I looked outside and saw the sun shining brightly through the trees. I kissed my wife and then my son. Next, I went to the bathroom to take a shower and shave. The warm shower hit my body and made me feel renewed like I was changing into a new person.

I dried my body and wrapped the towel around my waist so that I could shave by looking into the mirror. I lathered my face, picked up my razor, and stared into the mirror. What I saw in the mirror stunned me for a minute and I froze with my razor near my face. Rather than seeing my face lathered with shaving cream, I saw my father's face. It was then that I realized I looked so much like him that I had literally become him.

I was fifty-eight years old when my father died. The premonition of seeing my father alive again soon was complete. It was then that the tears began to fall from my eyes. We all mourn differently, and my mourning was in full effect.

I must have been in the bathroom too long, for my wife got worried and called out to me. I quickly finished shaving, washed my face, and opened the door to tell her that I was fine now.

During breakfast with my wife and son, I made a toast to my father. With a glass of orange juice in my hand I said, "This is to my father, a man who lived a full life and taught me how to love without saying the words. Sometimes unspoken words say more than realized, and spoken words say less than actually meant. I LOVE YOU, DAD!"

CHAPTER THREE

"THE RED BOTTOM SHOE MYSTERY"

I'm Lt. Fredrick Gamble of the Metropolitan Police Homicide Unit. The following incident is one of the most unusual cases we ever investigated.

With sirens and lights flashing, my unmarked car pulled up at Fox Run Apartments at 8:45 p.m. When I arrived at the crime scene, I was told by the overweight apartment manager that I was the second officer to arrive. The man, who identified himself as Mr. Aristotle Bivack, was holding a Big Mac hamburger in one hand as he pointed in the direction of my partner with the other hand. I noted his fingers were red with either ketchup or blood; he was also wearing black suede Hush Puppies with rubber soles that looked like two flat tires due to his body weight.

My partner, Lt. Rhonda G. Fleming, got there about thirty minutes earlier; she had radioed me and told me she was on her way to the scene. We had both been assigned as the leads on this new case. I liked working with Rhonda because she was smart and very thorough like me. We met at the academy and started on the force around the same time. Rhonda was a true detective.

I entered the door to the bedroom of the deceased and saw that the female body had already been covered with a lime-green fleece blanket. All I could see was the bottom of one of her shoes sticking out. Trying to be careful where I stepped, I called out to Rhonda to let her know I was there. She was busy checking closets and drawers, looking for clues that may lead to a motive.

I asked her, "Rhonda, what do we have here? Is this a homicide or self-inflicted?"

"I can't tell yet," she looked down. "It looks like the victim may have been bashed over the head with a solid object, or she drank too much and fell to hit her head. And by the way, she's only wearing a bra and panties and has one shoe on. I can't seem to find the other one. I just threw that blanket over her until the coroner arrives."

"One shoe... You mean, she was actually only wearing one shoe?" I questioned.

"Well, either that or someone else really wanted her red-bottom shoes and took the other one with them in a rush," Rhonda replied. "And...I know you can see the dancer's pole in the middle of the room."

"Yeah, I see the pole. She was either a dancer or a wannabe," I quipped.

I peeked under the blanket to get a look at the victim's face and body. She was very voluptuous with a heart-shaped tattoo on her left ankle. I made a mental note that her shoe looked like an expensive Christian Louboutin made even redder with blood near the bottom.

Looking at her notebook, Rhonda read off the few details she had collected.

"Her name is Conzie A. Rayford from Philly...age 26...been living alone in this apartment for two years. Never had a roommate. That's all I have for now."

Just then, the crime scene investigators and the coroner's office showed up and politely asked Rhonda and me to step out so that they could photograph and process the scene.

Rhonda and I both complied, but I abruptly asked the uniformed officer to let me know the results immediately after they conducted a forensic analysis of the corpse, the crime scene, and the shoe.

Officer Bowman snapped back, "Lieutenant, we always go by the rule book. Your department will get a copy of our completed report as usual...and you know that."

I apologized to the officer and thanked him for his cooperation and hard work. The coroner's office later loaded up the corpse and wheeled it away after the photographs were taken.

Once on the outside, Rhonda lit a cigarette and said, "You know those red-bottom shoes are not cheap. I wish I could afford them, but I can't on my salary."

"Who can? I understand they cost about a grand or more," I responded.

"Could be more, depending on where she bought them." Rhonda blew smoke into the air. "Had both shoes been there, I may have lifted them myself."

"Right, and I would have been investigating your stupid behind," I said as we both laughed.

* * * *

About four days later, we did receive the forensic report as promised. The report stated that: (1) Conzie Ann Rayford had worked as a dancer at The Bee Hive Night Club on Broad Street. (2) She was single with no children and had a college degree in Journalism from City College. (3) The gash on her head occurred when she hit it on a wine bottle after falling off the dancer's pole; her blood alcohol concentration was 0.15 percent. (4) The investigators found the wine bottle but were unable to lift any fingerprints other than the victim's own. (5) Interestingly, the report also stated that the red-bottom shoe she was wearing was not an authentic Christian Louboutin. It was traced back to a purchase she had made from a department store like TJ Maxx or Marshall's; it was hard to tell since both stores are part of the same chain. At any rate, she bought the shoes with black bottoms and either painted them red herself or had someone else do it professionally. In other words, the four-inch stilettos looked expensive, but they only cost her $99. The rest of the report was mundane.

Rhonda looked at me and said, "What? That girl was clever. I never thought about painting the bottom of my shoes red. Even I can afford $99."

"If you hurry, you may also be able to catch that same sale, and it might even come with a free dancer's pole," I joked.

"How do you know I don't already have a dancer's pole?"

I decided to let Rhonda have the last word on that subject and suggested we both drive over to The Bee Hive Night Club to interview the manager.

* * * *

After phoning them to advise we were coming, we met the club manager at the door. We flashed our credentials and she let us in. The inside of The Bee Hive Night Club smelled like cigar smoke, liquor, and sex, but not honey. Mrs. Angelina Talbert, the club manager and owner, appeared to be in her mid-sixties, but the makeup, the red lipstick, and the blonde wig made her look at least a few years younger. She took us to a back office and offered us something to drink. We both declined and started asking her questions about Conzie Rayford.

"How long did the late Conzie Rayford dance at this club?" Rhonda asked politely.

"Conzie had only worked here for about six months, but she didn't start out as a dancer. She was the coat check girl at first and wanted to make more money. She had a nice figure, so I let her dance." The club owner had a sparkle in her eyes.

"Do you have any video footage of her last night working here?" I interjected. "If so, we'd like to take a look to see if we may be able to identify any suspects in the club that night. You know, any secret admirers."

"Sure, I'm happy to let you see whatever video footage we have," Mrs. Talbert offered with a weird smile. "I want to help all I can... I really liked Conzie very much."

"Exactly how much do you pay your dancers?" asked Rhonda.

"Most dancers make $25 per hour plus they get to keep 50% of their tips. My best dancers like Conzie make a little more." She continued smiling.

"How much more?" inquired Rhonda.

"I paid Conzie $35 per hour and I let her keep 75% of her tips because she was that good and was very popular with both the men... and the ladies."

"That's an important statement," I said. "Are you suggesting that Miss Rayford was bisexual?"

"Aren't we all... I mean, isn't everybody?" replied the club owner with a smirk and a bigger smile.

I was visibly offended by her smug behavior and started to make an angry reply, but Rhonda quickly interrupted with,

"Ah...is it okay if we take a copy of the video footage with us? Thank you and we would appreciate your cooperation." Rhonda rolled her eyes at me to get me to calm down. Soon after, we left with the footage.

* * * *

We took the video back to the station and watched it over and over but couldn't spot anything or anyone who looked suspicious. Then Rhonda casually suggested we go by Marshall's and TJ Maxx to question the salespeople about the stilettos.

"Wait a minute," I said. "You want us to go to these stores to see if they have the same fake shoes she wore? What kind of a lead is that?"

"Well, what would you suggest we do next? We need to find out where she bought those shoes...they could prove to be material to the case," Rhonda suggested.

"I was thinking we go back and interview Mr. Bivack, the apartment manager. He might just have a shoe fetish, and I noticed that his fingers were red with something that looked like blood to me," I said.

"Or ketchup," snapped Rhonda. "There is no way that a slob like Bivack was involved with Conzie Rayford. That man weighs 300 pounds for a reason. He's probably eating right now!"

"Okay, you go to the department stores, and I'll go see Bivack. We'll report back to the station at 5 p.m.," I compromised.

* * * *

I drove back to Fox Run Apartments without calling to let Bivack know I was coming. I was hoping to prove Rhonda wrong, that Bivack would not be eating, and that he may have had a motive after all. I got out of the car and went straight to the manager's office. The time was 3:00 p.m.

"Mr. Bivack, you may remember me from last week. I'm Lt. Gamble. I just have a few more questions about your former tenant, Miss Rayford."

Mr. Bivack was seated behind his desk. He looked up at me and wiped his mouth at the same time. Then he took a big swig of his Big Gulp soda before he answered with,

"Pardon me Lieutenant. I'm having a late lunch, and I was just starting to eat my sandwich. Want some fries?"

"No, thank you. How well did you know Miss Rayford? Did you notice if she had any regular callers, like a boyfriend...or a girlfriend, maybe?"

"Uh, I usually mind my own business around here, but I do recall seeing a young man talking to Miss Rayford maybe a day before her demise," said Mr. Bivack as he stuck another French fry in his mouth.

"Really? Did you provide that info to my partner or any of the other officers who were here last week?" I asked.

"I don't recall... I may have. I didn't have any reason not to."

"Do you recall hearing the young man's name or know for sure who he was?" I questioned.

"No, but I know she let him into her apartment. He was tall with glasses, and he had on a hoodie. I couldn't see his face that well and I can't say how long he stayed inside," he said with a fry sticking out of his mouth like a cigarette.

"Mr. Bivack, have you ever been inside Miss Rayford's apartment? Do you know what her profession was?"

Mr. Bivack innocently answered, "No sir... I have never been inside her apartment, and I don't really know what she did for a living. Maybe a young schoolteacher or something like that?"

Usually, I can tell when a person is lying by his eyes, and Mr. Bivack appeared to be telling the truth. He wasn't nervous or evasive, and he kept on eating his food as we talked. I may have been wrong, but I couldn't see Bivack as a serious suspect. I decided to cut him a break, head back to the station, and leave him alone with his footlong cheesesteak. He ate all the fries as he was talking to me.

* * * *

Back at the station, I met up with Rhonda to see what she had uncovered. She said she went to both TJ Maxx and Marshalls but neither had the shoes on sale or in stock. She looked very disappointed; I could tell she really wanted a pair of those stilettos.

Rhonda reported that both stores claimed they never sold any shoes similar to the ones she showed them in the photo.

Then it hit her. I could see the lightbulb go on in her head. She smiled and said,

"I got it! Let's go check out H&M. I bet that's where she really bought them. Those shoes are just the kind of fashion statement that H&M is known for. Let's go, partner!"

* * * *

We drove to the H&M store closest to Miss Rayford's apartment building to see if Rhonda was right again. We went directly to the women's shoe department and Rhonda found the exact pair of black-bottom shoes that Miss Rayford was wearing. After talking to the saleslady, we confirmed that the stiletto shoes were a hot item and that they had been sold for $99 a pair about a month ago; they now cost $125. Excited, Rhonda pulled out her credit card and bought a pair on the spot in her size. Then, she sheepishly looked at me and said she only bought them to use as circumstantial evidence or probable cause in case we ever went to trial.

I smiled and said, "Of course, Rhonda. I can see that you LOVE those shoes. Are we stopping by the paint store on the way back so you can spray paint the bottoms red, too?"

When we returned to the office, we closed the case with these details:

Conzie Rayford was obviously someone who drank too much while pole dancing in her underwear; there was no foul play and no homicide.

The unknown guy in the hoodie was either a voyeuristic customer or a DoorDash food delivery man. Either way, he did not kill Ms. Rayford.

The only thing Mr. Aristotle Bivack was guilty of was gluttony – a deadly sin but not a deadly crime. He simply ate too much, and his only interest was food. We were never able to prove that he also had a shoe fetish, but we doubted it because the shoe was not edible.

Mrs. Angelina Talbert was also eliminated as a suspect. She was just a shrewd business shark trying to make money any way she could. Conzie Rayford was her cash cow, and she had no reason to want her dead.

In the end, the only mystery was that we never found the one missing red-bottom shoe. This case was never about the dead body, but all about the red-bottom shoes.

My personal theory, not listed in the report, is that my partner Rhonda may have removed the one shoe but heard me coming and got scared before she could get the other one. She was smart enough to make the evidence disappear. After all, authentic Christian Louboutin red-bottom shoes are expensive and everybody loves them.

Case closed.

CHAPTER FOUR

"FALLING OUT OF LOVE"

Falling out of love feels like skydiving without a parachute. Your body tends to free-fall aimlessly until sudden impact. Seconds before you fall to Earth, your soul leaves your body and looks at your silent corpse, wishing you had listened to your heart rather than your head.

Girls seem to fall faster than boys, but boys are believed to fall harder. My name is Sara Myles, and I am from Ozark, Alabama. I fell in love with Milton Gloster in second grade the first time I saw him. He sat behind me in class and pulled my ponytail to get a big laugh. I swirled around to slap his face but was stunned at how handsome he looked. Although I slapped him anyway, I admit that I didn't wash my hand for a week because it had touched his gorgeous body.

I adored Milton from afar all through elementary school, but he acted like he never even knew my name. It wasn't until the tenth grade that he first noticed me. We were in Biology class, and I dropped my book on the floor. I bent over to pick it up, but Milton beat me to the punch. He smiled when he gave me the book and returned to his seat without taking his eyes off me.

At first, I thought he was looking in my direction at someone else. His stare had a gaze that I had never noticed before. I smiled back with my eyes and returned to my seat, but not without saying, "Thank you." I wondered if he remembered that I was the same girl who slapped his face in second grade.

After class, he walked up to me and told me his name. It was obvious he didn't remember me from elementary school. I introduced myself as just Sara to make sure he did not recall the slap. He quietly walked me to my next class and then made a slow turn to go to his. Then he looked back at me with the same starry gaze, and I felt that he had finally noticed the "me" that I longed for him to see.

I wasn't sure what had caused the sudden change in Milton. I went to the girls' bathroom after class and looked in the mirror. I was the same flat-chested Sara with no makeup or lip gloss. My hair was still unstyled in a ponytail, and I was not a flashy dresser. I thought maybe if I arched my eyebrows and wore my hair a different way, I would be more attractive.

I confided in my best friend Denise Kelly about how I felt about Milton and my insecurities. Denise had known all along about my crush, but she was surprised to hear that I felt the way I did about my looks. She, on the other hand, was naturally beautiful without any imperfections. Most guys thought her hourglass figure was the result of consecutive days in the gym, but I knew that Denise had never worked out and she ate all the junk food she could find; she was just blessed with a nice body.

"Have you tried stuffing your bra with tissue to make Milton think you have a bust?" Denise asked.

"No!" I yelled. "I don't want him to think I'm artificial. I don't want any fake boobs."

"All the girls do it. Those are not Carla Turner's real breasts. That's just a push-up bra filled with socks," Denise declared.

"I don't care about Carla's breasts... I only care about mine, and I am not stuffing my bra with anything!"

* * * *

From the tenth grade to the twelfth grade, Milton and I maintained a mainly platonic relationship. We made small talk at school and at night we would talk on the phone for a few minutes; he would sometimes call me and I would sometimes call him. I felt that he liked me, but I didn't know how much until prom time came around.

By twelfth grade, I started to look different, more mature. My breasts had begun to fill out and for once other boys started to notice me, too. My sister, who was a cosmetologist, arched my brows and styled my hair with a sexy cut. Denise and I started getting our nails done together, and I even opted for a pedicure once during the summer so I could show off my new sandals.

Milton must have seen me out somewhere because he called me one evening and asked if I would go to the senior prom with him. I smiled a lot during the phone call and made it clear that my response was affirmative.

After I hung up the phone, I danced around my room until I felt dizzy. Next, I called Denise to tell her the news.

"Denise, Milton just called and invited me to the prom!" I exclaimed.

"Oh, Sara, that's great! You are finally getting your wish...and I know the two of you will have fun together. Have you thought about what you will do after the prom?" Denise asked.

"After the prom...what do you mean?"

"I mean, where you're going after the prom," Denise continued.

"I'm not sure what you mean. I just figured he'd bring me back home after the prom," I said excitedly.

"Oh, girl, we need to have a little talk like real soon," said Denise. "I'll stop by this weekend so we can have some girl talk."

"Okay," I said. And then I hung up, wondering what kind of girl talk she meant.

* * * *

Denise and I had a sleepover at my house the following weekend. That was nothing new since we had been having sleepovers at each other's homes since we were kids. Both my parents liked Denise and our parents were friends. My older sister was now grown and had moved out so our girl talk would just be between me and Denise in my bedroom.

"Sara," Denise began, "I think it's great that you and Milton are going to the prom, but are you prepared if Milton pops the question about having sex?"

"What?" I raised my voice, "Having sex...! Milton would never ask me that...he's not like that—"

"Not like *what*, Sara?" interrupted Denise. "Milton is a guy and guys do guy things. Like asking girls out for proms and hoping for more sometimes. I just don't want you to be caught off guard."

Calming down, I looked at her and stated, "No Denise, I was so excited that Milton asked me to the prom, I never even considered what could happen afterwards. I mean, you know I'm a virgin and the only boy I ever loved was Milton."

"I know Sara, that's why we're having this conversation...you're my best friend and I want you to be prepared for whatever happens," consoled Denise.

"I don't want to sound naïve, but I guess I am. I don't even know if Milton is experienced or has been with anyone else."

"Girl, not having sex after the prom is not a deal closer... I'm sure Milton won't think less of you for postponing what should be a special moment for both of you. I'm just saying..."

"Denise, are you saying that you have lost your virginity already?" I asked gently.

"Girl, Marvin and I started having sex a year ago." Denise smiled. "I mean, after all, maybe it's because my boobs started to grow way before yours that I started having sex before you."

"Wow! I had no idea..."

"Sara, I didn't tell you because I didn't want to pressure you into having sex before you were ready...I understand how peer pressure works. The only reason I'm admitting it now is because I want you to have your eyes wide open if it happens with Milton... and because I love you and care what happens to you."

I looked at Denise and said, "Thank you, girl, I love and appreciate you, too. My eyes are now open."

We popped popcorn and watched the movie *Waiting to Exhale* with Whitney Houston and Angela Bassett. We girlishly giggled at all the parts with gratuitous sex.

* * * *

Milton and I did attend the prom together and we had a great time. He looked fine in his black tuxedo, and I wore a strapless black dress; my dress stayed up without any artificial stuffing or push-up bras. Denise and Marvin smiled at us when we first arrived, and some of the others gave us looks of surprise. I assumed no one knew we were actually dating.

The car we rode in belonged to Milton's dad; it was a medium-sized macho sports car with leather seats. It smelled clean because Milton got it washed before he picked me up. I felt fresh and special when he walked around and opened the door for me.

We danced on the floor to every slow song as others marveled at how good we looked and how well we fit together. I happened to notice that Carla Turner was wearing a bright red strapless dress similar to mine and her boobs looked gigantic in it. I wondered if her bra was still stuffed with socks or her breasts had organically grown to that size.

After the prom, Milton took a detour out in the country on a long, quiet road and parked under an old fig tree. He knew no one would be taking this road and we would be alone. I suspected what Milton had in mind because I saw the picnic blanket neatly folded on the back seat. In case the backseat was too cramped, he was hoping we could sprawl out on the grass and let our passions run free.

He turned off the car's engine and its headlights and quietly looked over at me. I smiled because I felt I looked pretty in my prom dress, but the corsage he gave me was beginning to sag from all the dancing we did. He came close to me and kissed my lips.

Just when I thought he was about to suggest we move to the backseat, I said, "Uh, Milton, I've got something to tell you."

"Tell me what?" he asked. "Can't you tell me from the back seat?"

"Uh, that's just it... I've got company," I said shyly.

"Company? What are you talking about," he asked.

"It's that time of the month for me," I said.

"What time of the month?" he asked.

"I've got my period and we can't do anything tonight," I exclaimed.

"What???"

"Sorry, I didn't expect it to come this early," I cried.

And then he said to himself, "I was hoping to lose my..."

"Lose your what," I asked abruptly.

After realizing what he had said, Milton thought quickly to cover up his mistake.

"Uh, I was hoping to lose my cool and my self-control and fall deeply for you," he lied.

Sensing something was not right about his answer, I asked, "Milton, are you a virgin, too?"

"Me... a virgin? No, I've done it many times before," he quickly replied.

"With who?" I asked angrily.

"Uh... I'm not going to tell you that. I don't kiss and tell," Milton said, looking down.

"Okay, I can respect that since it's none of my business, but I thought we were..."

"You thought what, Sara?" interrupted Milton. "You think I don't know who you are?"

"Well, I meant I...I ...I," I stuttered.

"Sara, I have been in love with you since the second grade..."

"What???"

"Yes, ever since you slapped me after I pulled your ponytail. I didn't wash my face for a week because you touched my face. One of the reasons I wanted to have sex with you tonight is because I've always fantasized about being with you, and I think of you as my girl. The other reason is... well, I think I love you," Milton said.

"Wow, Milton," I managed to say. "I had no idea you felt that way about me."

"And yes," Milton murmured. "I am a virgin because I've been saving myself for you... I'm not embarrassed anymore because I suspect by the way you're acting that you've been saving yourself too...at least, I hope it's been for me."

My mind was blown but I managed to say, "Yes, Milton... I would love to lose my virginity right now with you, but I was not lying about having my period. Maybe we can try again next week?"

Milton smiled and snuggled really close to me. As he hugged me and kissed me softly, my corsage broke apart and fell between us in the car.

Without saying another word, Milton started the car and drove me home in silence. When we arrived at my house, he got out and opened the car door for me and walked me to my door. He kissed me on the jaw and waved good night, saying he really had a nice time. I wasn't sure if I had blown it with Milton or not, but I couldn't wait until my period ended so we could try again. I went inside and fantasized about losing my virginity to Milton.

* * * *

Denise called me the following day and asked if she could stop by for a few. Of course, I said yes because I wanted to tell her about what happened after the prom and that I felt really good about me and Milton.

After she arrived, we quickly headed back to my room to talk. I noticed that she was not saying much, but I thought she was just trying to wait until we were alone.

"Hey girl, what's up?" I asked.

"Sara, how was everything with Milton after the prom? Did anything go wrong?"

"Well, we didn't have sex if that's what you mean... I was on my period. Denise, why did you ask me if anything went wrong?"

"Sara, there's talk going around that Milton was seen with Carla Turner later that night...parked on an old country road. I thought you should know what I heard," Denise said quietly. She then reached out and grabbed my hands, locking her fingers in my fingers.

I was stunned into silence by what Denise said. I didn't know what to do or how to react. I felt like I had been gut-punched and started to cover my face to cry, but I thought better of that. I just looked at her and said, "Are you sure?"

"I'm only sure about what people are saying, but I did not see them myself," said Denise.

"But how could he do that? He told me he loved me and that he was a virgin too," I cried.

"Sara, sometimes guys say things to manipulate us into getting what they want and—"

"But he lied to me," I interrupted. "He looked me in my face and lied to me saying he fantasized about being with me when all the time he was just trying to get laid. I hate Milton and I never want to see him again!"

Denise moved in close and put her arms around me. I lowered my head and began to cry hard on her shoulder. It felt like the life had been sucked out of me and the world was coming to an end; I felt the sudden impact when my body fell to Earth.

* * * *

A week went by, and I never heard a peep from Milton. Each day I got stronger and felt more resolved about what I planned to do when I saw him again. Graduation was a week away and I was bound to see him then.

Denise and Marvin invited me out to lunch with them several times, but I declined. I needed to work on my self-control, and I did not want to break down in front of Marvin.

In hindsight, I was glad I was having my period when I went to the prom with Milton. It seems I dodged a bullet and do not have to be concerned about catching a venereal disease or even worse.

Unwittingly, Milton Gloster had taught me to distrust all men and to remain a virgin much longer than I intended.

* * * *

On the day of our graduation, I saw Milton walking up the steps toward the auditorium; Carla Turner was holding his hand. He glanced around and saw me staring at him. From a distance, I waved and smiled. I saw him say something to Carla as he let go of her hand and walked in my direction.

"Hey Sara, I've been meaning to call you, but..." he started.

"It's okay, Milton," I interrupted. "I haven't been waiting by the phone for your call. I can see that you've been busy. I get it... I'm a big girl whose eyes have been opened...It's all good and it was fun while it lasted."

"Sara, I never meant to..."

I interrupted again with, "But you did Milton...you did!" and quickly walked away before I started crying. We never spoke again.

Graduation went well. Our senior class made history by being one of the smartest classes to ever graduate from our high school. I did not attend the after-party. Milton had moved on and so did I.

Word had it that Milton and Carla eventually got married and had two bratty children, a boy and a girl. Carla became a voluptuous (big-breasted) nurse at the local infant's hospital because she was ripe for breastfeeding babies, and Milton became an egotistical (big-headed) manager at a DICK'S Sporting Goods store; their respective jobs were very prophetic and appropriate for both of them.

During the fifth year of their marriage, troubles in paradise began and Milton started to drink, becoming an alcoholic at the age of 23. I remembered thinking, "Girls seem to fall faster than boys, but boys are believed to fall harder."

Denise and Marvin got married and had three gorgeous children; they are very happily married together, and their children call me Aunt Sara.

After college, I got a job as a Special Education teacher in Dothan, Alabama. I am still single but dating a nice man named Walter Rich. He's very analytical and supportive of me in every way. He's not pushy and I've never caught him once in a lie. I like the way he looks at me as if I am his whole world. He loves me and I trust him. And because of that, I decided to lose my virginity to Walter – over and over again. It feels much better to fall in love than it does to fall out of love.

CHAPTER FIVE

"MY HARLEQUIN ROMANCE"

Harlequin Romance novels have been around for years. They are generally geared toward women, and they are known worldwide. Their published books number in the hundreds of thousands and have launched the careers of many aspiring writers.

As a curious reader and writer, I was familiar with many of the plots behind those Harlequin Romance stories because they were all very similar. You know, impeccably-handsome-man-meets-impossibly-beautiful-girl, then man-loses-girl or awakens to find it was all a dream.

Some of the surroundings in these novels take place on a dreamy, decadent island where there is a thin line between love and lust. Those kinds of books are not my cup of tea because something like that would never happen to a realist like me. I consider myself to be way too analytical to get caught up in such grown-up fairy tales.

Yet, while on a secret government mission in Costa Rica, I had sort of a Harlequin Romance. The flight was three hours and thirty minutes from Houston, and I traveled with a selective team of five male government employees. Although our mission and its details were highly classified, my romance was not. I was single, living on a budget, and had not yet met the girl of my dreams in Houston. I found the girls in Texas to be second to none and the ratio was twelve girls to each man.

Prior to traveling to the exotic island of Costa Rica, my government team was briefed on tactics used by some of the locals to entice Americans into embarrassing moments of seduction. The special briefing prepared us and made us astute to how some oblivious Americans can fall prey to many of the island's temptations; however, I was determined to remain focused on my mission and not be duped by any parasites or con artists.

To avoid the confusing hassle of currency exchange once we got on the island, we were issued government credit cards for spending. Although unofficially, many places accepted the U.S. dollar, the official currency there was the Costa Rican *colón*, named after the Spanish explorer, Christopher Columbus (Cristóbal Colón in Spanish).

Many innocent victims have succumbed to the friendly locals, the pristine coastline, the amazing wildlife, the delicious food, and the mesmerizing nightlife. Towards that end, the government gave us a list of things you shouldn't do while in Costa Rica. The list was extensive but not all-inclusive. So, I went onto the internet and found another list that the local Costa Rica Tourism Board published. It was specific and included such common "beware of" items as:

1. Don't feed the monkeys
2. Don't let your snake guard down
3. Don't forget to shake out your shoes
4. Don't stay at an international chain resort
5. Don't expect great coffee
6. Don't fall for parking lot scams
7. Don't go near the ants
8. Don't be lax about volcano alerts
9. Don't touch the tiny frogs
10. Don't take an unofficial taxi
11. Don't forget the insect repellent
12. Don't expect to see big cats in the jungle
13. Don't forget to bring sunscreen
14. Don't tip, but do tip
15. Don't disrespect nature
16. Don't forget to allot time for the departure tax
17. Don't neglect beach safety
18. Don't wait to buy souvenirs at the airport

19.   Don't forget to learn some basic Spanish

20.   Don't rely on travelers' checks

In hindsight, I probably violated most of these rules during the three days I was in Costa Rica. If only I had heeded the warnings I had been given.

After our first long day of work on the island, a few of us changed from our conservative clothes to fit in with the locals and went to a seaside eatery to get some food. We wore those brightly colored flower-print shirts with jeans and sandals. Some of the married guys took off their wedding rings and splashed on cologne just in case they got lucky. Since I was never that lucky in Houston, I assumed my bad luck would continue.

The island scenery was gorgeous, with a majestic backdrop of mountains and clear, rippling water cascading on the nearby beach. There are plenty of mountains and volcanoes in Costa Rica; the views from these heights are incomparable and unforgettable.

The sun was setting, and the clouds looked like billowy white pillows slow-dancing in the sky. Handsome, tanned-skinned male waiters moved in rhythm to the music of the five-piece steel drum band; exotic-looking women in tiny bikinis slowly walked by with smiles that encouraged our imaginations. This setting would make a perfect book cover for a Harlequin Romance book, I thought.

While seated at the bar with my back to the live band, I felt hands caressing my back and a soft, sweet voice whisper, "Ooh Papi, you look so strong and handsome. It is so good to see you again."

Then, I felt a kiss on my earlobe and a love bite on my ear; I felt hands caressing my body and simultaneously palming my butt near my wallet. I immediately thought someone was trying to pick-pocket me.

I spun around quickly and saw an impossibly beautiful five-foot-six-inch island goddess standing there smiling at me with teeth as white as ivory. The look on her face changed when she realized I did not recognize her. She embarrassingly dropped her eyes and her smile; I saw the disappointment in her humble demeanor.

I said to her that she must have me mixed up with someone else since this was my first time being on the island. I smiled to let her know I was sorry for the confusion.

She apologized and quickly moved away when she saw I was not her Papi. I turned to one of my more seasoned colleagues and asked him what "Papi" meant.

George Pryde, a twenty-year veteran, said, "Papi is an affectionate term that sort of means Daddy. In your case, she probably mistook you for her sugar daddy." Then he laughed with a big belly howl.

"*Sugar daddy?*" I questioned. "I'm nobody's sugar daddy. I can barely afford my apartment back in Houston. Besides, she was way out of my league."

* * * *

A tall, muscle-bound waiter appeared with a large tray of food for our table. We decided to order the Seafood Deluxe Platter and share it. The platter was humongous with steamed lobster tails, fried jumbo shrimp, pineapple-flavored rice, lush island-green vegetables, fresh fruit, and grilled local fish with the heads still on.

Many more drinks were ordered and soon my head started to feel dizzy. I was not a big drinker, but it was something about those sweet umbrella drinks that started calling my name. I think I may have had about six of them.

I looked at George and he was in no better shape than I was. In fact, George got up and started singing and dancing to the steel band music. George was a straitlaced shift supervisor who couldn't dance to save his life, but no one seemed to care.

Out of nowhere, the island goddess who had called me Papi reappeared and took me by the hand, saying, "Ooh Papi, I want to dance with you. Come on." She refused to take no for an answer and looked deep into my eyes.

I slowly got up and started dancing with her against my will. My dancing was no better than George's as I flailed my arms into the air when the band played their steel pan version of "Macho Man" by the

Village People. Then I smiled at her and said, "*Pura vida*," which sort of translates into *hello* or *nice to meet you*. "My name is Wade Randall."

She responded, "*Pura vida*, my name is Valentina" and then pulled me in close to smell her intoxicating perfume. She acted as if she knew me and we were not strangers. For the life of me, I did not understand her familiar behavior. I looked down and saw her 36Ds looking up at me with their high beams on; my drunken face plopped down into them.

✳ ✳ ✳ ✳

The next thing I remember, I was sitting in a small tub of warm water with someone washing my back. I looked around but did not recognize my surroundings.

A voice said, "Relax, Papi, this is a goat's milk bath. It is rich with nutrients and good for your body. It makes your skin sparkle and shine."

I blurted out, "Goat's milk…but I don't drink goat's milk!"

"No Papi, you do not drink it now. I bathe you in it."

"Where am I? Where are my clothes?" I managed to say.

"You at my home, Papi. I take good care of you tonight. You not worry."

"Where's George?" I asked.

"Who is George? There is no George here. Only you and me," she assured.

"But my mission… I have to go!" I cried.

"No, Papi. You not go. You stay with me tonight."

In a few minutes, she slowly helped me up out of the tub and started to dry my wet body with a huge, soft towel. She didn't seem to mind that I was naked as she carefully dried my body with attentive details below my waist. My six-foot-two-inch height next to her five-foot-six-inch body felt perfect as she stooped to dry my feet.

Looking up at my face from my feet, she smiled and said, "Ooh Papi, you smell so good. I bet you taste good, too."

When she stood up, she tip-toed to kiss me on my lips and coincidently dropped the wet towel on the floor. Wrapping her arms around my neck, she whispered, "Tonight, I will be your mission."

Then, in the missionary position, she laid down on a nearby bed and persuasively pulled me on top of her. I willingly allowed my naked body to free-fall forward like a man without a safety net; I surrendered and laid in her Garden of Eden.

I caressed her raven-black hair and quipped, "Papi feels good, but let's see who tastes the best." She smiled and acknowledged my witty double entendre by bringing her lips close to mine for another taste.

Her lips tasted like chocolate-covered mango and her touch felt like velvet; she used her tongue to lick the moisture from around my neck and ears like a kitten lapping up milk, and she added soft butterfly kisses to form tiny passion marks.

Bored with the foreplay, she reached her arms around her back to unhook her bikini bra while I worshipped her voluptuous breasts. She squirmed underneath me and managed to remove her bikini bottom without missing a stride. She moved like an acrobatic contortionist who flaunted her flexibility.

Government warning bells rang in my head to alert me that this may be a point-of-no-return seductive trap, but I blindly ignored the warnings and continued to go deep undercover.

I decided to test her flexibility by grabbing her smooth, long legs with the intent of putting them on my shoulders to touch my ears. When I did that, she accidentally kicked me in the balls, and I yelled out in pain. Like sticking a pin in a balloon, she deflated my ego and accidentally decocked my weapon. I felt my gun go limp and I knew it would take some time for me to reload my bullets. Realizing I was spent, Valentina headed south on me to help me out.

* * * *

The bright sunrise through the window served as my wake-up call. I tried to rub the sun out of my eyes as I realized I had to get up and report to work soon. I looked over at Valentina and she was still sleeping. I didn't know how far I was from my hotel, but I reasoned it couldn't be that far away because she had managed to walk me there.

As I was getting dressed, Valentina heard me buckle my belt and opened her eyes. She smiled and said, "Hola, Papi. Did you sleep well?"

I answered, "Hola, Valentina. Yes, I did sleep well...although I don't recall everything that happened last night."

She wittily replied, "You accomplished your mission last night very good!"

I wasn't exactly sure how to take what she said and assumed it was her attempt at using a sexual double entendre.

I said, "Thank you for a wonderful evening. I have to go get ready for work now."

"I understand," she said. "I hope to see you again before you have to return home."

I smiled and said, "Me too" as I waved goodbye to walk out the door buttoning my shirt. On the wall by the front door, I noticed a framed portrait of a couple that beckoned me to look closer. What I saw stopped me in my tracks. It appeared to be a photo of Valentina and me, holding hands and smiling at a national park.

"Who is this guy in this photo with you, Valentina?" I asked. "He looks like me."

She laughed, "You silly Papi...that is you. We took that photo the last time you were here. We went to the park to see the spider monkeys and the squirrel monkeys. Don't you remember?"

Looking dazed but realizing I had to go, I said, "Yeah, okay...see you later" and rushed out the door.

My mind felt cloudy, and I was feeling like I was either dreaming or still drunk from the night before. I must have a twin somewhere because there is no way I'd been here before, and no way I wouldn't remember meeting someone like Valentina. It was definitely not possible that I wanted to visit a park to see spider monkeys or squirrel monkeys. I decided I needed to talk to George to find out what was happening. I was beginning to feel like I was in the Twilight Zone.

* * * *

I managed to show up for work on time. I arrived soon enough to take part in a briefing that George was giving to the other male team members. At the conclusion of the briefing, George added,

"So, we've only got two more days to go, and I'm expecting everyone to accomplish the specific goals we came here to do... understand?"

"George, can I have a word with you away from the team," I said as I raised my hand.

"Sure Wade, I'm done here so let's go over there. What's on your mind" asked George as we walked away from the others.

"George, something very strange happened to me last night. Do you remember the girl that thought I was her Papi?" I said.

George laughed and said, "Of course I do, *Papi!*"

"Well, she really believes I am her Papi, but that's impossible because you know I've never been on this island before. She even has a photo with a guy that looks like me at a park looking at monkeys."

George got quiet, rolled his eyes around, and started looking down toward his feet.

"What is it, George?"

"Well, Wade, it's true that you've never been here before, but—" George said.

"But what?" I interrupted. "What are you trying to say?"

"Wade, the reason I'm being sketchy here is because the answer to your question is why we are here on this confidential mission," George replied.

"I don't understand what that has to do with what I just told you about Valentina and what she believes."

George stopped trying to be evasive, looked me dead in my eyes, and said,

"Wade, the other guy is your clone, but you are the real deal, I promise," George said, without laughing.

"What??? What are you talking about, George...how could I have a clone...I don't remember ever agreeing to..."

George interrupted. "Remember two years ago when you got sick and spent three days in the hospital in Houston?" George asked.

"Yeah, but what does that have to do with anything!" I exclaimed.

"When you signed the paperwork for them to run tests on you, you also authorized the doctors to take an extra tube of your blood," said George.

"What?"

"Furthermore," George continued, "the tube of blood was used to send to the doctors of a secret government program called DNA Acceleration and Regeneration at Hermann Hospital...and they were successful in cloning you. The other Papi that Valentina knows is really you, but not actually you... understand?"

I opened my mouth wide in disbelief at what George was saying. I kept waiting for him to break out laughing any minute and say, "Got you! I'm just busting your chops," but he didn't.

"But who else knows about this? Do the other guys on the team have clones too?" I asked.

Without batting an eye, George answered, "Yes, but they don't know it, either."

"Dang, how could this happen... This is wrong, George."

"Not really, Wade." George laughed. "After all, you know who we work for, and you know our agency is shrouded in secrecy. That's why you were selected for this team. You've got some great DNA, and the government has been cloning people for years. I have a clone living in Spain and one in Turkey, too."

"Will I ever see or meet my other self?"

"No, that is strictly forbidden. And Valentina will never know there are two of you either. When your clone was here last time, he took samples of Valentina's DNA and they put hers on a growth acceleration fast track," George said with a straight face.

I felt sick and didn't know what else to say. George told me to go do my job and forget about everything else. I obeyed his command and walked away to go to work.

The team concluded our work and prepared to leave the following day. I wanted desperately to see Valentina again, but George forbade me to do so. For some reason, I had grown to like her a lot and was developing a crush. Unfortunately, I was unable to relay any of that information to her because we were headed back to Texas before I knew it. I hated that I would never see her again.

During the plane ride home, I remembered how easy it felt being with Valentina. I had never felt that relaxed before. Although I had dated a few girls in Houston, none of them ever gave me a goat's milk bath. I banged my head against the window on the plane because I was unable to get to know Valentina better; I think I had fallen for her.

* * * *

A few days went by, and I felt unsettled and unable to get back into work in Houston. I was still unhappy with the way I found out about our secret DNA clone program. I needed a break from work to clear my head after returning from Costa Rica. I decided to put in a leave slip for a few days of vacation so I called my cousin Ruben in Manhattan and asked if I could visit him for a few days. Manhattan was very different from both Houston and Costa Rica, but I remembered it was on an island like Costa Rica.

When my plane arrived in New York at LaGuardia, Ruben was there to pick me up in his Mercedes. Ruben was a swanky Wall Street lawyer with a Rolex wristwatch that cost more than my car. Looking sad and dejected, I couldn't discuss my secret government work with Ruben, and he knew better than to ask me any questions about my work. For the first few days, I lazily lounged around his penthouse apartment and constantly thought about Valentina while he was at work.

On the weekend, Ruben suggested we go to a new hot spot in Manhattan where the women were off the hook. I eagerly agreed and felt I needed to clear my head with a new and different environment. I couldn't get Costa Rica out of my head.

When we got to the club, the music was pumping, the drinks were flowing, and the girls were as gorgeous as my cousin had said. Ruben was a great dancer and he loved to get out on the dance floor and prance; I mainly liked to sit at the bar and babe watch.

I ordered a light beer and was just about to put the bottle to my mouth when I spotted this beautiful girl from across the room who looked very familiar. I set the beer bottle on the bar and walked over to get a closer look.

She was wearing a tight, shiny blue dress with heels and a familiar body. Her raven-black hair flowed in the wind as she bounced on the dance floor. When she turned around and faced my direction, I almost had a heart attack. It was Valentina.

I walked up to her and said, "Valentina?"

She stopped dancing long enough to answer, "No, my name is Tracee, not Valentina...sorry!"

I just stood there and looked at her dumbfounded as she continued to dance alone. She had to notice how I kept staring at her without moving an inch. Then I said,

"Tracee, please forgive me, but you..."

"I know," she interrupted, "I look just like someone you know. I've heard that pickup line many times before." She laughed and kept on dancing to "I'm Every Woman" by Chaka Khan.

"No, no," I said, "That was not a pickup line. I'm serious. I do know someone who looks exactly like you. My name is Wade Randall, and I'm here from Houston visiting my cousin," I said with a smile.

Tracee stopped dancing and carefully looked me up and down as if she was measuring me for size or something. Then, with her New York accent, she said,

"Well, if that was not your pickup line, it should have been, because I like what I see."

I smiled and returned the favor by admiring and acknowledging her hourglass figure.

Then, she said, "I'm Tracee Costa... I was born and raised here on Manhattan Island... I love to dance...and this is my spot."

Without skipping a beat or missing another opportunity, I quickly said, "Okay, Tracee, why don't you let me buy you a drink so we can get to know each other better? And then, if you're okay with it...I can invite you back to my spot."

"Oooh, let's talk about that…and by the way, what's so enticing at your spot?" she flirtingly asked as she smiled and grabbed my hand as if we were old friends and lovers.

I answered, "Music, wine, dancing, and…"

She interrupted, "Wade, have you ever had a bath in goat's milk before?"

I lied and quickly answered, "No," because I wanted to have a repeat bath experience with Valentina's clone. I was ready to drink a glass of goat's milk if she asked me to.

I knew then we were either going to her place at some point or we had to stop and buy some goat's milk on the way to a hotel. I tried to get Ruben's attention on the dance floor, but he was having way too much fun.

Tracee then asked me what kind of work I did, and I jokingly told her I was an undercover body mechanic who specialized in tune-ups, front-end alignments, and oil changes.

She laughed hysterically while caressing my arm as we walked toward the bar. I was expecting to have more sweet umbrella drinks and more fun as we got to know each other better; there was no way I was going to let any trace of Valentina get away from me again. For real and for once, I was going to fall in love.

I then thought to check my weapon to see if it was fully loaded because I suspected I would need a lot of ammunition tonight. I checked. It was cocked and ready to go.

CHAPTER SIX

"REINCARNATION OF A ROMANCE"

When I learned my girlfriend Erica had died in a car accident, I wanted to die, too. Every Sunday I would put fresh flowers on her grave; the ones from the week before wilted and drooped from a loss of vigor just like me. She loved sunflowers almost as much as I loved her; nonetheless, the heat from the sun withered the flowers away every week.

I had never considered suicide before and wondered what it would feel like. I no longer wanted to live after my soulmate, Erica Jane, died and left me all alone. We had planned to be married after we graduated from college, but now I would never get to hold her hand or smell her perfumed hair again.

I was ready to die now and imagined it would be like playing hooky from life without ever having to go to school again. I hated to disappoint my parents and my friends, but I felt lifeless and wanted to just disappear.

All my friends noticed the dark clouds constantly over my head and tried their best to help me in any way they could. Thinking they could cheer me up, they invited me to a campus fraternity party. I really didn't want to attend the party, but they kept saying,

"C'mon Danny, you'll have fun. There'll be plenty of food and girls!"

I wasn't in the mood for fun or food and I didn't want to meet another girl. All I wanted was Erica back, but I knew that was impossible. Every time I'd mention her name, my friends would respectfully remind me that it had been a year since she'd left and it was time for me to move ahead.

"She didn't just leave," I'd always snap back. "She died and she's not coming back, ever."

"Okay, but there's nothing you could have done, Danny. She had an accident, and you can't go on feeling sorry for yourself forever. Let it go, man, and let her rest in peace. There's no reason to live the rest of your life dying," said my best friend, Richard.

Deep inside I knew they were all right. Maybe that's why I relented and went to the stupid party anyway. But a moment after I arrived, I wished I hadn't come. All college fraternity parties were the same old stuff. The house was jam-packed with students I didn't know, and the speakers were vibrating off the walls with loud dance music. I was not in the mood to mingle and dance at all.

I saw guys huddled along the walls, rehearsing the lines they planned to use on the girls, and the girls were excitedly running in and out of the ladies' room giggling and rehearsing their planned responses to the lines they hoped to hear. It seemed everybody came to party except me.

Pushing my way through the crowd, I made it to the refreshment table. Just to be sociable, I chomped down a few chips and gulped a glass of punch. Looking at my wristwatch, I decided to give it five more minutes before I bounced.

Just then I felt the strangest sensation I was being watched, but I didn't know by whom. I wondered if they had spiked the punch with something. My eyes scanned the room to see if I could spot anybody looking at me. From across the room, I saw a cute girl quickly look away when she thought I was looking in her direction. I waited until she looked back in my direction, and I watched her eyes dance away to avoid my stare. The more I looked, the more beautiful she became.

When she looked again, our eyes seemed to be in sync. My eyes penetrated her skin to see her shy, illusive soul. It was so weird and uncanny. My heart felt funny, and it started to develop a crush on this beautiful, familiar stranger. She made me wonder if I'd gotten mixed up in another world somehow with people I've known in a different life. It was my first time seeing her, but I could have sworn I'd loved her before.

Trying to get closer to her without being too obvious, I casually made my way in toward her through the crowd. Although the house was full, no one else saw our private stares or our supernatural connection. She froze without moving until I reached where she was standing.

In a surprise moment, we were actually meeting at a very common place. A place no architect could design with wood or stone, but a very special place somewhere deep within our hearts. When we finally got close enough to touch, her hand gently reached out and grabbed mine. We quietly stood together holding hands and not wanting to let each other go.

Holding her generated so much warmth and electricity inside me that I began to perspire. Everyone else seemed to magically disappear and nothing or no one else mattered.

Never uttering a word to each other, we danced to a slow song and our feet were already familiar with the movements. Our bodies moved like they were possessed, and our hearts kept perfect time like a two-faced clock. With fingers that felt like they belonged to a concert pianist, she touched my face and caused my broken heart to play and to heal.

I smelled her perfume and my nose recognized the fragrance; the way she smiled let me know that I was right. She then rested her head on my shoulder in a familiar way, and I naturally secured my arms around her waist.

I had never felt so strange in all my life. It was both eerie and wonderful to feel like I was falling in love all over again with someone I'd just met. She knew me and I knew her. We never exchanged names because we both knew. We were far too familiar with each other for this to have been a coincidence.

When the music stopped playing, we kept right on dancing and swaying our bodies to the melody inside our hearts. No one else seemed to care that we continued to dance alone. Now they all knew we were in love.

I wasn't sure if it was proper to kiss her on our first date, but I felt I'd kissed her many times before. The way she looked into my eyes made me know that it was alright. When we kissed, our lips parted as if to allow our spirits to come forth and reunite within each other. We became a part of each other, yet separate.

At first the kisses were soft and wet, and then they became slow and long. When my lips finally left her mouth, I kept my eyes closed. I was imagining an instant replay, trying to make the moment last forever. When I opened my eyes, she had the same look of self-confidence in her eyes too. We both knew without a doubt at that moment what this was.

"What a great party," I shouted out to Richard as we kept dancing. He smiled and waved his hand as he watched me change in front of his eyes and return to the best friend he knew. His eyes said, "Danny's back!"

After the party began to break up, I sensed it was time for her to go, but no way was I going to lose her again. I touched her face to assure her I would never leave her side, and she smiled with her eyes to let me know she knew.

We stood for a moment and just stared in each other's eyes to be sure this was no dream. It was so strange; it seemed we only needed a few moments to renew a lifetime of loving each other.

I turned and waved at my friends, thanking them for inviting us. We then clasped hands and walked outside into the fairytale moonlight. We looked up and saw a full moon with a smile on its face. The man in the moon winked at us.

I unlocked the door to my car and held the door open for her to get inside. She got in, and together, we cruised off into the moonlight, sitting extremely close to each other and feeling very good. Driving over the hill in my orange Volkswagen Beetle, we must have looked like two enchanted lovers leaving a supernatural ball in a huge, magical pumpkin. I knew then that we both had been given a second chance, and our love had been reincarnated.

CHAPTER SEVEN

"EAVESDROPPING ON A LOVE LETTER"

When I was in college, I was a proud member of *The Dead Man's Suit Fraternity*.

I was a poor, struggling student who could not afford to buy a suit at regular prices. My parents were not rich and were barely able to cover my full tuition. I had to get an on-campus job with a Work Study Program in order to supplement what my folks could pay.

While reading the newspaper one day, I came across an announcement regarding an estate sale that was close to the college campus. Having more curiosity than money, I decided to walk over to the nearby house. When I arrived, I met a silver-haired lady who proudly introduced herself as Mrs. Celestine Palmer, a widow. She said her husband, the late Mr. Lawrence Palmer, was the reason for the estate sale. She pointed to a distinctive portrait of a well-suited man with a glint in his eyes. Mrs. Palmer modestly bragged she and Mr. Palmer had been happily married for over 50 years. All of the proceeds of the estate sale were being donated to his favorite charity.

I introduced myself as Leon Willis, a student at the nearby college. Mrs. Palmer looked me up and down carefully with a gentle smile and told me to take my time browsing around. I smiled back and said, "Thank you." By the look of everything at the house, the man had been fairly well-off. Subsequently, I learned he had been an attorney.

I came across a clothes rack full of expensive-looking suits. As I looked closely at them, I noted that all the suits were tailor-made and had the deceased man's name stitched on the inside. The more I looked at the suits, I surmised that the dead man and I were about the same size and possibly wore the same size suit. I wondered if that was why Mrs. Palmer had looked at me the way she did with a smile.

Realizing I would never be able to afford a suit like those, I asked Mrs. Palmer how much she wanted for the suits. She told me she was going to ask $100 each for them, but she would let me have them for $10 each. Astonished, I asked her to hold the suits until tomorrow and I would return with the money.

I ran back to the dorm and rounded up all my friends. The next day, we all went back and purchased the whole suit rack. For me, the suit fit perfectly, but the others had to get simple alterations made so that they could fit them properly. We all turned this one experience into a regular thing by commonly searching newspapers for estate sales. Soon, we became known as the best-dressed men on campus and jokingly dubbed ourselves *The Dead Man's Suit Fraternity.*

Before walking away from the sale, I noticed a stack of old books. I actually found some real classics and most of them cost about twenty-five cents each. I loved reading and ended up with about ten books that came to only $2.50. I was in heaven and couldn't wait to take them back to the dorm and start reading them.

One day during the week, I picked up one of the books, a book of poetry that looked very old and interesting. It smelled a little musty and its back cover was torn from wear. I opened the book and out fell a folded-up piece of paper onto the floor. I picked it up, opened it, and realized it was a handwritten letter dated Wednesday, March 29, 1967.

Scanning the letter with my eyes, I quickly understood I was holding a long-lost love letter that had not been mailed to its intended party. I was unaware if the letter had intentionally not been mailed or if it had just been forgotten. The handwriting was legible and strong, and it carried an urgency with it.

I sat on my bed and began to read the letter to myself. The letter read:

Dear Katherine,

I hope this letter finds you well and rested. Our moonlight rendezvous last night proved to be a fitting end to our ill-fated beginning. Due to our current circumstances, we can no longer continue in this manner.

Although it will break my heart and cause a deep void within me, I have to leave you my dear and never see you again. My sanity has become brittle and my soul feels like it is on the offering plate. Please allow me to submit this final, sensuous missive to you.

This letter is dressed in black and laced with poetic imagery to remind you of the forbidden love that we have made. It is necessary for me to leave so that each of us can get on with our obligated lives – if that makes any sense at all. Living, I thought, is what life is all about. I guess life sometimes has different connotations and motivations for some, especially in our special case. We each have vowed to love others in front of God. Yet, behind their backs, we have flirted with Satan once too many.

I have to leave you, for to love you like this would mean that someone else would not have all that is rightfully his. And you have to leave me also, for to stay would mean to wrongly share my love and my guilt for this – our illicit covenant.

I don't know why fate allowed us to meet like this at this time. Whether this is heavenly or sinful, I am not certain. We met for a reason but I can't sort through the silver or the sulfur to see which side the scale leans to for me to be sure.

But I do know that I will never forget you or what you gave me through knowing your soul for this brief and small grain of time. Your place is deeply embedded in my heart, although leaving is so hard and hurting. We were happy together.

Bridges burn quickest when made of paper or wood; the most difficult bridge to burn is one constructed of that rare, human-contrived steel called love. And if we never meet our special way again, we'll always have the memory and the legacy of the time

when we were made as one – natural, harmonious, and a cappella – without any musical instruments other than the human touch.

There is nothing more intimate or sexier than a handwritten note to the one you love. Sometimes store-bought cards seem impersonal and quick; they can't express what we really feel. However, a handwritten love note preserves the feeling and the scent of love.

I love you but I cannot bear to ever see you again. Please know that I'm leaving my heart folded within the pages of this letter just for you.

With all my love,
Lawrence

I didn't know what to think. It was clear that the man who wrote the letter was in love because it seemed painful for him to write. Love letters are a thing of the past, as evidenced by the date on the letter. I looked at the man's signed name again, and it hit me where I had recognized it.

I jumped up from my bed and went straight to my closet; I wanted to check the name stitched inside the estate sale suit I had purchased. I located the suit and looked at the name. The name inside the suit was Lawrence Palmer.

But who was Katherine? The contradiction was clear: Mrs. Palmer's first name was Celestine. I spent the rest of the day trying to process what I had read without making any judgments.

I came to the conclusion that falling in love is a huge sacrifice, especially when you are married to someone else. I would never know the real story behind the love letter from Lawrence to Katherine, and it was really none of my business.

I decided to burn the letter so that no one else could ever find it and face this same dilemma I was experiencing. But before I burned the letter, I read it over in its entirety once again. I focused on parts in particular that made me smile:

> "We were happy together. Bridges burn quickest when made of paper or wood; the most difficult bridge to burn is one constructed of that rare, human-contrived steel called love."

Something now was telling me not to burn the letter and to dig deeper into the significance of why I was chosen to find it. Being a criminal justice major, my curiosity was raging to solve the mystery.

I researched the major events of the day on the internet for March 29, 1967, and learned that the number one song in America at that time was a song by the American rock band The Turtles called "Happy Together."

I then searched for the song and listened intently to the lyrics. I was sure that Lawrence knew the lyrics too and included the reference in his letter for a specific reason. It was clear he loved Katherine and she made him very happy when they were together, but there was something else there. They both knew that their love was taboo, and they had to keep it hidden forever.

Who was Katherine and what ever happened to her? There was no way that I was going to easily find enough public information to locate an unknown person named Katherine from fifty years ago. I didn't even have a last name.

* * * *

A month or so went by, and I was getting busier with my schoolwork. I had a research paper that was due in my English class with Dr. Vasser. She'd quickly become one of my favorite professors due to her longevity at the college and her intimate knowledge of so many things outside of English class. She had a pretty face, and one could easily tell she had been a beautiful girl growing up and originated from a good family. Her husband also worked at the college in the administrative office as the dean of financial aid, a stuffier position than a college professor.

On a whim, I stopped by Dr. Vasser's office to see if she was in and could clarify the research paper I'd been assigned. I knocked on her door and she answered, "Come in." Once she saw it was me, her face lit up and she said, "Hi, Mr. Willis, please come in."

That was another thing I liked about her. She always referred to her students as either Mr. or Miss, which made us feel like she equally respected us. Other professors usually called us by our first names.

"Dr. Vasser," I said, "I was hoping that you could clarify our research assignment a bit for me. Are we allowed to use research we obtain from both the library and the internet?"

"Why yes, Mr. Willis, you can use either or both together. There's nothing wrong with using the internet as long as you can verify your sources. In my day, we didn't have anything like the internet." She laughed and took her glasses off to clean them.

I returned her smile and said, "Thank you, Dr. Vasser," as I started to walk away. Then I quickly spun around and thought that I might pose another question to her regarding the letter I found in the book.

"Dr. Vasser," I asked, "how would I go about locating information on someone in the past if I only have scant details about them?"

"Well, that's difficult to say. It depends on what kind of information you are seeking. Is this a local person or someone from out of state?"

"Actually, I'm not entirely sure, but I think the person could be a local...well, at least they were about fifty years ago," I replied.

Dr. Vasser put her glasses back on. "I think you are going to have a difficult time researching someone unless you can find some more intimate details about the person you are searching for."

When she said *intimate details*, I thought about the love letter I had found, but I dared not say anything to her about that, especially since the details were so intimate.

I smiled at her again and turned to walk away, saying, "Thank you," as I opened her door to walk out.

Behind me, I heard her pleasant voice say, "You are welcome, Mr. Willis. Drop by again if you need my help."

* * * *

While doing research on my assigned English topic in the library for the paper that was due, I remembered an off comment that Dr. Vasser had said while I was in her office: "In my day, we didn't have anything like the internet."

So, I thought, if things like the internet and Facebook were not around in 1967, what did people use to search for others? The phone book was the first thing that popped into my head, but I knew that would be a real long shot and last resort with hundreds of people named Katherine in it.

The word "book" stuck in my mind as I looked around at the thousands of books in the library; then it finally hit me. What if Katherine had been a student at that time attending college here, and her photo is located in one of the school's yearbooks?

I thought my idea was brilliant and began searching for past copies of the college's annuals. The school's name for the yearbooks had remained the same all these years: *The Catamount*, which was a cross between a mountain lion and a bobcat.

I located the shelves for the past annuals and started with the ones beginning in the 1960s. It struck me as funny as I looked at the books lined up by years in different sizes, colors, and smells. I laughed to myself when I realized I was looking at a bunch of smelly old Catamounts for a girl named Katherine whom Lawrence had written to say, "A handwritten love note preserves the feeling and the scent of love."

I took my time going through the books, carefully looking at the names under the photos of all the girls. There were plenty of

"Catherines" but not that many "Katherines." The yearbook for 1967 had only two girls named Katherine; there was Katherine DiAngelo and Katherine Greenwood.

I went through all the past annuals from 1960 to 1970, theorizing that one decade of books should be sufficient if Katherine had been a student during that time. I finished with thirty-three girls named Katherine during that period. I then Xeroxed all the girl's photos at the nearby copier and took them back to my dorm room for further study.

With a list of possible suspects, I then searched for each name using the internet to see if I could locate any current information about these names. After spending about an hour scouring the web, I found obituaries for twenty of the Katherines, which made me feel sad to know. It left me with the possibility that the Katherine I needed to find may be in that deceased number.

The remaining thirteen names were scattered throughout the country, with most of them relocating after college and never returning to the area. I may have glossed over Lawrence's Katherine without even realizing it. Although I started with a good idea, I had not made any real headway in finding the mysterious Katherine, whom I now nicknamed Katherine Doe, like the infamous Jane Doe. I gave up and went back to working on my research paper.

* * * *

Over the next month, I put my search for Katherine on the back burner and decided that would be something I could do over the summer when school was out. I turned in my research paper and received a "B+" from Dr. Vasser. I was okay with my grade after realizing I would have done better if I had not gotten sidetracked by my other research.

Then, after passing out all the papers, Dr. Vasser made an announcement to our class. She said that she would be retiring at the end of the semester after fifty-three years of teaching at the college. She laughed when she reminisced that she had just been a young graduate student when she began teaching here; she said she graduated from

Harvard and moved here to be with her husband, Frank Vasser, the dean of financial aid.

Many of us, especially me, were saddened by her announcement, but we respected her enough to be happy for her. I went up to her after class and gave her my personal congratulations. She thanked me and said that it was time, and that both she and her husband were retiring together and moving to Maine.

At the end of the semester, the college scheduled a very nice retirement party for Dr. Vasser. It put on a huge public celebration with food and music. Both faculty and students were invited to say farewell to Dr. Vasser. The biggest surprise came when the college chancellor announced the college was naming a new girls' dorm after Dr. Vasser.

It blew me away when the chancellor said, "We are proud to name our new female dormitory after our own Dr. Katherine Vasser."

While others clapped and cheered wildly, I froze like a mummy. I could not believe it. All these years, I had only called her Dr. Vasser and never thought she also had a first name. And in my yearbook search for Katherines, I did not think to look at faculty members. Wow, I thought, could Dr. Vasser be the Katherine that Lawrence Palmer wrote about?

* * * *

The next day, I went back to the library and found the yearbook for 1967-68. I looked at the faculty and there she was: Dr. Katherine Vasser, a first-year professor in the English department. It was unbelievable. She was beautiful with long hair that covered her shoulders; the photo was black and white, so I could not determine her real hair color, but her smile was luminous.

The chances that I had found the right Katherine had narrowed significantly. I fantasized about the way she and Mr. Palmer had met. Mr. Palmer, being a handsome young attorney, probably saw Katherine walking on campus, or maybe she came to his office to get something notarized and he saw her then. The ideas of how they met were endless, but the end itself had come in a love letter that touted a love that was endless, too.

I was beside myself and wanted to know if Dr. Vasser was, in fact, Katherine Doe. I tried to devise a way to secretly find out if Dr. Vasser ever knew Lawrence Palmer, but there was no easy way without getting caught. I liked Dr. Vasser way too much to reveal to her that I believed she had been unfaithful to her husband at one point. And then there was the dilemma of whether I should show her Mr. Palmer's letter after all these years. Surely, that could backfire on me big time, even if I thought I was doing the right thing.

I went home and picked up the book of poetry that I had found the letter within. I never even thought to look at the book's title to get a clue for a connection to the letter. The name of the book was *Leaves of Grass* by Walt Whitman, first published in 1855. A quick search on the internet revealed to me that "Whitman's book was controversial when it was published because it was notable for its discussion of delight in sensual pleasure during a time when such candid displays were considered immoral."

Mr. Lawrence must have been very familiar with the poetry in Whitman's book when he wrote his letter to Katherine or Dr. Vasser if it was her. His love letter was very lyrical and sensuous, like poetry; he must have admired Whitman to try to copy his style. One of the lines in his letter to Katherine actually read, "Please allow me to submit this final, sensuous missive to you."

Everything was beginning to come together and make sense, especially if it turned out that I was right about my suspicions. I decided that if I could verify that Dr. Vasser and Katherine were one and the same, I would try to find a way to surreptitiously give her the book with the letter inside as a going-away present; however, I would not connect myself to the book in any way.

At Dr. Vasser's retirement celebration, I decided to go on a fishing expedition; if my little trick worked, I would set my plan into motion. When I went up to Dr. Vasser to wish her well in her retirement, she thanked me and asked me about my plans for the summer.

I told her that I was planning to go home and get a temporary job working with my uncle, who was an attorney in New Orleans.

Dr. Vasser said, "Oh, that would be nice, and it would give you a chance to develop your research skills, Mr. Willis."

And then I threw in my uncle's fake first name just to see her response; of course, this was my fishing expedition plan.

"Yes, Uncle Lawrence has been an attorney for years, and he's told me I could work with him to make some extra money," I said, waiting for her reaction.

It was amazing. Her eyes sparkled, and her face glowed with a reminiscent smile.

She said, "Your uncle's name is Lawrence? I once knew someone named Lawrence who was an attorney, but that was many years ago before you were born."

After I received my confirmation, I quickly changed the subject so as to not arouse any suspicion.

"Well, I really hope you enjoy your retirement, Dr. Vasser, and I am going to miss you so much since you are my favorite teacher," I said. I walked away to let the others congratulate her.

Now that I had confirmed that Dr. Vasser was the same Katherine in Mr. Palmer's letter, I needed to figure out how to deliver his love letter to her without tying it back to me. In thinking about it, I really was not sure if it was the right thing to do or not. What if I gave her the book and she never found the letter inside, or what if her husband Frank found the letter first? Furthermore, what if the letter threw her into a state of depression or guilt about her illicit affair and her indiscretion?

In the end, I decided to give Dr. Vasser the rare book as a going-away gift minus the love letter. I did not want to take the chance of ruining her happiness in her retirement. I wrapped the book and dropped it by her office later that day; I wrote a note that said I had found Whitman's book of poetry at a garage sale and thought she might like it. I provided my return address in case she wanted to stay in touch.

At the beginning of the new school year, I received a handwritten thank you note in the mail from Dr. Vasser, who was now living in

Maine. She had a beautiful handwriting, and I was touched to get it. The note read:

Dear Mr. Willis,

Thank you for your kind, rare gifts of poetry and of your friendship. I am very familiar with Whitman's book as I had read it many years ago as a young graduate student. In fact, a close friend of mine used to read poems from the book to me. The book brought back many pleasant memories that I had long forgotten. Thank you for reawakening in me something I had relinquished.

"Bridges burn quickest when made of paper or wood; the most difficult bridge to burn is one constructed of that rare, human-contrived steel called love."

Your friend,
Dr. Katherine Vasser

CHAPTER EIGHT

"LOCKER GIRL 2: WHAT'S HER NAME?"

Believe it or not, but I plan to ask Locker Girl to go on a date with me. At least, I thought I might. I realized I didn't know her real name, so I needed to find that out before I asked her.

After she left her perfumed note in my locker, I decided I would look inside her locker to see if I could find anything with her name on it. I spotted a biology book and opened it real fast. I saw the name Mary Ann Dobson written in cursive on the top left side of the book. I quickly closed it and slammed her locker shut before anyone could see me.

I smiled as I thought how pretty and feminine her handwriting was. I loved the way she swirled her letters to make it look like she had a famous signature. I couldn't wait to tell my best friend Billy what I was planning. Billy and I had been friends since kindergarten, and I knew I could trust him with all my secrets.

In P.E. class after lunch, I spotted Billy in the locker room. I moved over to him and punched him on the shoulder with a playful hit. He saw the grin on my face and asked me what was up.

"Man, I've got something to tell you, but you can't breathe a word to anyone about it," I whispered.

"Okay, man, you know me... I won't say a word. What is it?" Billy asked.

I tried to keep my voice down, but I blurted out, "I'm asking Mary Ann Dobson out on a date." Thank goodness there was no one else in the locker room but us.

Billy looked at me and said, "Are you serious... MARY ANN DOBSON?"

"Yeah, man, but I haven't asked her yet. I plan to do that tomorrow." I grinned.

Billy was still stunned by my news, and he just kept looking at me in amazement.

"Man, are you sure you want to do that?" Billy asked in a weird tone.

"Yeah, why not? She's a girl and I'm a guy. I think she likes me and would say yes. She left a note in my locker to say that I was handsome," I bragged.

"Mary Ann Dobson left a note in your locker to say that you are handsome?"

"Yeah! I'm not lying. I'd show you the note, but I keep it at home in a secret place."

"Okay, if that's what you want to do, it's okay with me. I hope you guys have a great time together," Billy said as he got dressed and went outside to the gym floor.

I finished getting dressed too and followed right behind him.

* * *

The next morning, I got to my locker early, hoping to meet Locker Girl there. As luck would have it, I saw her standing next to her locker, getting ready to open it.

I walked up behind her and said, "Hi!"

She turned and replied, "Hi back" with a smile.

I then looked down, trying to find the right words to ask her out. She looked at me and asked, "Is something wrong?"

I said, "No, I was just wondering...wondering if...I mean..."

"Are you trying to ask me out on a date?" Locker Girl interrupted.

"Uh, no... I mean, yes, I was wondering if you would like to go on a date."

"With you?" she asked.

"Oh, yes, with me," I nervously replied.

She said, "Okay, but aren't you going to ask me my name first?"

"Uh, your name? Yes, I already know your name…it's Mary Ann Dobson," I said assuredly.

"MARY ANN DOBSON?" she angrily asked. "Where did you get that from?"

"Uh, I looked in your locker and saw your name written in your biology book."

She said, "That was not my biology book! I borrowed that book from another classmate because I left mine at home. My name is ASHLEY CHRISTOPHER!"

I got that deer-in-the-headlights look again and said, "Uh, oh… I'm sorry. I made a mistake. I just thought…well, I would still like to take YOU out, Ashley."

She just looked at me and didn't say another word. Then she walked away without confirming if she would go out with me after my foul-up.

I yelled after her, "Uh, my name is…"

"EDDIE MURPHY!" she yelled back.

"Uh, no, it's DARYL… DARYL JARRETT."

She kept on walking.

* * *

I ran home after school to get to Billy's house to make sure he had kept our secret. When he came to the door, I said, "Man, let me in. We need to talk."

"What's up," he said as he walked me back to his room.

"Uh, you didn't tell anyone about our little secret, did you?"

"What secret?" Billy asked with a funny look on his face.

"The one about me asking Mary Ann Dobson out on a date," I said.

"Er, I mean…I may have said something to Greg about it, but…"

"You told loud-mouthed Greg Dickens about our secret?"

"Well, not really told him…I just said I thought Mary Ann Dobson was going on a date with my best friend," Billy said, looking at the ground.

"But Billy, everyone knows we are best friends!"

Billy said, "But Daryl, you acted like you were happy to be going out with Mary Ann. What's the problem if I told a few people?"

"The problem is that I made a huge mistake. I thought the girl's name I was asking out was Mary Ann Dobson, but that's not her name at all. Her name is Ashley Christopher," I exclaimed.

"ASHLEY CHRISTOPHER? But she's one of the prettiest girls in the whole school. Are you serious…. you sure about that?"

"Yes, her locker is right next to mine. I asked her today, thinking her name was Mary Ann Dobson because I looked inside her biology book to learn her name. Turns out the book belonged to Mary Ann Dobson, not Ashley Christopher," I explained.

"HOLY SMOKES, that's not good," Billy said.

"If the word gets out that I plan to ask someone other than Ashley out on a date, I'm going to be in big trouble. I don't even know what Mary Ann Dobson looks like."

Looking down at the ground again, Billy said, "Er, Daryl, let's just say Mary Ann Dobson does not look anything like Ashley Christopher… not even close. But she might not look too bad if she lost some of the tattoos on her arms."

"What?"

"Man, that's why I couldn't believe it when you first told me that you were asking her out on a date. You may recall the look on my face and my asking you if you were serious," Billy stated.

"I do recall that, but I just thought you were jealous or something," I said.

"Jealous? No, man, I was thinking different strokes for different folks. Mary Ann Dobson was all yours."

* * *

I waited at my locker the next morning to try to explain to Ashley exactly what happened. I waited for an extremely long time, but she never came. The bell rang, and I had to go to my first class without seeing her.

As soon as I walked into the classroom, everyone started clapping. Greg Dickens stood up and said, "Here's the man of the hour himself."

Darlene Jackson shot me a middle finger and said, "You dirty dog, you. I can't believe you treated my best friend like that."

Having no idea what she meant, I said, "What are you talking about?"

"Everyone in the school is talking about you and Mary Ann Dobson going out on a date together. How could you diss my girl Ashley like that? You know she likes you," Darlene exclaimed.

"Uh, but I didn't… I mean, I never asked Mary…"

"You liar!" said Darlene. "Billy Scott told my boyfriend that you told him you were asking Mary Ann Dobson out."

"But I don't even know Mary…"

"Liar, liar, pants on fire," Darlene interrupted. "Ashley stayed home from school today because of you." Darlene shot him another middle finger.

"But I…"

"Sit down and take your seat, Daryl Jarrett," said Mr. Reese, the teacher. All the girls booed me as I walked to my seat. Greg Dickens booed me, too.

* * *

After school, I was desperate to contact Ashley to apologize for the mix-up. I didn't know where she lived or her phone number. The only thing I could do was write her a letter in hopes that she might get it from her locker. It took five pages to complete the letter and explain everything in detail. I was sure I had covered everything, including how Billy let the cat out of the bag by mistake. I sprinkled some of my dad's Midnight Madness cologne on the letter and put it in a long white envelope.

I got to school a half-hour early the next day so I could sneak the letter into her locker. Ashley must have had the same idea because I met her at our lockers and she had a white envelope in her hand.

"Ashley," I said. "I am so sorry for the mix-up. I never wanted to ask anyone else out but you. I had never even heard of Mary Ann Dobson before I saw her name in that book, and I've never even been on a date with a girl before. I made an honest mistake because I was trying to impress you with knowing your name. I should have just asked you!"

"Yes, you should have, Daryl," Ashley said.

"So, can we start over? I'd like to ask you to go out...with me."

Ashley smiled. "Well, Greg Dickens did ask me to go out with him after he learned you were going out with Mary Ann Dobson."

"What? Did you tell Greg you were going on a date with him?"

"Not exactly...but I did tell him I wanted to go on a date."

"With whom?"

"I told him I wanted to go out with Eddie Murphy...but if Eddie was unavailable, I wanted to go with you, Daryl Jarrett."

I smiled, looked at the white envelope in my hand, and tore it in half. Copying my exact move, Ashley did the same thing with her letter.

Since it was still early and no one was around, Ashley came close to me and kissed me on the mouth. I surprised myself and stepped forward to kiss her back.

We held each other close only for a second. Then she asked me for a favor.

"You name it," I said.

"Can I be your Locker Girl?"

"Yes, and I'll be your Locker Boy."

"Thanks, Locker Boy. Can't wait for our first date."

CHAPTER NINE

"CAROL, MY FELINE LOVE"

I have always been indifferent to animals, especially house pets. I was never mean to them, but I mostly just acted like they didn't exist and never saw fit to develop any type of special rapport with them. Although I grew up in rural Alabama, my family could not afford to own and feed any extra mouths, much less dogs, cats, or even goldfish. Rats, mice, roaches, and water bugs didn't count because they normally came with the real estate on our side of town.

When I first met the lady who became my wife in New Jersey in the mid-1980s, I was an adult working for the federal government. She had a huge dog and two cats; I was afraid of them but tried not to let my fear show. My new lady grew up with pets and around pets; she even went to college to become a veterinary technician, where she spent years working with all kinds of animals. She had a unique knack for communicating with them.

When we first met, she briefly told me she had pets and gave me a cursory introduction to them. Frankly, I saw them but I didn't *see* them because I was mainly interested in dating her – not her pets. During the time we were dating, I recall staying over at her place on a work night. She got up early, mentioned something about leaving a key and letting myself out on her way to work, and left me alone with her three feminine four-legged children.

I woke up to see Sigma, Essence, and Chelsea all staring at me as if I were their buffet breakfast. They didn't know me and were unaccustomed to seeing a strange man-person in their habitat. They began to mark their territory by cornering their prey – me.

Essence, a black domestic shorthair and self-appointed spokesperson of the group, stuck her nose in my face to sniff my breath to see if I was drunk or something. I was not and had not been drinking.

Chelsea, the white Maine Coon cat and matriarch of the bunch, sat on my feet to prevent me from getting up and running away. She acted as if she was demanding to know what my intentions were with her mother, my girlfriend.

Sigma, a ninety-pound German Short-Haired Pointer, was the canine intimidator and natural protector; she frightened me with just her looming presence. I needed to get up and go to the bathroom to pee and shower but I was scared all three would attack me and then claim it was self-defense since I was an unwelcomed intruder.

Looking-at-them-looking-at-me, I felt like I could hear their thoughts. I always wondered if animals could talk to each other when humans were not around. Feeling like Dr. Doolittle, I finally got my answer.

As Essence sniffed my face, I imagined she said to the others, "He doesn't smell drunk, but his breath doesn't smell too swift either. He needs to brush his teeth."

"Well, I'm not getting off his feet until he tells us something! I'm not even sure I like him. He doesn't look all that smart to me... Let's scratch him," Chelsea seemed to boss the other two.

"No, let's not get over-anxious here," barked Sigma. "He may look dumb, but he wouldn't still be here if she didn't see something in him."

All got quiet as they kept looking at me. Finally, I couldn't lie there any longer and had to get to the bathroom quickly. I slowly moved my feet to indicate I needed Chelsea to get up so I could get up. She lazily took the hint and moved to the side but kept gazing at me.

I finally spoke to them and said, "Look, I just need to get a shower so I can leave and go to work, too. I'm sorry for any inconvenience, but I was given permission to be here."

Then I felt dumb when I realized I was addressing three pets who all just looked at me with unblinking stares. Suddenly, Sigma moved out of the way so I could go to the bathroom, and the other two acquiesced and stood down from their cold reception.

When I got to the bathroom, I was expecting to see a shower. Instead, there was a white clawfoot bathtub. I had to fill the tub and take a bath, which took a little longer than I wanted. After the bath, I hurriedly got dressed and walked out to see all three lined up by the front door. I wasn't sure if I needed to do or say anything else for them to let me leave.

With quick thinking, I removed my FBI credentials from my pocket and proudly flashed my badge, saying, "I'm with the FBI and I'm one of the good guys… I wouldn't do anything to hurt your mom…or you. Honest, I promise!"

Essence turned her back and walked away toward the kitchen as if to say, "We'll see."

Chelsea looked as if she said, "What makes you think we know or care what the FBI is? It probably stands for Female Body Inspector from what we saw last night."

Sigma barked to indicate she understood I wanted to leave, and she moved so I could walk out the door. Once I got outside, I locked the door and thanked God that I was alright and they didn't attack me.

When we got married in 1990, I was adopted by her three children and they gradually came to accept me. She had mothered these pets for a lifetime. Essence lived to be twenty years old, Chelsea lived to be nineteen, and Sigma lived to be thirteen. They all carried my wife's last name as if she had delivered them at birth. Over time, it was devastating for her to lose her three closest friends and family members. It became obvious that I was her fourth closest family member.

During our marriage, my wife got heavily involved with Spay and Save, an organization that cares for stray and sometimes abused cats to help find them a home. She would routinely use our home to foster cats to get them ready to move in with a willing and compatible family.

My wife housed the cats in an adjacent bedroom near our son's bedroom and would always introduce us to them and tell us their names. Like I said before, I was never really interested in getting to know these furry houseguests because they were all temporary; besides, I couldn't remember all the different names they had. There may have been something slightly wrong with each of them, too. A few may have been crippled, one was blind, a couple were newborns, etc. At any rate, when they left our home, they were always in much better shape after my wife's expert rehabilitative care.

After many years of seeing these cats come and go, my wife brought home this one little brown tabby kitten named Carol, who was also a domestic short hair. I noticed that Carol was very small with wiry hair that literally stood up all over her body. She didn't have a loud voice, but she had a very big attitude and a lot of character. We later learned that Carol had inflammation of the tissues behind her teeth that required many of her teeth to be removed by a veterinarian. As the disease persisted, she had all of her teeth removed.

One evening, my wife had Carol in our bedroom as she played with her on the floor. I was lying in bed watching TV. I didn't mind the cats staying with us, but I had some very strict rules regarding these pets. One, they could not take my last name under any conditions, and two, they could not be in the bed with us – at any time.

My wife assured me that Carol was too small to climb up or jump up on our bed and that I didn't have anything to worry about. We had a California King bed, and it must have seemed like an Egyptian pyramid to Carol. Sometimes, when my wife would take a shower and leave Carol playing on the floor near me, I would look down and see her looking up at me, wondering who I was and what I was doing up there, but she couldn't get to me. She meowed and looked at me with longing, but there was no way she could scale our bed. I smiled and teased her, knowing I was safe from her clutches.

As time went by, Carol seemed to stay longer than most other feline guests, and she grew to be bigger and more agile. We had her for more than a year. During her long stay, my wife took her to many veterinarian appointments. The veterinarian clinic had a file on Carol with her name listed as having my wife's last name; my wife had maintained her maiden name with our marriage. I was okay with that as long as the cat didn't have my last name.

On another occasion, my wife went downstairs to the kitchen and left Carol on the floor in our bedroom while I watched TV. I must have dozed off without realizing it. The next thing I knew, Carol was on our bed trying to gnaw my fingers with her gums since she had no teeth. I woke up and screamed loud enough for my wife to run upstairs to see what was going on. My screams scared Carol, too, because she jumped back down on the floor.

When my wife entered the room, I was alone in bed and she thought I was having a nightmare.

"James, what's wrong with you? I could hear you all the way downstairs," she said.

"Carol got up on the bed somehow and was trying to gnaw my fingers," I exclaimed.

In disbelief, my wife looked down at Carol, who was wearing a halo on her head like a model citizen. Carol looked back at my wife and purred and meowed with, "Nightmare!"

"You must have been dreaming...are you sure Carol was on the bed?" my wife laughed.

"Yes, I'm telling you the truth. Carol was on this bed!"

My wife just shrugged and went back downstairs, saying, "Well, she's a cat and cats can climb... I think she likes you!"

I looked down at Carol, and she looked up at me with a toothless grin. I knew I hadn't imagined that she was on the bed. I waited for her to do it again, but she laid low.

A few nights later, Carol did an instant replay when I had dozed off again. Of course, I yelled again for my wife to come and see. And by the time she got there, Carol had scampered back down to the floor. I gave up trying to convince my wife.

Then, on the weekend, my wife and I were in bed watching TV together. We heard some strange scratching sounds on the side of our bed. We looked over and saw Carol scaling the bed with her sharp claws firmly dug into the bed comforter. So, that was how she was able to get on the bed. Once on the bed, she could jump off, but she had to climb the bed using her claws and our comforter. What a little scamp!

We both realized that Carol had violated one of my strict rules by being on the bed. My wife said to Carol, "Daddy doesn't want you on the bed, so I'm going to have to put you back on the floor."

"Hey, don't tell her I'm her daddy because I'm not," I snapped.

Both of them looked at me. My wife looked like she wanted to reply to my comment, but Carol interrupted her with a loud meow as if to say, "You got that right!"

In the coming weeks and months, Carol learned how to jump on the bed at will. When she did, she came straight for me and started in on my hands and fingers. I didn't know what her fascination was with trying to bite me with no teeth, but it started to get comical and I was beginning to enjoy watching her do it. In fact, I would sometimes come home from work, pick her up, and put her in the bed with me so we could play. She would snuggle up next to me and purr loudly; then, I would let her go under the covers so she could tickle my feet.

I could look at my wife's face and tell that she knew I was violating my own rule by purposely putting Carol in the bed with me, but she didn't say a word. She actually thought it was cute. Carol, on the other hand, acted like she was cheating on my wife and did not want my wife to know that we had developed a deep love for each other. When we were alone, she would snuggle up and love on me like a secret girlfriend, but when my wife walked in, she would quickly scamper away from me as if she didn't even know me. My wife would die laughing when she caught Carol doing that. Carol would just give her that innocent look like, "Hey, I wasn't messing with your man. He pulled me over to ask me something and that was all!"

Soon, it became obvious to both my wife and my son that Carol and I were inseparable and that she was daddy's girl. I couldn't understand it. I found myself falling for Carol like a ton of rocks; she just had a strange effect on me that made me love her like a family member. Carol became the daughter I always wanted, and we were literally wrapped around each other's fingers.

Not long after Carol stole my heart, she became very ill. My wife took her to the vet for an exam, but the news we received was not good. My wife later told me that we were probably going to lose Carol soon. She was used to losing pets over the years, but I was not. My son liked Carol, too, but no one loved Carol like I did.

When I finally got the news that Carol had passed away, I was crushed; my 195-pound body went limp as I thought about how this ten-pound bundle of joy had changed my whole view of animals and pets. However, I did not want another pet; I only wanted Carol.

Rather than have her cremated, we decided to bury Carol in our backyard. The three of us picked the right spot, and I dug the hole. We wrapped her real nicely and placed her in a decorative box. We all began to weep, but I was the loudest. I'm sure our neighbors were trying to figure out what we were doing in the backyard with the freshly dug grave.

I opted to say a few words over Carol and thanked the Lord for her short stay with us. My wife and son placed some small flowers over the top of the grave before we filled the hole. We all went back inside without saying anything. It took a while before we did discuss losing Carol, but we all agreed that she had brightened our whole house when she came.

A few weeks later, my wife came home from work and I couldn't wait to show her and our son what I had purchased. I took them outside to Carol's resting place and pointed to a plaque I had placed on top of her. The plaque read: Here lies our C.A.T. (Carol Ann Thompson).

CHAPTER TEN

"FIRST PROMISE RING"

When I was in high school, promise rings were a big deal. Presenting a promise ring to a girl was akin to a pre-engagement ring about five years before the marriage was expected to occur. Puppy love was a serious matter, and it was not considered to be premature when it came to putting a claim on the one you dreamed of marrying to signify a commitment.

At sixteen, I was deeply in love and had found the girl I was going to spend the rest of my life with. I won't reveal her real name, but it reminded me of Stevie Wonder's most popular love song from the 1970s.

School was out for the summer, and we could spend all our weekends together. Over the weekend, while courting her on a date at her house, we made a covenant with each other to be together for the rest of our lives. We pledged to have a big family that consisted of two girls and two boys. We wrote down the names of each of our children and kept them close to our hearts. Then we pictured our dream house with a white picket fence around it; we added a dog with its own house in our backyard. Strangely, we never discussed getting jobs or how we would finance our dreams.

To seal the deal, we pulled ourselves close and gave each other the start of many eternal kisses. After I opened my eyes from the kisses, I knew what I had to do next. I secretly planned to buy my love her first promise ring to make her forever mine and to make it seem legal.

On Saturday morning, I rushed downtown to Lorch's Jewelry store to look at some rings. I didn't know exactly what to look for because I had no experience with rings and jewelry. The lady behind the counter approached me and offered to help.

Politely, she asked, "Young man, do you need some help?"

"Yes, ma'am, I'd like to look at some rings, please," I proudly replied.

"What kind of ring are you looking for?"

"Uh, I think they call them 'first promise' rings."

"Oh, yes, we have a nice selection over here. What price range would you like to see first?"

"Price range? Uh, I don't know. Something that looks pretty would be nice," I said.

She frowned and said, "Well, all of our rings are pretty. Take a look at these in this case. They start at about $25 and go up from there."

"$25? Uh, do you have anything cheaper...uh, less expensive?" I replied.

The lady took in a deep breath and sighed, "We have a basket full of costume jewelry over there that you can look through. There's some in there for less than $10."

I looked through the basket of rings until my eyes spotted the prettiest one in the bunch. Then I said, "I'll take that one. Can I put it on layaway?"

The lady rolled her eyes and said, "This ring costs $9.95. To put this ring on layaway, you will need to put some money down on it to hold it and then pay weekly payments until it's paid for."

I smiled and pulled out a dollar bill and gave it to the lady.

She said, "A dollar downpayment leaves a balance of about $9, not including tax. We can only hold this for one month, so you will have to pay at least $2 a week to have this paid in full."

I smiled and said, "Okay!"

"What size ring does she wear so that we can size it for you?"

"What size? Uh, I don't know what size. How do I get that?"

"Well, you have to measure her finger because one size does not fit all."

"Uh, okay. I'll bring that in later. Thank you."

"Wait, I need to give you a receipt book. Please bring this with you every time you come so that we can write down your payments."

"Uh, okay, thank you."

I walked away thinking about my love's finger size and wondering how I was going to get that without spoiling the surprise.

* * * *

All week, I tried to figure out a clever way to get my girl's ring finger size without her knowing my plan. When I saw my dad light up a cigar to take a smoke, I came up with a brilliant idea. I would use one of those paper bands around the cigar to place on her finger to get the size; I would make her think I was just playing a joke.

And then I thought, *what if that doesn't work?* I needed a backup plan.

Next, I thought about using one of those aluminum rings found on soda and beer cans. It kind of looked like a ring with a pointed diamond sitting on top.

Armed with both the paper cigar band and soda can ring, I waited for the weekend to go visit my girl.

It weighed heavy on my mind how I was going to make the weekly payments for the ring. I reasoned that I could collect glass bottles and aluminum cans to get money from recycling them. Then, I thought I could get about fifty cents from mowing my aunt's lawn; I wasn't sure how or where I was going to get the rest of the money since my parents were unable to give me an allowance. I would get the money from my piggy bank if I had one. I was not allowed to have a glass piggy bank because my parents thought that I would get cut from the broken glass every time I tried to get the money out.

On Friday evening, I marched to my girlfriend's house for our weekend courting date with my pocket filled with two substitute promise rings.

We sat on her porch swing that evening and rocked back and forth until the moon came out. Then, I removed the fake rings from my pocket. I looked in her eyes, got down on one knee and said, "I have a surprise for you!"

She laughed at me and asked, "What is it, silly?"

I took out the paper cigar band first and tried to slide it on her finger. She laughed real hard, thinking I was being foolish. The paper ring was too small; it broke apart as I tried to stick it on her finger.

"I know this is not your idea of an engagement ring," she laughed.

"No, I am just practicing for when the real day comes," I replied.

Then I pulled out the soda can ring and attempted to slide that one on her finger. This time, the aluminum ring fit perfectly on her finger, but I could not get it to come off; it seemed to be stuck on her finger.

As I tried to pull the ring off her finger, I slyly asked her the size of her ring finger. She said she didn't know because she never had a ring before. I never thought of that. I kept on pulling until the soda top ring finally came off.

Putting the ring back in my pocket, I got up from the floor and sat back on the swing with her. She smiled at me and kissed me on the cheek.

"What's that for?" I asked.

"For wanting to give me a ring," she said.

"But I was just messing around...you know I can't afford a ring now."

"I know, but if you could, you would buy one for me... I know that." She smiled.

I looked at her and she looked deeper into my eyes until a tear fell from hers. With the full moon glowing and her hypnotic stare, I couldn't help myself from saying, "I love you with all my heart, and I plan to marry you when the time comes."

She simply said, "I know," and kissed me like it was the last kiss on earth.

* * * *

The next day, I was hard at work trying to find as many chores as I could so I could get paid. The weekend was coming fast, and my next ring downpayment would be due. I had collected about one dollar and thirty-five cents already, but not enough for the total payment. I went door to door with a large plastic bag, asking neighbors if they had any recyclable pop bottles or cans. At the end of the day, I had about fifty cans, which would probably net me another twenty-five cents.

I thought about getting a job at one of the fast-food hamburger places. The minimum wage was about $1.45 an hour then. There was no way I was going to pull that off because I didn't have any transportation to get to and from work. I got so desperate that I started checking each of the public pay phones nearby to see if any money was left in the coin slots. I got lucky and found a dime in one of them. I now had a total of $1.70.

Then, it suddenly hit me how I could make enough money to buy the ring for my girl. My good friend Rambo made money from washing cars; I figured I could wash cars, too, to make some extra money. I asked my mother if I could wash cars at our house to make money, but she promptly said no, citing an increased water bill.

Next, I thought of getting a paper route, but then I remembered that paper boys have to get up early and sometimes stay out late delivering newspapers. Besides, our newspaper was only ten cents, so I would have to sell a hundred to make any money for myself. I was running out of ideas to make enough money to pay for the ring I had on layaway. Hopefully, the jewelry store would not keep my ring if I missed the first payment.

* * * *

I walked toward Mr. and Mrs. Mayo's house and saw Mrs. Mayo sitting on the porch in a lounge chair, smoking a cigar with her feet on a foot stool. She was the first woman I ever saw smoke a cigar in town, and she was right proud of that fact. Her husband, Mr. Curtis Mayo, worked at the local meat-packing house where they slaughtered and packed beef, pork, and chicken. He regularly wore a meat apron and always smelled like fresh meat.

As I usually do, I smiled and waved at her and said, "Hi, Mrs. Mayo. How are you today?"

"Not bad for an old woman, James. How are you?" she said as she blew smoke rings in the air. The smoke rings reminded me of the ring I had on layaway going up in smoke if I couldn't come up with the money.

I replied, "I'm fine."

"Would you like to come over for a glass of lemonade to get out of the heat?" Mrs. Mayo offered.

"Uh, okay… I mean, yes, ma'am."

I slowly walked up the steps toward her porch. As I got closer, she said, "What's wrong? You look sad today, boy."

"I've got a big problem that I'm trying to work out," I said.

Mrs. Mayo laughed and said, "You're too young to have big problems. How can I help?"

"Well, I got my girl a ring on layaway downtown, and I'm trying to earn enough money to make the payments," I said.

"How much is the ring?"

"About $10, and I already paid a dollar on it. I have a downpayment due soon."

Mrs. Mayo looked around her yard and thought for a minute as she blew more smoke rings in the air as if she was on cue with my thoughts.

"I've got it," she said. "How about mowing my lawn every week until you pay for the ring? I'll pay you two dollars a week, and Curtis will be glad to take a break from cutting it."

"Wow! Would you?" I asked.

"Yes," she said. "And you can start today if you like because Curtis is at work. Our lawn mower is around back, and you'll see the gas can there, too. How about you be here every Saturday morning after today?"

"Okay. Thank you, Mrs. Mayo," I said.

"I know how it feels to receive your first ring. Curtis gave me one when I was around your age, and I still have it. It probably only cost ten cents back then, but we've been married for fifty years now, and it's still my favorite because it was my first," Mrs. Mayo said with a smile.

"Fifty years is a long time... I hope we can be married that long, too," I said.

"You will if you love each other like we do," Mrs. Mayo said, still smiling.

* * * *

I walked around to her backyard and found the lawnmower. I checked to see if it needed gas and it did; I filled the tank from the gas can and set the can way back away from the mower. After three tries, I was finally able to crank the mower to start cutting the grass.

Mrs. Mayo didn't have a huge yard, but it was a nice size. There were more trees there than I remembered, which meant I had to also rake up the fallen leaves with the grass I cut. The Alabama sun was much hotter in July, so I removed my shirt; I was done cutting the grass in about forty-five minutes, and then it took me another forty-five minutes to rake and bag all the grass and leaves.

Mrs. Mayo seemed happy with my work and promptly paid me the two dollars she promised. Putting my shirt back on, I thanked her and started my walk home, which was only a few blocks away. I was sweating profusely.

"Thank you, and see you next Saturday, Mrs. Mayo," I said as I walked away.

She said, "You're welcome, James," and lit up another cigar.

* * * *

After a month of cutting Mrs. Mayo's lawn, I had enough money to make the final payment on my ring. As luck would have it, I found another dime in one of the downtown payphones on my way back to the jewelry store.

I walked into Lorch's Jewelry store with my receipt book in hand. The same lady who waited on me before was behind the counter.

"Hi, I'd like to pick up my ring from layaway, please," I announced to the lady as I put my money on the counter.

"Well, I see you were able to make all the payments. Did you ever get the proper ring size?"

I reached into my pocket and pulled out the aluminum soda top ring and placed it on the counter, too. The lady looked at me and asked, "What's that?"

I said, "My girl's finger almost fit perfectly inside this ring, so can you make it a little bit bigger than this size?"

The lady frowned and said, "Well, I never! I have never heard of such a thing, but if that's the size you want..."

"Yes, ma'am, that's the size I want," I interrupted her with a grin.

The lady snatched the soda ring off the counter and said, "Come back in an hour, and your ring will be ready."

An hour later, I walked out of Lorch's Jewelry store with a pink paper bag and a neatly wrapped box inside. I couldn't wait to surprise my girlfriend with the ring.

* * * *

That evening, I went over to my girlfriend's house with the ring box hidden away in my back pocket. As usual, we sat on the porch and talked for a while before the sun began to set. When I thought the light from the full moon was romantic enough, I pulled out the box and gave it to her.

She said, "What's this, another practice ring? Is it a paper ring or another soda ring?"

"Open it and find out," I said with a big smile.

She cautiously pulled the ribbon off the small box and opened the top slowly as if she expected a jack-in-the-box to pop out. She smiled when she saw the ring sparkle from its case.

"Oh my, James, this is lovely. You actually got me a real ring," she exclaimed.

"It's a first promise ring," I said. "I saved up until I could afford it. I hope you like it." I beamed with pride.

She quickly looked around to see if her parents or siblings were nearby before she pulled me close to kiss me on the mouth with a long kiss. Then she jumped up to run and show her mother.

I sat there glowing and listened as her mother and siblings screamed with excitement. Then she came back on the porch and asked me to place the ring on her finger.

"Should I get down on one knee?" I joked.

"No, silly, this is not a wedding ring. It's a promise ring!"

I took the ring out of the box and slid it on her ring finger. It was much looser than I expected.

"If it's too big, I can take it back and get it re-sized," I said.

"No," she replied. "I'm not letting this ring out of my sight. I like it just the way it is...thank you, honey. I love you."

"I love you, too," I replied. We smooched and relaxed on the porch swing.

We just sat there smiling and looking at her ring as we reconfirmed our commitment to each other and revisited having a big family and a dog. This time, we finally gave the dog a name that we would always remember: *Ringo.*

* * * *

When school started again, I was eager to let everyone know that my girl and I were promised to each other, and her first promise ring was the proof. I waited in front of her homeroom on our first day back to school to see if she would be wearing her ring.

As she rounded the corner near the lockers, I waved to let her know I was waiting for her. I knew something was wrong when she didn't wave back or smile at me.

"What's wrong?" I asked as she met me face-to-face.

"I have some terrible news to tell you, James," she said.

"What is it," I asked, hoping there had not been a death in her family.

She replied, "I don't know how to tell you this, but..."

"But what?" I eagerly asked.

"Last night after dinner, I was washing the dishes, and..." she said.

"And what?" I asked.

"When I finished washing the dishes, I noticed that my ring was missing," she said as she dropped her head.

"Which ring? You're not talking about the first promise ring I just gave you, are you?"

"Yes, that's the only one I have."

"You mean you lost the ring that I worked so hard for the whole summer that cost me over $10?"

"I didn't lose it on purpose," she said.

"Well, isn't your dad a plumber? Ask him to get it for you," I snapped.

"My dad is a brick mason, not a plumber," she said.

"What's the difference...they're practically the same thing!" I raised my voice.

She looked up at me and ran into the girl's bathroom crying. I felt terrible and wanted to apologize for the way I acted, but it was too late. I waited for her to come out, but the bell rang and I had to go to my homeroom.

My girl avoided me the whole day at school. During lunch, we usually sat together, but this time she sat with her twin girlfriends, Ethyl and Bethyl Ramsey. They were not identical twins but fraternal twins. Ethyl was okay, but Bethyl was too bossy for me.

I went through the whole school day without getting a chance to apologize to my girl. I walked home alone and went straight to my room without sitting down to eat with my family. When my mother asked me what was wrong, I told her I had a terrible headache and needed to rest. She said she'd keep my plate warm in case I changed my mind.

I lay in my bed and just looked at the ceiling, hoping I could figure out a way to make things right with my girl. I closed my eyes for a second, and then I dozed off to sleep.

I dreamed I was now married and living in our dream home with a white picket fence. I looked outside and saw our four kids playing in the backyard. They were all chasing Ringo, trying to remove a shoe that he had in his mouth.

It was late morning, and I was dressed for work. Wearing a big white apron, I was headed for work at the local meat-packing house where I carpooled with Mr. Curtis Mayo. My wife was rolling her hair in our bedroom, and I went in to kiss her goodbye on my way to work. When she turned around to kiss me back, it was a different face; I was married to Bethyl Ramsey.

It felt like I was dreaming inside a dream of being married to Bethyl. She was wearing the first promise ring I bought her on one hand and a wedding band on the other. It was the right ring but on the wrong hand of the wrong person. I tried to scream, and I woke myself up in the process. I then sat on the side of the bed and was determined to see my girl and finally apologize for my earlier behavior.

The next day at school, I made a point to catch her alone before anyone else came around so we could talk. Before I could say anything, she held up her hand to show me she had my promise ring on.

"Wow, how'd you get the ring back," I gently asked.

"My dad, the brick mason, loosened the drainpipe underneath the sink and pulled it out for me."

"Oh...honey, I want to apologize for the way I acted. I didn't mean to get so excited. It's just that..."

"I know," she interrupted. "You wanted me to have your ring just as much as I wanted to have it. Just as much as I want us to get married and have a family one day," she emphatically stated.

"Thank you for understanding and for accepting my apology," I said.

We both smiled, held hands, and walked to our homerooms. On the way, we saw the twins Ethyl and Bethyl, and I frowned to think I could ever be married to Bethyl. I started to tell my girl about the nightmare I had, but I decided to keep it to myself. I had learned my lesson and was ready to work hard to buy my girl a second promise ring, which would be the last ring that I would ever buy.

CHAPTER ELEVEN

"MY HEART TRANSPLANT"

In the fall of a year that I have long forgotten, I was felled by a bullet straight to my heart. It was a love bullet!

It wasn't meant to kill, but it almost did. It was a slow, painful misery that took me almost a year to succumb to.

As I lay dying, I contemplated suicide because I didn't want to chance surviving and having to face the consequences of the truth. Was it an accidental shooting, or was it premeditated? Since all love comes from God, I looked up to the heavens while holding my chest. I asked God what the difference was between his holy bullets and the ones fired by friends and family, not strangers.

I never received an answer, but does it really matter if the bullet was from a loved one or from a gangbanger's gun? I was still dying and wondering if it was just God's way of letting me know my time was up. If this was an act of God, then does that mean God sometimes sends holy bullets instead of lightning bolts?

Waiting to die, I looked up again toward the ceiling, expecting to see a bright, white light or my life flashing by before me on a video screen. On that fateful day, there was no bright light, and the movie projector that shows your life flashing by must have been broken.

Then, I thought maybe my life had not been worth a movie. Nothing I did was important enough to rate having a story to tell. I felt numb, cold, and dead through and through. Everything and everybody had deserted me, including my soul.

I wanted to get it over with and just disappear into dust with no memory of ever having existed. In short, I willingly closed my eyes, gave up the ghost, and wanted to rest in peace.

But then something happened. I heard a voice whisper, "Get up. You do matter, and your life is worthwhile. If you let me, I will give you a heart transplant and teach you what love really is."

I opened my eyes, and my heart slowly brought me back with love. It took a while for me to believe in myself again before I could fully believe in someone else, but I did. Instead of being guarded, I allowed myself to be open, vulnerable, and free to feel without fear; this was something I had obviously never done or known about before.

I was no longer afraid, and I did not care anymore that others may have wanted me to die. I accepted the fact that I fell down, but I also relished the fact that I got up again.

Since that time, I have grown into a different person, and I have spawned a family with offspring who will continue the story and the legacy of life with love instead of a restful death without love.

Anyone can lie down and die to be forgotten, but it is the ones who get up that survive like the phoenix, regardless of the odds against their survival.

After all, living in peace and love allows one to finally rest in peace and love when the time comes. Until then, may we all live in peace. I am thankful for my heart transplant and being given a second chance at love.

CHAPTER TWELVE

"The Man Who Was Caught by a Butterfly"

One day while strolling through an enchanted forest, a tall, dark, and handsome man was lit upon by a beautiful butterfly. What a wonderful butterfly it was. It was decorated with lovely velvety wings and a long, sleek body. Its body was perfectly sculptured to match its angelic wings, and a rainbow of colors adorned the butterfly's head like a halo. The man was so awed by the butterfly's courage and graceful manner that he harmlessly allowed it to remain perched on his arm. Determined to make this prize catch a cherished possession, the butterfly quickly but elegantly introduced itself to the man.

"Hello, my name is Arual. I come from an enchanted land far, far away. Where are you from, and what is your name?"

More amazed by the butterfly's beauty than by her ability to speak, the man nervously answered.

"Uh, my name is James. I take this path all the time, but I've never seen anything like you before. I mean, you're so...so beautiful. Oh, please excuse me for being so forward. I hope I didn't embarrass you."

Not able to believe what she had actually heard, Arual replied,

"Thank you, kind sir, but it is you who are truly handsome. I am very much aware that you come this way often, for I have watched you before. As a matter of fact, I was wishing to see you come this way today. I hope you don't mind my being so fresh by lighting upon you like this."

Astonished, James wittily replied, "No wonder they call you a butterfly. You really know how to butter up a guy."

They both laughed and continued to talk. After laughing and talking for what seemed like days but was actually only an hour, James apologetically advised that he had to leave. He stood, bowed, and complimented Arual for being such an enjoyable acquaintance. It was then that Arual thanked James for his kindness, gentle ways, and warmth that allowed her to touch him. As James was walking away, Arual could not stand the thought of not seeing him again. She panicked and screamed, "But wait, will I ever see you again?"

James smiled and said, "Oh, I certainly hope so. But until then, let me give you something that will help you to remember me."

Although Arual already knew that she would always remember James, she waited for James to surprise her. James gently kissed Arual on her tiny head and continued his stroll toward his destination. Arual smiled, waved, and hovered in the sky until James was out of sight. She wished so hard to be a human. With that, she flew away in hopes that she would once again see James.

James was a man whom she, a gentle butterfly, had captured and loved, if only for a moment. It was then that Arual knew this precious moment would last a lifetime, for she, too, was caught. Not by a guy and his net, but by a gentleman and his love.

CHAPTER THIRTEEN

"THE RUNAWAY"

The feeling of abandonment is never a good feeling, especially when you are really all alone with no one else with you. I had never been so frightened in all my life. My mommy had left me alone many times before, but never at such an eerie time and place as then. As I sat still in the strange, dark, cold, smoke-scented room of rectangular fear, I felt so helpless and unloved, like a motherless child.

I listened, I looked, but I could hear very little and see only a short distance in front of me. All was still except my imagination, and it wandered like a homeless lamb. I jumped as my stomach growled from hunger because I was afraid that something might hear me. Like a roach hiding from bug spray, I hid in a corner as the wind whispered through the cracks in the wall; it sounded like a scary ghost outside was trying to come inside. As the darkness shaded me from the sight of the unknown, I held tight to my only possession, a little red handkerchief.

Outside the window, it was pitch black. I was not as afraid of the dark as I was of the time. I didn't know how to tell time, but I couldn't remember ever being up so late. Mommy had always told me that the Sandman would get me if I didn't go to sleep at bedtime. I didn't know what the Sandman looked like, but I imagined he was big and ugly. I could only guess that it was past nine o'clock because it was getting darker and darker. I was left without supper, and I didn't have anything to eat. I felt as if I were being punished again. Without really thinking, I nervously tied my little red handkerchief around my fingers so that it, too, would not get lost in the dark. I would have been twice as scared if I didn't have my little red handkerchief with me.

Because Mommy told me to sit still and wait until she came back, I was afraid to get up or even look out the window for her. Inside me, my bowels were beginning to feel full. With my back against the wall, I sat there for a moment to think. The seconds seemed to go by in slow motion like snails with suitcases. I didn't know whether to untie my little red handkerchief and set it free or let it stay and be afraid with me.

I suddenly remembered some cookies that Mommy had given me before she left. Of the seven that she gave me, I think I had only three left. I remember eating two before she left and one later. I reached for the others in my pocket, but they had disappeared. I figured either the Sandman or the Cookie Monster had taken them. The wind's whisper had turned into a slow, spooky moan, and the dark had gotten darker. It sounded as if something outside had finally made its way inside.

My eyes widened and shot upward when I heard an odd, thumping sound on the ceiling. I couldn't see anything, but I felt something was there. It was a weird kind of noise; I imagined it was huge bugs playing ping-pong or giant bats tap-dancing upside down. Either way, I felt like I was in for a real surprise and that something was going to kill me. I used to think that being dead was like playing hooky from school and never having to do homework again. Then, I didn't think doing homework was so bad. I pulled my feet in and tried to tuck myself into a ball. I could only clench my little red handkerchief tighter and wish for Mommy. I was so afraid.

My body started to shake in fear. I could feel my little red handkerchief tremble as I held it in my hand. I began to talk to it and beg it not to be afraid, but it wouldn't listen. I felt the darkness standing over me, watching me, staring at me. I closed my eyes so I couldn't look. When I remembered my little red handkerchief, I shielded it with my face and hands. I don't know how long I held it up to my face, but it felt like a real long time. At least my little red handkerchief could feel safe from the dark. We had never been so frightened in all our lives.

The light shining through the window let me know it was another day. I froze, I waited, I listened, as everything was quiet again. I slowly opened my eyes and found the darkness gone. Nothing else was there now except me and my little red handkerchief inside the familiar, cool, smoke-scented room. I was no longer frightened. I wiped my face with my left hand instead of with my little red handkerchief because it had been my comfort and my one and only friend. Without it, I would have been twice as scared. I LOVED my little red handkerchief because that was all I had.

I rose from my seated position and looked out the window for Mommy. I noticed a big white sign out front in the yard. I couldn't read too well, but the big red letters were K-E-E-P...O-U-T...N-O...T-R-E-S-P-A-S-S-I-N-G, whatever that means. Mommy must have been working late or gotten lost or something. I couldn't understand why a sign would be in front of our very own house. Maybe Mommy wanted to sell the house so we could move into a bigger and better one. Yes, that must have been it. She just forgot to tell me.

When I stooped to pick up my little red handkerchief, I felt a damp spot on one of its sides. I guess it had been crying because it had been so scared. I said, "Don't cry, little red handkerchief, don't cry. We're going to find Mommy." And without looking back at our very own house, we left to find another place to stay or another Mommy.

CHAPTER FOURTEEN

"The Hands of Mr. Cleed Spurlock"

I have very fond memories of an old man I knew growing up as a boy in the South. He had a very unique name, and he was also a very unique man in a nice way. His name was Mr. Cleed Spurlock, and he was a wood craftsman; he worked with his hands making things from wood and restoring old things into new.

All the adults just called him Cleed, but kids like me were required to call him Mr. Cleed out of respect. He was a rather short man with slow movements, which made some people consider him odd. He had a ready smile, and his hands were like large leather baseball gloves; his hands looked comic and out of place on his nimble, energetic body.

I assumed his hands were magical since everything they touched turned into a work of art. Mr. Cleed was not book-educated, but he knew things about wood and other things that no one else knew. It was as if he were born with wood in his blood – he knew everything about all kinds of wood.

He was also an usher at our church, so I would see him on Sundays wearing the same black suit and ready smile. Mr. Cleed lived alone and had no wife or children. He didn't talk much, but he was well-known because of his wood craftsmanship. He kept to himself and didn't allow others to watch him work in his little shop except for me. For some reason, he liked me and wanted to teach me some of the secrets of his special craft.

My parents named me Lonnie, but everyone nicknamed me "Loonie" except for Mr. Cleed; he just called me Boy. I was certain that he didn't know how to read, but I still liked him a lot. He was insistent on making me his apprentice whether I wanted to be or not.

To be honest, I really was not interested in working with wood or doing manual labor with my hands. Every time he would tell me that he was going to make me his apprentice, I would snap back, "No, I'm going to college to be a writer." I was only about fourteen then. Mr. Cleed would just smile and say, "Well, Boy, at least you'll still be working with your hands!"

Once, he invited me inside his small house for lunch when he took a break from working. He offered to share some of his homemade lunch with me: a fried Spam sandwich with cheese and mayonnaise, a bowl of Ramen noodles with peas and carrots, some green boiled peanuts, and a tall glass of buttermilk. I politely thanked him and lied that I had just finished eating. I always thought that buttermilk was disgusting and couldn't understand how anyone could drink it. I didn't like boiled peanuts, either.

"Boy, you don't know what you're missing," he said as he took a bite of his sandwich and then chugged down a big swallow of buttermilk. After hearing my stomach growl loudly, Mr. Cleed fetched me a small bag of Golden Flake Potato Chips and a short bottle of Coca-Cola. Side by side, we sat and ate our separate lunches together. It felt good sitting there next to my old friend, Mr. Cleed.

That same summer, I watched Mr. Cleed work on an old dresser that looked fit for the trash. When I asked him why he bothered with such an antique, he said, "There's a good piece of wood under there, Boy. You just have to know how to strip it down to its core, and then you'll see its beauty." I had no idea what he meant but I continued to watch him over the next few days as I witnessed him turn the old relic into something that looked brand new. It was indeed like magic, and if I had not seen it with my own eyes, I would not have believed it. As a matter of fact, when I looked around his shop, everything looked new. He told me that each piece in his shop had once looked just as poor as the piece I had just witnessed him restore. He said he just seemed to have a knack for making things beautiful, and he didn't know how or why.

Most of the things he restored he said he found in the trash or along the side of the road. "Just a little sanding and polishing is all she needs," is what Cleed would always say. Whatever money he made from selling them to people was pure profit. Sometimes, he sold the pieces back to the same people who had discarded them; they didn't even recognize that it was the same piece they had thrown away.

When I finished high school and was ready for college, I got plenty of gifts and encouragement from my friends and family. I was college-bound and couldn't wait to leave home. When I went by to tell Mr. Cleed I was going to college, he surprised me with a small gift box wrapped with a handmade bow. I opened the box and took out the contents – it was a small metal chisel, just like the ones he used in his shop to chisel wood. I must have looked perplexed because Mr. Cleed said, "Just in case you change your mind about working with your hands or if you want to come back and be my apprentice." I didn't know what to say because I couldn't tell if he was serious. Then he laughed and said, "Congratulations, Boy! Go make us all proud...and don't forget all I taught you about working with your hands."

During my first semester in college, I eagerly declared my major to be English as I had planned to become a writer. One of the first assignments we had in class was to write a narrative story with comparisons or contrasts. I didn't know exactly what the instructor meant, so I asked him for more information. Mr. James Curtain, our English professor, said that he wanted us to tell a story and include something that shows a comparison or a contrast. He said the story could be a true story or it could be fictional, something we make up. Since this was our first writing assignment, he told us we could make it only three typed pages but that it was due in two days.

I spent all day wondering what to write about and how to get started. I didn't have a clue, and every time I thought I had a good narrative idea, I couldn't find a comparison or a contrast. It seemed I had developed writer's block at an early stage in my writing career, and that was not good. That evening, one of my new classmates came by my room and invited me to a freshman class party at the Adams Center. I decided to go and stay for a little while to try and clear my head.

I was having a good time at the party, laughing and joking with friends, until I noticed a shy boy sitting down, looking lost. I walked over, introduced myself to him, and asked his name. He said his name was Lex, short for Lexington – an odd name, I thought.

Lex told me he didn't want to attend college but that his parents made him. He said he didn't think he belonged there. I sensed Lex was suffering from an inferiority complex. I was dumbfounded and didn't know what to think. Lex seemed just the opposite of me. While I was highly encouraged to attend college and was eager to be there, Lex wasn't.

As I searched my mind for words of wisdom to offer him, I again developed writer's block. I couldn't think of a single thing to say. And then, Mr. Cleed and his chisel popped into my head.

I looked at Lex and said, "Just a little sanding and polishing is all you need, Lex."

He looked at me and said, "What?"

I smiled and said, "You just have to strip yourself down to the core, and then you'll see the beauty."

I pointed to my head and said, "You've got a good piece of wood under there, Boy."

The way Lex smiled let me know he understood. We became the best of friends, and subsequently, Lex went on to make the Dean's list his first semester.

When I got back to my room, I had my narrative story with its comparison and contrast. I decided to write about my experience with Lex and the comparison and contrast I made to Mr. Cleed's wood. When I turned in my paper, I was eager to have Mr. Curtain read it. He asked us to read our stories out loud in class, and I volunteered be first.

Everyone enjoyed my story, and they admired the clever way I used Mr. Cleed's wood in it. Needless to say, Mr. Curtain was impressed and I got an A. I seemed to be on my way to learning how to be a good writer, and I owed some of that to Mr. Cleed.

I called home to tell my mother about my good news. I was so excited as I told her about the A I received on my first narrative, and I owed it all to Mr. Cleed. I asked her to tell Mr. Cleed that I would stop by to see him on my next break; the college I attended was only about fifty miles away from my hometown.

My mother got quiet on the phone and then said, "Loonie, I'm sorry to tell you this, but Cleed died yesterday morning from a stroke. I wanted to call and tell you, but I didn't want to upset you. His funeral is this coming Saturday."

I drove home early Saturday morning to attend the funeral. While standing in front of Mr. Cleed's casket with tears in my eyes, I didn't know what to say or do. He had on his black suit and a ready smile, but the undertaker had covered up his hands with large white gloves. With everyone looking, I removed the gloves one at a time and then stuck a copy of my narrative in his hands for him to keep.

I turned around and told everyone in the church that the gloves hid the best part of Mr. Cleed because his hands were like magic. No one argued with me, and my parents smiled as I sat down. Without realizing it, Mr. Cleed gave me something special by sharing his special gift with me, and I wanted to give him something back in return. I will always remember the hands of Mr. Cleed Spurlock. Although I never wanted to be his apprentice, he did teach me a lot about working with my hands – maybe not so much as a chiseler, but definitely as a writer.

"I LOVED that old man!"

CHAPTER FIFTEEN

"LITTLE PIECES OF CONVERSATION"

The rap has been around since the dawn of time. Over the years, some smooth-talking, silver-tongued devils have perfected it to the point that they do it without even thinking about it, especially when they see a beautiful girl.

The following is a realistic scene at a party where a loquacious man is trying to make a pick-up while using some of the oldest lines in history. You might notice that the girl can't get a word in edgewise since the man is speaking in run-on sentences. The only thing missing is the look on the girl's face as she endures this onslaught from a gift-of-gabber and his little pieces of conversation. One can only imagine that her facial expressions are priceless.

--The Scene--

"Now baby, you know I'm telling you the truth. We can leave right now and go over to my place, and nobody will ever miss us. I ain't lying. I'll give you a backrub when we get there if you want me to."

"You know I'm crazy about you, and I've always been crazy about you. I would never think of looking at another girl because no other girl has your charms or your beauty. I would pass over ten girls just to get to you."

"Your parents would love to have me as their son-in-law because I'm a good catch. I'm handsome with good teeth, good hair, and not a bad catch.

"I drive a brand-new car with a sunroof top and a diamond in the back."

"I promise if we leave now, I'll have you back in a few hours. I just want to show you my shell collection and my goldfish bowl. I got a big, tropical goldfish that's very rare. There's only two of them in the whole world."

"You like wine? I got a bottle of French wine that I bought when I went to France last year. That was right after I got back from Greece. You ever been to Greece before?"

"I think Vyena is a beautiful name. And you look just like your name sounds."

"Yes, you look like your name could be Vyena, and it sort of rhymes with … well, never mind that."

"From the very first time I saw you, I knew we had a lot in common and could be good for each other. We both got those same rare qualities, and we're both very stylish."

"I didn't want to say anything for fear of sounding like I'm bragging, but this suit I'm wearing was tailor-made just for me."

"The shoes I'm wearing were just shined by that shoeshine boy down the street. I always give him a big tip when he shines my shoes because that's just the kind of guy I am."

"Boy, you smell so good. Is that a special fragrance, or is that just the way you smell?"

" You seem real shy and not that talkative, but I can get with that. I'm kind of shy, too."

"Can I get your number?"

"I'm going to call you every day and send you a dozen roses every week."

"It's kind of noisy in here. Why don't we go outside and sit in my car?"

"I promise not to drive off without your permission. Here, I'll even let you hold my car keys."

"What flavor of lipstick is it that you're wearing? Can I taste it for myself?"

"Look, I'm putting my cards on the table. I'm not even married, and I swear it."

"I don't have any kids or baby mamas...well, I don't claim any, anyway. Billie Jean is not my kid."

"That was a joke. But just because they say that baby looks like me, it ain't necessarily so."

"Girl, I love you! When we get married, I'm going to give you a bubble bath every night."

"And I'm going to bring my paycheck home every week and give it straight to you."

CHAPTER SIXTEEN

"MR. AGNES"

Decades ago, in the 1950s and 1960s, before we ever heard the letters LGBTQ, we knew about Mr. Agnes in our close-knit community in Dothan. Mr. Agnes was a woman who wore men's clothing and gender identified as a man. Everyone in our small community embraced him as ours, and we respected him just the way he was because he was an important part of the Baptist Bottom. If the Bottom was a microcosm of the larger city of Dothan, I suspect there were others like him around.

Agnes was his first name. In secret, most people referred to Mr. Agnes as a *bulldagger*, but we kids didn't exactly know what that meant. Years later, we came to realize it was a derogatory name used for describing a lesbian or masculine female in the Black community. Mr. Agnes walked, talked, dressed, and did everything as a man; he even dated women who were very pretty. He wore oversized men's shirts to hide his breasts from plain view, and he often smoked cigarettes and wore expensive wing-tipped shoes with cuffed dress pants.

The Bottom landscape also had several men who were deemed *sissies* because of their effeminate ways and actions. They were publicly visible and served in very prestigious positions like church musicians, schoolteachers, seamstresses, cooks, and hairdressers. In hindsight, the fact that these gay men were so prevalent meant that there were probably straight-looking men who were on the *down-low* back then, too.

However, there was only one Mr. Agnes that we knew about who was also in-your-face public minus any shame. Mr. Agnes owned and operated a pool hall or billiard parlor in the Bottom. He always wore his hair in a ponytail or a rolled-up bun underneath his hat. His facial hair consisted of a thin, neatly trimmed Clark Gable mustache and a small goatee; he was known for carrying a .22 caliber pistol in his back pocket to protect himself against anyone who bullied him.

Many folks said Mr. Agnes was an unbeatable pool shark as he was always winning games against unsuspecting suckers who took his feminine looks for granted. He actually lived at the pool hall in a small room in the back of the building. He spent most of his leisure time playing pool and making impossible shots that no one else could imitate.

On the weekends, we would often see many of the local uniformed Fort Rucker Army soldiers crammed into the pool hall with fists full of money, betting that they all could beat Mr. Agnes. One by one, Mr. Agnes would usually let them win the first few games to suck them in; then, he would chalk up his favorite cue stick and run the whole table in a few minutes. All the soldiers would leave crying and broke, but they never threatened to harm Mr. Agnes because they had heard about the gun in his back pocket.

Mr. Agnes and my dad, known as Mr. Shack or sometimes just Shacklebones, were close friends with a seemingly love-hate relationship. They could always be seen arguing or calling each other bad names inside Shack's Grill Cafe, but everyone knew they were good friends; they never fought for real. There was a mutual respect between them and they had each other's backs, especially in a time of real need. There are plenty of humorous stories about Ol' Shacklebones and Mr. Agnes and their outlandish public battles.

A favorite neighborhood story is one about the time the Renaissance Men's Club and the Men's Civic Club had a championship softball game. My dad played for the Men's Civic Club, and Mr. Agnes was on the opposing team. Softball and hotdogs were everywhere during the summers in Dothan, and the Bottom was no different.

On this particular day, the two teams were playing on a field at the Lincoln Community Center. Mr. Andrew Bell was in charge of refereeing this championship match since both teams were hugely popular. Mr. Gipper T Berry was the star pitcher for the Renaissance Men's Club.

The bases were loaded, and Mr. Agnes's team was ahead by one run. Shacklebones was at bat for the Men's Civic Club, and he was expected to hit a home run to bring all his teammates home to win the game. Mr. Agnes was the defender on first base. The baseball jerseys worn by Mr. Agnes's team were old and ill-fitting, especially on Mr. Agnes, who was heavier up top than most; also, one of the top buttons on his jersey was missing.

Gipper T stared at Shacklebones for a minute, and then he threw a fast underhanded pitch to him. Shacklebones decided to play it safe and bunt the ball. The ball rolled between second and first base. Second baseman Sweet Willie Hayes quickly scooped up the ball and pitched it to Mr. Agnes just as Shacklebones was barreling his way toward first base.

Right before my dad reached first base, Mr. Agnes unbuttoned his jersey to flash his naked titties. My dad stopped on a dime and stared at Mr. Agnes's titties, which gave Mr. Agnes time to run forward and tag my dad out before the runner on third base could reach home plate. Mr. Agnes's stunt became a legendary story that exaggerated the Renaissance Men's Club win by one run and two titties.

Reportedly, my dad quickly turned around after being tagged out and stormed past home plate without stopping. It was said he went home, found my mother, and they had family relations on the spot. People theorized that either my father was scared to death when he saw Mr. Agnes's breasts, or he was so turned on to the point that he ran home to impregnate my mom.

My dad's position was that he didn't want anyone to think he was attracted to another man, so in order to protect his manhood, he went home and had sex with my mother. Regardless, my youngest sister was born nine months later.

I also liked Mr. Agnes because he always gave me a nickel to buy candy and two-for-a-penny cookies without my asking. When he wasn't playing pool, he had a part-time job working at Hawk's Funeral Home across the street from the pool hall. I never knew what he actually did at the funeral home, but I suspected it had something to do with handling the dead bodies, of course. I just assumed he assisted in the embalming room since he sometimes smelled like formaldehyde. He was afraid of dead folks and would never be in the funeral home alone; his hands always trembled when he lit his cigarettes after leaving there.

Sometime later, Mr. Agnes became the self-appointed caretaker of Homeless Jake. He would make sure Homeless Jake had food to eat, clean clothes to wear, a bath, and an inside place to sleep to keep from sleeping on the streets. He also made sure that Homeless Jake went to church on Sundays; however, Mr. Agnes never went to church with him.

When pranksters would bully Homeless Jake in public, Mr. Agnes would pull his pistol and threaten to shoot them if they didn't stop. He was so convincing that most bullies ran away in fear that he would actually pull the trigger; I believed that he would, too. Mr. Agnes's caring actions toward Homeless Jake demonstrated to all how his natural motherly instincts overcame his need to be a man all the time. Everyone was shocked to learn years later that Mr. Agnes had once been married to a man and actually had a biological son who lived elsewhere with many children.

I like remembering how everyone and everything peacefully co-existed in the Bottom during the turbulent times when the rest of society was dealing with so many pervasive and invasive ideals. Because of all the real turmoil that these ideals caused, we were forced to be close-knit and depend on each other regardless of the unimportant differences regarding gender and lifestyle. We didn't feel it was anyone else's business outside of the Bottom who loved whom.

When Mr. Agnes died, he was in his late nineties and had lived all of his life hiding in the Baptist Bottom. After his death, it was reported that Varner's Funeral Home, a new funeral home in the Bottom that had his body, discovered that Mr. Agnes had female genitalia. In the absence of any family members, the funeral staff wanted to dress the corpse in a beautiful white silk dress with a pearl necklace and sparkling earrings. As soon as the Bottom citizens learned about this ordeal, they all protested the idea of burying Mr. Agnes in anything other than his favorite suit and tie with his pretty wing-tipped shoes.

On the day of the funeral, Homeless Jake sat in the front pew at the church and cried, looking at the casket of his friend and protector. Many other Bottom citizens cried too, including Shacklebones. This was the first time I ever saw my dad cry in public. Had Mr. Agnes lived long enough to see the arrival of the LGBTQ movement, he would have been a pioneering member but still carry his gun in his back pocket.

CHAPTER SEVENTEEN

"UNMAILED LOVE LETTERS TO MY DNA"

Being a law enforcement officer is a scary occupation, especially these days. When I was an active federal agent, I traveled constantly and was always concerned about not being able to make it back home again. I was forty when my son was born, and thoughts about my mortality were normal then.

Carrying a gun on a daily basis added to my fear of getting shot or killing someone else in the line of duty. Knowing that tomorrow was not promised to anyone, I decided to write my only son a letter and leave it for him in a location that he could easily find in the event I could not make it back home.

He had recently turned fourteen and was beginning to resemble the son that I had always wanted and was so proud of in many ways. He knew that I loved him, but he probably couldn't gauge how much.

I remember when he was around eight, he asked me how it felt to be a parent. I'm not sure I was able to answer his question to his satisfaction, but I wanted him to know that my love for him was immeasurable and reached to the moon and back.

So that he would never question or wonder if I loved him to the moon, I decided to write him a letter without a stamp. I wrote the following letter and left it in our basement in a box marked with his name.

Dear Son,

I love you and always will. Like a doting father, I have watched you grow and change over the years from a suckling infant to the intelligent teenager that you've now become. You are truly a gift of life and an example of your mother's undying love for me, as she gave you to me fourteen years ago.

When your mother and I became "twitterpated" with each other, we learned about the birds and the bees firsthand, thereby conceiving you and making our lives whole and complete.

Over the years, your mother and I have changed your diapers, taught you how to eat, talk, walk, and read, but most importantly, I hope we have taught you how to love. I've watched you excel in such sports as swimming, soccer, karate, and tennis. In karate, you learned to speak words and phrases of Japanese, and in school, you are learning Spanish – something I could never do easily.

Even as a child, you exhibited a sharp mind and were adept at putting things together, such as Legos, puzzles, building blocks, etc. Today, you are an avid reader, a promising writer, and a distinguished honor roll student; if you stay on course, you will have a very bright future.

As you grow, please remember to stay close to God and family. In this life, all that matters are family and friends – nothing else. Not money. Not cars. Not houses. Not careers.

Your mother and I have tried to make you feel safe, loved, and free to grow into your own person. I wanted you to have your own name and identity and not name you after me, making you the third James.

Just like anyone else, you'll make mistakes in life, but just be man enough to accept them and move on. When you fall, get back up and continue. Our family is not a family of quitters, and we believe in working our way through to success.

Wherever you go or whatever you do, let this letter be a reminder to you that you are loved for who you are and for what you mean to me. A father's love for his son is nothing new. My love for you is eternal, regardless of what you do, where you go, or what you become in life.

May your love for animals and humanity continue to rule your heart and make you an individual who is not afraid to care for others, regardless of who they are or what they look like. I am so proud of you, and I always will be. Thank you for being my son.

Love always,
Your Dad

Next year, my son will turn thirty. He has far exceeded my expectations with what he is doing with his life, and I am continually amazed at his maturity. Our father-son relationship is quieter and more laid back than most. He knows that I'll always be there for him like a safety net, and I know he'll be there for me like a lifesaver. If he needed a kidney, I would gladly give him one of mine.

We do verbally tell each other that we love each other. I often wish I had that same rapport with my late father, but I didn't. We felt we both loved each other, but the words were harder to materialize. My father died at age eighty-nine, just three months short of his ninetieth birthday. I wish he had left a letter for me to read. He didn't because of the limits placed on his education by the southern signs of the times during his lifetime.

My son was about eighteen when my father passed away. They didn't develop a close kinship because my father lived in Alabama and we lived in Pennsylvania; my father also didn't do telephones.

Since I was unable to articulate my love for my father like I have for my son through this letter, I have penned a special love letter to my father to also be sent without a stamp and mailed through the universe.

Dear Dad,

You've been gone for over a decade now, and I still miss hearing you laugh and smelling the smoke from your cigar. Since you have been gone, I have continued to develop into my own person and done many things that would make you proud. Most importantly, I have raised a son in your image with your same core values, who will extend our family name into the future. My family is intact, and we understand why family matters and why you worked so hard to create our family. Thank you for teaching me how to be a man.

Your grandson is kind and smart, and he remembers you fondly as a man who cared for him even though the communication was non-verbal. He is strong, creative, resourceful, and giving. He understands that life is fleeting; he believes in getting all he can out of life while realizing that he can't get it all. He has become a force for the world to reckon with in his own right.

Next year, I will turn seventy, but I still feel like a child at times. The most important change in me has been my mind or my perception of things. I now realize that listening is more important than talking and that it is better to give than to receive. While on a cruise to Bermuda years ago, I stood atop the ship's deck and marveled at how vast the sky was; we were surrounded by so much water that land was not visible.

I realized then that I was merely a grain of sand to God and that my problems were insignificant in the sea of all things real. In other words, I came to realize that everything is not about me; making it about everyone else is the key to a life full of balance.

If I am afforded the opportunity to meet you again in the afterlife, I will tell you I love you for all the times that I didn't and make you feel that without your giving me life, I would never have been. You never abandoned me or made me feel unloved, ever.

Although your life was hard and full of denials and declinations, you made sure that my life was easy and full of acceptance. You once told me that if all you had was one peanut, you would take half and give me the other. That was your way of telling me that you loved me to the moon and back.

In closing, I would like to add that you went away at a good time on Good Friday. The world you once knew has become a difficult place to navigate now with the invisible dangers all around us. Although my faith is still strong, I sometimes wonder if there really is a divine being watching over us and preparing a home for us elsewhere.

Thank you for giving me life and for giving me a purpose. Lately, I've made sure that everyone now knows who *Shacklebones* was to me. May you continue to rest in peace and know that your family is representing the life you created for us all.

Love always,
Your Son

CHAPTER EIGHTEEN

"THE SCENIC ROUTE"

The Houston traffic was super congested with bumper-to-bumper gas-guzzling carbon monoxide dispensers as we stood frozen on the interstate. The city's crime rate was skyrocketing, and I had to escape. My stress level had reached an all-time high, and I was headed to Atlanta for vacation. I was way past burnout on my job and couldn't wait to get out of the city.

Even though I had a long, boring drive ahead of me, I knew it was just what I needed to relax my mind. It would give me a chance to cool down and get away from it all, if only for a few days. It was autumn, and the leaves had already begun to change from green to golden brown. As I gazed out my car window at the different-colored trees, I realized just what I needed – a change.

Amidst all the assorted cars and trucks, I didn't see anything remotely scenic about the highway route I took. I regretted not taking the backroads. The more I stared out the window, the more my mind bounced back and forth from memories to fantasies. They soon took control of my environment. My car's windshield suddenly became a wide screen for my visions, like a portal into space. I moved my face closer to the windshield to get a better look like a Peeping Tom.

I envisioned my first year as a salesman when I was on a legitimate business trip to Las Vegas. I walked into the lobby of the Golden Nugget Hotel and was amazed to see slot machines everywhere with all types of people hovering over them like zombies. It was hard to tell which ones were the robots, the machines, or the people.

Since I'm not a gambler, I usually don't pay too much attention to the slots or the people attached to them, but there was this one lady who readily caught my attention. She was trying to seduce a one-armed bandit into giving her all its money. Dressed in a tailored, navy blue suit, she looked like an airline stewardess. Her skin was a smooth, caramel color, and her hair was short and sassy. I was in Vegas only to meet with a client and was not looking for an affair, but I couldn't resist looking at her.

I quickly registered and asked the desk clerk for change for a fifty-dollar bill. Then I gave my luggage to the bellboy to take to my room as I decided to see my room later. I was in such a hurry to get to the vacant slot machine next to the pretty lady that I gave the bellboy a twenty-dollar tip without realizing it. I then rushed over to try my luck.

The lady looked over at me, smiled, and said, "I hope you have better luck than I'm having. I can't seem to win a thing tonight."

I studied her pretty face and fine body for a moment and then smartly replied, "Depends on what you're trying to win and how bad you really want it. I feel I've already won the lotto by just standing here next to you. Who knows, maybe I've got the Midas touch."

"Maybe you have," she said, looking me up and down. We both smiled and freely flirted back and forth until we forgot about the lottery inside the bandits; it seemed we were now playing another kind of lottery. After we introduced ourselves, we opted to get some coffee in the hotel café to continue our flirting. She was a single flight attendant, and I was a recent divorcee. We soon realized there was some hot chemistry brewing between us. I've often heard people say, "Blame it on Vegas," and it was a little scary and exciting how well we connected so quickly.

It wasn't long before we began to confide in each other; we traded fantasies and seduced each other into believing we could make all our fantasies come true in one night. Later, in her room, we tried our best to make as many fantasies come true as possible. Afterward, we made a pact to meet every year to try and top the fantasies we had transformed into reality. I had to meet my client at 9 a.m., and she was flying out around the same time. Although I hated to leave her room, I had to go to my room, take a shower and get ready for my appointment.

The following year, we met in San Diego, then New York, then Denver, then Boston and Atlanta. I remember when she first introduced me to chocolate syrup, honey, and whipped cream. I initially thought those were only things used to top ice cream or pie for dessert. Of course, I found out later I was very naïve; however, she did use them like dessert toppings with my body as the main course.

She turned me on to such interesting body dessert toppings as fresh fruit, strawberry jelly, nuts, and ketchup. I remember saying, "Ketchup? Yuk, how odd." And she replied, "Why not? I always put ketchup on all my meat – hamburger, steak, and foot-long hot dogs." She then looked down at my crotch, giving me one of her trademark grins as she licked ketchup off her fingers. She had a kinky sense of humor, but she was also very imaginative, sexy, and inventive. She invented all kinds of pet names for her favorite body dessert toppings she put on me. The most memorable ones were the "Nutty Buddy" and the "Chocolate Fudge Sickle."

As I continued to drive on cruise control, I smiled at the thought of it all and my mind suddenly switched channels. Now, I saw myself when I was ten years old. My father and I were at our first major league baseball game, and we were sitting in the bleachers with all the other screaming fans. Just like in 3D, I heard a bat crack as a ball whizzed over my head. The smell of hot dogs, roasted peanuts, and popcorn was all around me. I remember eating four hot dogs, a box of popcorn and a huge drink on that day. My father was amazed at how I ate everything and did not get a stomachache. I felt really special then.

On the way home, my father and I had a man-to-boy talk. He told me he loved me and would always be my father. Then he told me that he was going away and wouldn't be living with us anymore. He used a big word I had never heard before called *divorce*, which I didn't understand at the time. He further explained that he and Mom didn't love each other anymore but that they both loved me. I cried when I finally realized what he was telling me. The next day, my father went away and I never saw him again. I didn't feel special anymore. As an adult man now, I wiped the tears from my eyes and continued watching the windshield.

Next, I saw myself pledging my college fraternity along with my other brothers. We were being tortured and teased by the more senior members. One of them blindfolded me, tied my hands and feet together, and stood me up on a chair. While on the chair, someone briefly took the blindfold off and told me to look down. I glanced down and saw a large box filled with blood and broken glass. The brothers re-blindfolded me, took off my shoes, and told me to jump down into the box of broken glass. When I hesitated, someone pushed me off the chair into the box of what my feet thought was broken glass. I screamed like a banshee, but the glass in the box turned out to be just cornflakes and the blood was ketchup; this trick was nothing more than a test of my bravery or my stupidity, but it captured my imagination and my fears.

Finally, I looked down at my gas gauge and noticed my tank was almost empty. At the next exit, I pulled away from the crowd and into a dimly lit gas station; I could hear crickets singing as I pumped gas into my tank. It was a quiet night, and no other cars were filling up except for mine.

I finished filling up my tank and went inside to pay the attendant. As soon as I walked inside, I realized why things had been so quiet. Two masked gunmen held a gun to the attendant's head as they ordered me to get inside and be quiet. Before I could protest, one of them threw me down and took my wallet, all the while pressing the gun to my head. When they were finished robbing the store and me, they turned and shot us. In slow motion, I watched the bullet enter the station attendant's headfirst as his eyes rolled back in his head. I opened my mouth to speak but could not before they shot me in the head. I didn't feel any pain, but I abruptly woke up in a cold sweat. I then realized I was at home in my bed dreaming the whole time. It was all a series of dreams. I got up, got dressed, and started my long drive from Houston to Atlanta, but this time, I took a different route through the country back roads.

CHAPTER NINETEEN

"THE WEDGE OF ALLEGIANCE"

The stated mission of the Boy Scouts of America (BSA) is to prepare young people to make ethical and moral choices over their lifetime. The BSA does this by instilling in them the values of the Scout Oath and Scout Law. Scout Law requires the young person to be trustworthy, loyal, helpful, friendly, and courteous, among other things.

The member's motto is to always be prepared, and the Scout Oath asks them to obey the Scout Law at all times and to keep themselves physically strong and morally straight. Many of these young people will spend their whole lives being great stewards of the BSA and changing their lives by positively changing others' lives along the way.

Reggie and Harold were members of the same local Boy Scout troop. Their troop consisted of eighteen boys from ages twelve to seventeen who all lived within the same community; most of the boys had been together since Cub Scouts and had known each other forever. Harold and Reggie, both seventeen, were next-door neighbors and best friends.

Reginald Daniels was the taller of the two friends and stood 5 feet, 10 inches tall. He had a natural athleticism for sports, but he enjoyed fishing just as much. Many of the girls at school sighed when he walked by due to his muscular build and friendly smile. Harold Huntington, 5 feet, 8 inches, was a talented musician, mainly because his parents insisted on him learning music; they were afraid he might not find his academic equal in school. Harold played keyboards, saxophone, and drums and was a leader in the school band. It was hard to find two better friends who complemented each other's talents as well as they did.

The town they lived in was diverse and had scores of other talented boys and girls; however, there was no equivalent Girl Scout Troop to rival the BSA. To remain socially engaged, many girls pursued academics and sports interests like the National Honor Society and gymnastics; however, there is an exception to every rule, and the exception to that rule in this case was named Cenethea Beaumont. Cenethea, a seventeen-year-old, leggy, biracial beauty, was more interested in boys than academics or sports, and she was very good at how well she played them.

It was the Fourth of July weekend, and Scoutmaster Stevie Watford was leading the boys in their daily Pledge of Allegiance to the flag as they crossed their hearts. He formed them into special teams so they could earn more merit badges. Merit badges were awards earned by members based on activities assigned in a particular area of study or assignment-oriented tasks. The badge allowed the boys to study worthy areas that they might consider doing as a hobby or even a career later on, and they motivated the boys to become better scouts and better individuals.

Both Reggie and Harold chose the Exploring Program as a guide to help them determine the kinds of careers they might be suited for as adults. They had both earned an equal number of merit badges in their long affiliation with the BSA. The Explorer Program contained a multitude of resources and adult mentors to help them navigate from youth to adulthood by performing fun activities.

Mr. and Mrs. Beaumont, parents to Cenethea, were new adult mentors with the BSA Exploring Program. Mr. Beaumont was a high school guidance counselor and Mrs. Beaumont was a lawyer; she graduated from Howard University Law School. For this July event, they brought their daughter along with them so that she could meet some new people her age.

Cenethea smiled brightly when she saw Harold, Reggie, and the crowd of boys surrounding her; her gaze primarily focused on Reggie, but Harold was the first to walk over and introduce himself.

"Hi, my name is Harold Huntington. Welcome to Troop #210 of the BSA." He smiled.

"Hello, Harold, my name is Cenethea Beaumont, and I'm—"
"And my name is Reginald Daniels, but everyone just calls me Reggie," Reggie interrupted by extending his hand to shake hers.

"Hi, Reggie," she said, with a bigger smile as she reached out to grab his hand.

The smile on Harold's face weakened when he saw the warmer reception that Cenethea gave Reggie.

Mr. and Mrs. Beaumont stepped up to introduce themselves to the boys and said they were grateful to be volunteering to help them explore new opportunities. Mrs. Beaumont then asked them the way to the bathroom so that she could powder her nose, at which point Mr. Beaumont asked the boys to tell him what kinds of things they specifically wanted to explore. The Scoutmaster motioned to the boys to answer the question.

The boys shouted all kinds of answers like cars, business, cooking, birdwatching, painting, building, etc. When Mrs. Beaumont came back, she asked the boys if any of them ever thought of going to law school.

Arthur Clarke raised his hand and said that his dad was a lawyer, but he wanted to be a curator for a museum.

"That's a pretty unique and exact occupation, son," responded Mrs. Beaumont. "What led you to that particular career choice?"

"I like going to museums and thought it would be a good occupation," said Arthur.

Harold quickly raised his hand and added, "I'd like to have my own band one day. I'm a musician."

"Oh, what instrument do you play?" asked Mr. Beaumont.

"I play keyboards, drums, and saxophone...in our school's stage band," bragged Harold.

Cenethea looked over at Harold and gave him a flirty smile slightly bigger than the one she had given Reggie. Reggie noticed and frowned to indicate his disapproval and his jealousy.

By the end of the day, it looked like Harold had gained the upper hand with Cenethea as she was now laughing at all his jokes and touching his arm when she laughed. In basketball terms, Harold was playing the inside court and slam-dunking on his competition; Reggie was left with shooting three-pointers from the backcourt that all hit the rim and bounced out of bounds. Reggie's anger toward his rival Harold was beginning to show.

Literally standing between them in the crowd of boys, Cenethea symbolized a wedge between the two best friends, who were beginning to act like enemies vying for her attention. The tenets of the Scout Oath and Scout Law were far from their thoughts when they competed for Cenethea's affection; her only goal was to win boys over regardless of the collateral damage it caused.

As the summer went on, Cenethea continued to tease both friends by secretly going out on dates with each of them. Reggie took her to the movies, and Harold took her to a concert. When they each learned what was going on, they met up to argue about how the other was being a traitor and a backstabber.

"Look, Reggie, it's clear that Cenethea likes me better than you because she told me," said Harold.

"She told me the same thing, Harold, so you must be lying," replied Reggie.

"You calling me a liar?" snapped Harold.

"I am if you said she likes you better than me!" yelled Reggie.

Harold balled up his fist and swung at Reggie's head. Luckily, Reggie ducked and avoided his punch. Before another punch could be thrown, Arthur Clarke intervened and pulled the boys apart.

"I don't ever want to be friends with a backstabber," Harold said and stormed away.

Reggie yelled after him, "That's fine by me!"

Arthur just stood there in disbelief as he witnessed the breakup of two of the best scouts and friends in the world. The common denominator that caused the friction between the two was named Cenethea Beaumont, who had become the straw that broke the camel's back.

Word quickly spread that Harold and Reggie were no longer best friends. Reggie quit the scouts and focused on trying to gain a football scholarship to college. Harold let his hair grow long and managed to join a band.

In the aftermath, Cenethea married Arthur Clarke after high school and started a big family; Arthur changed his mind about being a museum curator and became a lawyer instead, like his father before him. With four children, they needed the extra income.

Over the years, Reggie and Harold saw each other in passing but never spoke. The two men had become strangers, which was very different from their closeness at BSA. Their broken pledge of allegiance to each other had caused a lifelong fracture that was never mended. Neither of them got the girl they both wanted.

They long abandoned the Scout Law that required them to be trustworthy, loyal, helpful, friendly, and courteous, among other things.

The Scout Oath asked them to obey the Scout Law at all times and to keep themselves physically strong and morally straight.

In the end, their pledge of allegiance was transformed into a wedge of allegiance caused by jealousy, one of the deadly sins that was paid for on the cross.

II

POETRY

48 POEMS ABOUT LOVE (MORE OR LESS)

Poetry – Literary work in which special intensity is given to the expression of feelings and ideas by the use of distinctive style and rhythm.

I concur with that definition and try to distinguish my poetry with my own distinctive style and rhythm. I view my poetry as a concise snapshot of a special feeling, thought, or idea that urges one to think exponentially about the words they see. Sometimes, I use a few words to communicate a bigger picture of the same idea.

I hope you enjoy the words and pictures that I have assembled and labeled as poetry. Some are short, some are longer, but they all bear a striking resemblance to reality as they address the contradictions of art imitating life and life imitating art.

CHAPTER TWENTY

1.

"LOVE IS LIKE GLASS SLIPPERS 2"

Fragile, rare, and crystal clear
Oh, how I wish you were still here
You left me without a safety net
And a broken heart filled with much regret.

Do I follow you and see where it may lead
Or allow my broken heart to continue to bleed
Not sure how I manage to get you back
And put our love firmly back on track.

A broken heart and a broken shoe are alike
They both abandon the body and go on strike
Both can be repaired with the right glue
I can live without the shoe, but not without you.

You are the shoe that I long to wear
I continue to search for you everywhere
I won't give up as I continue to sit
Waiting for the shoe that once did fit.

Love is like glass slippers and so is my heart
Fragile, rare, and crystal clear from the start
It easily breaks when love slips away
I won't stop crying until you're back to stay.

2.

"CHAMELEON LOVE"

Love changes like a chameleon,
It becomes whatever it touches;
Love bloats us up like helium,
And holds us tight in its clutches.

Falling in love offers no guarantee,
Your heart serves as the thermostat;
Falling in love is usually free,
But your body becomes an acrobat.

Your mind becomes a spinning wheel,
And your life becomes a whirlwind;
It's hard to tell if love is real,
When love becomes your only friend.

A chameleon is best described as a lizard,
It charms its prey into submission;
Love was created by a wizard,
Who casts his spells without permission.

Chameleons and love are synonymous,
It's the nature of who they are;
Love and chameleons are autonomous,
It's their duty to be bizarre.

3.

"UMBILICAL CORD"

Matthew 19:6
speaks of a model marriage without divorce –
a modern-day miracle, to say the least.
Yesterday, Adam's rib was enough to sustain Eve
after the serpent appeared in the garden with the poison apple.
Today, when the serpent appears,
all the ribs in the kitchen can't keep us from
cutting the umbilical cord – that vital lifeline
which connects Husband and Wife at the birth of a marriage.
Everyone knows a vowed marriage can only be severed by death,
but the serpent modernized and changed the shape of his
poison apples to the form of legal misnomers.
The tasty red ones are dubbed "irreconcilable differences."
The delicious yellow ones are called "incompatible lifestyles."
And the green tart ones are named "non-commensurate educations."
They are all equally poisonous but convenient alibis to legally sever
the umbilical cord of marriage when troubles appear.
Fortunately, Matthew 19:6
does not share the same legal opinion.
It simply says, *"Wherefore they are no more twain, but one flesh.*
What therefore God hath joined together, let no man put asunder."

4.

"BLACK GOLD"

Like Abraham, Martin, and John
Tupac, Michael, and Prince are gone;
They, too, left in their prime
We mourn their deaths as a crime.

Young death is a mystery
It often comes before victory;
Their return is a fairy tale
Their legacy of good will prevail.

Whitney, Aretha, and Tina
Three queens departed the arena;
Their talent set a gold standard
In them, our pride was anchored.

They all answered the call
To excel before their fall;
The world is not the same
Their fame was not to blame.

Talent, Love, and Praise
Are accolades that we raise;
We lift our glasses and toast
The ones who meant the most.

Their short stay here on Earth
Was unequal to their worth;
Yet, we thank Him for their stay
And for their souls we always pray.

5.

"BEFORE JUNETEENTH"

Listening to the lazy dawn
Feel like skipping work today
Stretch my arms wide and yawn
And relax on a bale of hay

    Working on a big farm
    Is my daily occupation
    Hangover headache is my alarm
    And the reason for my vacation

Will pay dearly if I procrastinate
My chores will go undone
Plowing will have to wait
And this day will not be won

    Been working since I was nine
    And now I am fifty-two
    None of this farm is mine
    This is what I was bred to do

Working hard is the rule
Vacation is not to be had
No forty acres and a mule
No mom and no dad

    My vacation was a fantasy
    My tardiness was unreal
    This farm depends on me
    I'm off to plow the field

6.

"After Juneteenth"

Listening to the quiet dawn
My life is nice and warm
Stretched out on the lawn
For a picnic on our farm

Worked hard to own this land
To extend our family roots
We crossed the burning sand
In bare feet without boots

Kids growing big and strong
It's hard to believe my eyes
What could ever go wrong
In our man-made paradise

Our children are our currency
Our forty acres and a mule
We cannot afford complacency
We believe in the Golden Rule

We toil with blood, sweat, and tears
Our tractor plows our field
We work all through the years
For this dream that we build

We celebrate our ancestors
And picnic every year
They and God were our protectors
And made our freedom sincere

7.

"LOVE LINES TO AN ICEBERG"
(A COLD LOVE)

Trying to unthaw frozen affection
is like licking a gigantic popsicle,
Confucius might say. What a protection!
Why must love be so cold? A mere obstacle
blocking the way to a truthful heart
and causing one to fake what is felt.
A popsicle is still cold when torn apart
and sweet when it begins to melt.
But a person who is always cold
will never melt anything except away
and probably alone, never to unfold
the mystery of those who stay
     In love rather than strive to be
     That cold part of the iceberg you can't see.

8.

"MY SIGNIFICANT OTHER"

What's significant about us
Is that you belong to me and
I belong to you, forever.
No matter what society says,
We were meant to be.
I am yours and you are mine –
S I G N I F I C A N T L Y.

Call what we have a common law marriage or two soulmates who are equally yoked.

We may not be legally married, but you were meant for me and I was meant for you. I knew it instantly when we first met.

The most profound thing that I've ever experienced in my life was when I first met you. When you rode your bicycle past mine, I was drawn to you like a firefly to a lantern. My world got really small and very large simultaneously.

You complete me and we can usually finish each other's sentences. My soul feels like it's known you forever, although it's only been a few years.

It is impossible for anyone to tear us apart. I would rather lose my life than to lose you.

You are my safety blanket. You are my pacifier. You are my umbilical cord, my lifeline.

I cannot see myself going through life without you. There is nothing or no one more important to me than you.

In my world, there is only you and me. We control our own universe and guard each other with our lives.

Until the end of our time here on Earth and beyond that, I will only give myself to you.

What love has joined together, let no one else put asunder, literally.

And I do love you with no fear of our love ever fading. I significantly thank you for being my significant other.

9.

"LIFE PARTNERS"

In Life
Everyone needs a partner –
Someone to talk to
Confide in
Walk with
Believe in
Hold onto
Someone to –
LOVE.
In this life
YOU are MY
Life Partner

People often talked about the two of them when they were together in public, but they didn't seem to care. They were life partners who were oblivious to the world around them. They lived within their own matrix, which served as their whole, special world.

Unlike others who go through life unfulfilled, they were unashamed at openly displaying their affections in public, and they defied anyone else who wanted to define their relationship. They knew that going through life solo was not meant for them.

They had no limits and would not be limited by others' social mores or moral codes.

Every day, they lived the meaning of ride-or-die lovers, and they knew that in death, they would still prefer to be together – wherever they landed. They were unconcerned about the afterlife because they knew their love had been ordained by the universe.

A life partner is like a birthmark: a skin-deep designation that develops soon after a person is born.

In the end, it may finally prove that these life partners were in perfect harmony while everyone else was out of tune.

10.

"Heroes and Lovers"

Heroes
are best remembered
by their incredible
feats;
Lovers
are best remembered
by their indelible
words.
Both are immortal.

Heroes may always
save the day;
while lovers always
come what may.

Lovers do work
to steal our heart;
Heroes give us
a brand-new start.

Lovers give love
for us to keep;
Heroes we dream of
when we sleep.

Lovers can be
from either gender;
Heroes can too
with names like Brenda.

In the end,
Heroes always win;
Lovers win too
when love begins.

11.

"TODAY I MET A GIRL"

Today, I saw a Girl –
Young, Pure, and Impressionable.
Warmly, her smile singed my soul
as her beauty fondly made me reminisce
how it feels to be infatuated:
> It feels just like love
> so right, so genuine, so magical,
> yet the magic often fades when the mysteries unfold.

Flowers, candy, and kisses are initially
cherished above all, but even they yield
when true love does not exist.
I suppose candid convictions are preferred more
than candied rhetoric, kindly coated with sweet, elusive truths.

Today I met a Girl –
Inexperienced, Eager, and Optimistic.
Softly, she held my hand and her touch
made me wonder what makes love real:
> If true infatuation is manufactured feelings
> manifested by fickle emotions, then
> real love must be made of that which is
> divine: blind trust, faith, and prayer.

Today, I let a Girl –
Loving, Original, and Stable
enter my world through an invisible door.
Gracefully, she walked in and again,
I placed the reins in my heart's hands:
      Starting anew with a new love is never easy
      when hurt lingers freshly, but to start over
      is to love again. New faith gives way
      to new trust and old hurt becomes healed with forgiveness.
Although today I saw, met, and let
A Girl singe, touch, and enter my world,
I feel I have just discovered a new Lady.

12.

"Premeditated Sex 2"

Murder and love can both be
spontaneous, impulsive, and premeditated.
Love can be murderous
and murder can be lovely –
If expertly done by professionals.

When I first saw her,
I knew what had to be done.
She simply must be taken out,
but it had to look like an accident –
It must appear to be a natural cause.

I sharply turned my vehicle
and began to secretly stalk her every move.
Down one aisle and then another –
I wanted to avoid any detection for as long as I could.
Suddenly, she turned her vehicle in my direction.

It seemed she became suspicious
and began to stalk me, so I purposely careened off course.
I could no longer see her, but I could feel her presence.

Then I spotted her again farther away down the aisle;
she seemed ready for a face-off.
I rushed my vehicle toward hers
and made a quick impact.
She spun her vehicle around quickly and stared at me.
I now suspected my cover was blown.
She stretched out her hand
and told me to reach for it –
She stuck her weapon of choice in my face.

Looking at her lusty cleavage, my weapon
hardened and brushed against my thigh –
she had beaten me to the draw.

She gave me a friendly shot and walked away
before I was able to trigger my weapon.
Now that I had her business card in my hand,
I knew this murder was going to be easy.

13.

"Hey Man, I Love You"

Yesterday, I wrote my best friend a letter
and signed it, "Yours truly."
After I mailed it, I wondered why I didn't sign the
letter with love.
After all, he is my best friend and I do love him.
Then I wondered if my stubborn male pride had made
me too ashamed to tell another man I love him.
But he's not just another man; he's my best friend.
I suppose I was trying to find another way to tell him
I love him without actually saying I love him
so that my meaning could not be misconstrued.
But how can love be misconstrued?
Why didn't I just say what I felt?
We've been friends for over 25 years.
It might have been easier when we were younger,
but I never told him then, either.
I may never get another chance to tell him than now.
After all, he is my best friend and I do love him.
Today, I'll write another letter, and this time I'll say,
"Hey man, I love you!"

14.

"WHAT IS BROTHERLY LOVE?"

I love my brothers in a special way
I'm not talking about the way others say
This love is true with room to grow
Unlike the quiet love only the down-low know.

Loving your brother is like loving yourself
For self-pride is required for mental wealth
To be free to love your brother is God's plan
There's nothing wrong with loving another man.

My brothers unconditionally love me back. I feel
Our blood is thick and our bond is real
Others may question or even doubt
But I know what I'm talking about.

What is brotherly love, you may inquire?
It's the burning inside like a warm fire
To know your brothers will always be there
Whenever you need them, and they'll always care.

15.

"The Walls That Love Built"

My treasure is now safe!
As far as the human eye can see,
An impenetrable wall encircles my well-guarded treasure –
My heart.
Is it a fort or a fortress?
It makes no difference to the attackers.
These walls were built as a defense mechanism
Against those who trespass and plunder—
Against those who leave pain instead of pleasure—
Against those who rob and leave the lights on—
Against those who…well, against everyone!
Burning these walls with fiery old flames
Yields no instant admission.
Scaling these walls with intent to do malice
Provides only a rungless ladder to descend.
Smashing these walls with sticks and stones
Reflects no visible scars on its force field.
Robbed once before, this treasure will never be robbed again,
And my walls guarantee that it won't.
Built by a very shrewd but foolish architect,
These walls not only keep others out,
But they also keep the treasurer hidden from other treasures.
Are they diamonds or fool's gold?
It makes no difference to these walls.

16.

"The Wisdom of Understanding"

Sometimes,
unspoken words say more than realized
and spoken words say less than actually meant.
But when the wisdom of silence and understanding
touches lips, words disintegrate and matter very little.

Beautiful women can make men do crazy, stupid things.

A handsome man can reduce the most mature woman to become girlish and giddy.

When Mother Nature is at work, no one is safe from her magic charms and spells.

Opposites attracting each other is the way nature planned it, and everyone is susceptible to falling in love.

Soft music, sweet perfume, a starry night, and a full moon are just convenient enablers to help set the mood or stage the environment but are not required when true love is upon us.

The wisdom of understanding understands and appreciates the wisdom behind falling in love. It is an indescribable feeling that surpasses anything else on Earth or beyond the universe when caught up in its rapture.

People have fallen dramatically in love with just a glance or a mere touch of a hand without uttering any words. Words are not necessary to fall in love. Only a complete understanding and acceptance of the experience that transcends one's life into something otherworldly is required.

Being blind or deaf does not hinder one from experiencing true love.

When someone special comes, our heart opens up like a door and pulls the welcome mat safely inside.

And when someone special leaves, that same heart shrinks to the size of a pin and sticks itself to bleed.

17.

"CLOSE ENCOUNTERS WITH AN ANGEL IN FIVE PARTS"

(Part One)

"Nobody Else New"

Like the covered bridges of Madison County,
I eagerly wait to be re-encountered;
aliens may possibly exist,
but I know angels do.

Nobody else knew
about the angelic starship
that once transported me
into another space and time.

Nobody else new
has ever given me such
an out-of-body experience
that also probed my mind.

Nobody else knew
about the picnic in space
with my alien love
that picked my heart apart.

Nobody else new
knows that what happens in space
stays in space
until the end of time.

(Part Two)

"Cold Turkey"

Cold turkey to a junkie
is like a walk in the park
on a summer's day
compared to the jones that has me.

My aching body is doubled over
trying to regurgitate a taste
that refuses to leave me
due to being under my skin.

One does not have to believe in aliens
in order to be captured;
my close encounter was yesteryear's summer,
and I never saw it coming until it was too late.

The starship that snared me was unadorned
with flashing lights and whirring sounds,
but it was quietly beautiful with a noble shell
shaped like an angel with ebony wings.

Ever since then, I yearn to see my captor again
to ease my pain and restore my balance;
the line was cut and I was disconnected
from the normal lines of communication.
As the temperature plummets,
I sense that I will never be the same –
not until I get a new fix
or until I am thawed out by another close encounter.

(Part Three)

"Separate Dreams"

What do angels dream of?
Or do they dream at all?
When we were made as one,
my dreams were suspended in space.

While my body is in the present,
my mind swims beyond the stars
like floating on a magic carpet
upside down and inside out.

It's complicated, but it's also relative
because life is best lived on the edge,
not knowing what makes your heart beat,
but knowing who has the key to it.

Separate but equal dreams are fine
when I sense I am being dreamed about, too;
our shared experiences make for a
once-in-a-lifetime covenant.

Dreaming of a time when I was free
could never be the same as freedom
because my mind was imprisoned
by the rapture of the moments.

Separate lives with separate dreams
equal one conjoined heart of memories
vast enough to stay strong until confirmed
by the reality of it all – Lust Never Sleeps!

(Part Four)

"The Da Vinci Code Revealed"

Deeply embedded between the paint and the canvas,
lie secret mysteries only known to a few;
the code da Vinci used to communicate
his love of art has always remained in plain view.

To the casual eye, the embedded messages mean very little,
yet to the one who understands, much is revealed;
decoding art is a function of the mind,
but feeling art is a purpose of the heart.

A single word paints a thousand pictures
for the mind's eye to see and the heart to feel;
"a picture paints a thousand words"
is a cliché that unlocks all our 5 senses plus 1.

Simply put, no one else can make sense out of human art
that only has one for its intended audience
except for the one who holds the second key to
unlocking the secret mystery of yesterday and tomorrow.

(Part Five)

"The Road"

The road of regret is a long road
full of doubt and second guesses
that, in the end, serve no purpose
because life is short and precious by the second.

The road is a lonely place for two weary travelers,
but it keeps them safe from the rush hour of reality;
they carry the fire that others seek
by seizing the opportunities of the day.

On one hand, timing is everything,
but on another, it is not;
sometimes, time marches out of step
between what is real and what is desired.

The angel who took my hand
and led me away was as real as I am;
yet I never expected to be reborn
during a virtual yet mutual midlife crisis.

As our swords touched,
we danced around the real issue
until it was too late to be on guard;
she *touchéd* my heart and left me wounded.

So, I say that nobody else new
could ever inspire a cold turkey like me
to have separate dreams intertwined with
Da Vinci codes and lonely roads like my angel.

18.

"L.U.S.T.

(LOVE U STILL TOMORROW)

I've loved a thousand women,
but mostly in my dreams or theirs;
the touch of your virgin lips
pushed my odometer back to zero
when we met and made our covenant

I've never known anyone like you before,
Or anything like you made me feel;
the electricity of you inside of me
revived my heart to a level unknown
by modern medicine or sexual healing

Wherever I go, I think of you,
And I feel you inside of me;
two hearts beat inside my chest
and the love I feel is protected
by the secret of you in my soul

The difference between love and lust
is something I will not reveal;
your secret is safe with me,
and your unmatched love for passion
surpasses all to become my one desire.

19.

"LOVE ME BECAUSE I LOVE YOU"

Sometimes, it's not enough to just love someone,
Especially when you feel love is not reciprocal.
And it's no fun loving just for fun
Unless you're expecting a miracle –

Although I can't make you love me,
Please love me because I love you.
I promise to always make you feel free
To do the things you need to do –

Loving me is not a quantum leap,
For my love is honest, real, and true.
I pray for you before I sleep so
Please love me because I love you –

20.

"SECRET SECRETS"

No one has ever known that I love you –
Not even myself.
I guess my feelings felt that I would betray
Them by telling someone else.

Because no secret keeps its secrecy
When it's told,
Even my feelings know that –
That's why they keep themselves under control.

Like a window, my feelings look at you
From both sides with much regret,
For I long to tell you I love you,
But to keep things quiet, it remains a *secret* secret.

21.

"SCATTERED REFLECTIONS"

Scattered reflections mean more than viewing
    thousands of pieces of broken glass;
Collectively, they represent thrown-about thoughts
    and fleeting images of past golden days.
A solid love affair can very well be
    shattered when troubles in paradise pass;
Trying to pick up the pieces after it's broken
    becomes a hard task to repair in many ways.
Tattered lives and *battered* emotions are often the result
    of fragile hearts made broken;
Even the love and memories of good days gone by
    cannot replace the heartache now felt.
Remembering that it is better to give than to receive,
    is only an old adage that serves as a token;
For efforts in rekindling an unwilling candle are futile,
    if they, like wax, begin to melt.
Scattered reflections never reassemble themselves after being broken.

22.

"TALKING TO A TREE"

I rarely talk to a stranger, but I often talk to a tree.
Maybe God created trees just like me in his own likeness.
The old oak in my backyard told me it wants to be free
I told the oak that its search for freedom is a mutual quest.

When I talk to the tree, I'm talking to an old friend,
Another child of Mother Nature's standing tall before the sun;
What we have in common is our innate ability to bend
The oak is free to grow, stretch, breathe, but it cannot run.

The freedom it seeks is to be appreciated and respected,
And to always know that trees and humans have a common link;
The oak in my backyard does not want to be neglected for
It communicates back to me and it causes me to think.

We both can bear witness to life and the beauty it brings,
And our roots serve to honor our ancestors with leaves and seeds.
Being one with nature is the way God planned things,
For the tree was made to provide for us and support our needs.

Talking to a tree is not as strange as it may appear,
After all, it is alive with God's spirit and majesty.
When I talk to my oak tree, I feel God is near
I rarely talk to a stranger, but I often talk to a tree.

23.

"The Rose Inside of Us"

We give the rose to profess our love
It blooms in our heart and makes it red
Its smell is heaven-scent from above
It helps celebrate the words we said
We may forget, but roses never do
Those three little words – I Love You!

Red, white, yellow, and pink
Roses tend to make us think
Roses have a very short lifespan
Secretly, they're God's message to man
Orange, blue, black, and gold
All God's miracles for us to behold!

Our heart is the red rose inside
The part where love resides
Its thorny stem serves to remind
It hurts sometimes to be kind
Roses are special and so are we
Roses and love should always be free!

24.

"DREAMS AND WISHES"

Dreams and Wishes
most often come true
when the Mind and the Heart
are joined with Faith.

Wishes and Dreams
fill our Heads and
our Hearts alike
when we Believe in them.

Wishing on a Star
and Dreaming on the Moon
are both based on Love
Given and Love Received.

25.

"Perception"

Who would perceive life inside a peanut,
Or look to find freedom inside a shell?
Probably one who believes that honey is in a coconut,
Or the color of a rose does not determine its smell.
And what in him sparked HIS interest to make him see?
Possibly his belief and his humbleness,
Or maybe his genuine sincerity.
Whatever HE had perceived, he went on to confess.
The life of the peanut was soon illuminated,
But freedom was still far behind,
Yet, HIS spark of interest was communicated,
As it forever remained in his mind.
For just as the sheep of the shepherd are spread in herds,
He used the peanut (among other things) to spread HIS words.

(Written upon leaving the Dr. George Washington Carver Museum in
Tuskegee, Alabama, 1977)

26.

"SOLO"

At times we may have to sing alone in order
To be heard above the others. It's not
The song that we sing that will make us known,
But the way that we sing it.
Not too soft and not too high.
Or not too low and not too loud.
Even though life may seem like a solo for some,
It is a song worth singing.
For who can tell,
It may finally prove that you are in perfect harmony
While everyone else is out of tune.

27.

"PLEASE, TUNE ME BACK IN"

Lately, it seems we are on different wavelengths.
Our signals are strong, but we are going in two different directions.
Our fuzzy logic is no longer logical,
and our latitudes and longitudes have been lost.
Maybe it's just me. Am I too far out of range to receive your signals?
If so, will you adjust my antenna, wiggle my dish, play with my remote,
Or whatever it takes to tune me back in?Please tune me back in so that
I can be on your frequency.

28.

"Forbidden Fruit"

From afar, I admired the beautiful tree,
and I longed to get nearer for a better look.
From behind the fence, I adored the luscious fruit,
so I climbed the fence to get even closer.
The warning signs were all around,
but I ignored them to get even nearer.
A piece of the forbidden fruit
broke loose by itself and rolled next to me.
I picked it up and held it in my hands
p l a t o n i c a l l y.
With no intentions of eating it,
I began to crave a piece and then I took a small bite.
As I devoured the fruit, I became the fruit
and it became me – we were one.
From then on, I was ripe with desire,
and I longed to be with other forbidden fruit.
The only thing forbidden now is
my will to return to the innocence I once had.
I am the sinful, forbidden fruit,
and I will be here forever.

29.

"THE GOLDEN WATCH"

Time watches over our carefree days of infancy
with peace, calm, and tranquility.

Our invulnerable adolescent years are lavishly spent
without stress or worry, and they remain forever gold.

Yet, the precious, quiet moments of maturity are not
perpetual – they only last until the silence breaks.

A *peace* of time that elides the clock and renews
our youth is one that is rare and prime.

Like the proverbial needle in a haystack, it seems
impossible to find until we look inside and behold it.

This inner peace is both timely and timeless –
Its silent music uplifts our spirit and awakens our soul.

Nothing escapes or enters our mind when we're
reflecting on a piece of time suspended.

The golden watch does not symbolize retirement –
It symbolizes the full circle of our youthful life.

The golden watch was not made to be rewound or reset –
Yet, it keeps perfect time by how well we live.

30.

"A Peace of Time"

The carefree days of newborn babies, so calm and tranquil,
cleverly evade capture by staying suspended in time –

Thus, a peace that eludes the clock and renews
our youth becomes one that is rare and prime –

And, like the proverbial needle in a haystack, seems
impossible until we look inside and behold –

This inner peace, both timely and timeless,
Gives us an uplifting and our spirit it awakes –

As we listen to the soothing music of every silent thought,
it harmonizes our soul and makes us feel sublime –

With our eyes closed and our minds open,
nothing escapes or enters during this period when dreams unfold –

Quiet times cannot be bridled or broken into pieces,
but to know oneself inside is all that it takes --

31.

"Today I Saw the Wind"

Not far from where I was sitting in the sun,
I saw a miracle happen right before my very eyes.
The wind seemed to be playing merry-go-round in a sand pile
and a bee was darting and gliding overhead like a small plane.
As the bee dove toward the grassy ground,
a boyish image faintly came into view;
its hand fanned the bee back up toward the sun.
Breezing off after it, the childish wind raced and
escorted the bee over the tops of the trees,
and they disappeared beyond the sky.
What a miracle! Who would believe me?
Today, I saw the wind take time out to play with a bee,
and I wondered if, again, I would ever see anything
else so breathtaking.

32.

"Capturing The Day"

Oh, if only I could make this day last forever
and take it out when I need it again.
The wind is blowing freely through to my soul –
The sun is shining brightly through to my soul –
The rain is showering lightly through to my soul –
    I feel so very good, so alive, so blessed!
And I'm cherishing every second of this day's rare gifts.
If every day was like this one, we wouldn't have to worry
about trying to capture the days and keep them forever.
But every day already is special and rare;
why don't we feel good all the time?
Today I feel very good.
      What day is this?

33.

"Free Spirits"

Broken perches, changing climates, and hungry minds
are general reasons why birds take flight.

Seeking strands of straw to build their nest or
food to feed their minds, they sometimes land near us.

Possibly, birds are like us. And if they are, I'm
sure there are other things that make them soar to higher heights.

Although they don't stay long and they're not ours to keep,
it's nice to see one land in our backyard; thus,

Birds connote freedom just like children, heaven,
and flags on poles.

Birds are meant to wander, to fly solo, and to
frequently change their homes.

Like them, we are often compelled by an inner
drive to reach our goals.

And when we do, yesterday becomes a pathway
to much greater domes.

No one can surely know if the birds' flights are
ever in vain,

Or if their searching will lead them back this way
to our door.

But for our sake, let's pray that the birds will
come back to us again,

And that they will take us with them, wherever,
on their next soar.

34.

"WITH NEW EYES"

When I first saw You, I didn't notice the real YOU;
    I only saw a familiar face attached to a fatigued body
Like mine: worn, weary, and withdrawn.
    In You, I saw a mirror image of myself more than I saw
The face that represented You. But now, after knowing You better,
    My vision has been enhanced by Your individual beauty.
With new eyes, I see You as a humble friend who
    Unselfishly puts others before Your own special needs.
I see you as a soft candlelight that touches others
    With your care and causes a chain reaction similar to
A Domino Effect.
    I can see through You, to Your soul, and know that
Your heart is pure; I can actually feel your aura as it
    Encircles Your face and permeates your body.
And I see you tomorrow as You change only to remain
    The same, realizing that love is a renewed faith in life.
With new eyes, I see You, I see Me
    Walking together, hand-in-hand, heart-to-heart,
Looking forward to the day that we become ONE.

35.

"SPACE"

Sometimes
I need mine
and you need yours,
I understand.

Occasional breathers
are good for any
relationship
so neither one
ever feels crowded.

However, I hope the
breathers are brief,
for I wouldn't want
anyone else to ever crowd my
S P A C E.

36.

"FIREFLIES"

On almost quiet
crickety summer nights
of dimly lit skies
that resemble both solitude and despair,
tiny bursts of light *flicker* about like
flashes of new inspiration or like
ideas of hope conveniently appearing
so we can *see* that all is never lost.
Where do fireflies come from?
Where do they get their light?
I wonder if fireflies ever experience *burnout*?

37.

"CONSEQUENCES"

I once watched an excited little boy
launch a small paper boat into a beautiful lake.
The small boat peacefully waded along
until it came upon an unexpected waterfall.
When the boat reached the waterfall,
it fell out of view and the little boy cried.
That whole scene made me think of the word
C O N S E Q U E N C E – that which naturally
flows from a preceding action or condition;
result; a logical conclusion.
You see, the boy, the boat, the lake, and the waterfall
were each operating as created to be.
The young boy's natural wonder
caused the boat to sail on the waters with an unchartered course
until it reached its logical but unexpected conclusion – the waterfall.
If the boy or the boat had control over the lake or the waterfall,
things may have been different.
I don't know what actually happened to the small boat,
but I like to imagine that it landed safely upright
and continued its sail until it reached another logical conclusion.
Life is full of consequences and lessons learned,
but all of them don't have to be
painful or fatal.

38.

"A SOMETHING-FOR-NOTHING WORLD"

The human quest for an endless favor
Without offering a hand to repay the deed done,
Makes this world four-seasoned with savor.
That selfish myth deceives almost everyone,
But there are some still chivalrous,
untainted by the thought of money and material things
being obtained through means that are often hideous
and with the desire to truly earn their wings.
Still, there are those who seek the light load and
Low-risk street, never to give, only to receive;
but soon, judgment will come and we all must stand
on our own two feet and begin to heave
    Our way into the coal yards or the vineyards as payment
    For something for nothing is only a figment.

39.

"A SENSE OF HUMOR"

With nothing else to do, I started a rumor
That the key to life is a sense of humor;
Laughter is the best medicine to prescribe
Regardless whatever ailments one can describe.

Laughing at ourselves is even more key
for being less serious makes us most free;
To be comfortable within our own skin
gives us the ability to always win.

A sense of humor makes us howl and
laughing gives us a beautiful smile;
Laughter increases our days on Earth and
Maximizes our potential and human worth.

40.

"The Psychology of Preaching"

Yelling out to us on how we should live
Making us feel guilty so we will give
Lightning will strike if we don't pay
'Cause the Lord will get his anyway.

Giving us a real, big, scary look
While reciting to us from The Good Book
Telling us all our ways we must mend
Or the world will surely come to an end.

Promising us that if we are pure
We might go to heaven, but not for sure
Because only God knows how to choose
The sandals from the alligator shoes.

And after we're through with all our giving
We can go back to our regular living
But don't forget my people to pray
That you'll have more money next Sunday.

For it is better to give than to receive
And easier to be scared than to believe.

41.

"WHEN I HAVE FEARS"

When I have fears of the world coming to an end,
I hang my head and my evil ways I try to mend.
But I don't get far because soon I know,
That I must reap all that I sow.
So, I start right back just like before,
And to my list of sins, I add a bit more.
But soon all of this will come to a halt,
My actions – not my fears – are all my fault.

42.

"Things That Make Me Cry"

I don't like to see one person hurt another
    By calling him a name,
Or watch my little brother lose
    When he's playing his biggest game.

I don't like to see people starving
    When there's enough food to share,
Or see a father neglect his child
    And make him turn for love elsewhere.

I don't like to see grown-ups fail to understand
    That children have feelings, too,
By letting them grow up in a world
    Without love and truth.

I don't like to see a person keep himself
    From loving by hating his brother,
Or violate the Commandments
    By killing another.

Somehow, all these things and more
    Make me wonder why,
Maybe one day I'll understand their meaning
    And cease to want to cry.

43.

"LOVE INDIGO"

Love changed from red to blue
  In the wink of an eye;
What happened to our romantic glue?
  Why did it say goodbye?

Up and gone means love indigo,
  I wonder where it all went
Hide and seek is love incognito
  Something more than a hint.

My heart leaves, my body stays
  Our love is now suspended;
Love lasts forever, not for days
  Yet Cupid has been apprehended.

You - I don't love anymore
  My love has run its course;
You - I no longer adore
  My love requests a divorce.

44.

"WEDDING DAY DUET"

On this day
We will be joined by the songs we sing
As we tune our voices for this melody.
We both sing solos for the King
But today we will sing in harmony.

Your solo is a song of Beauty
And mine a song of Love.
Together we will make a rhapsody,
And continue to sing for God above.

There will be no need for two solos,
For we will make one duet.
There will be all joy on this day
That we will never forget.

45.

"Jumpin' the Broom"

When we first jumped the broom
My laces were untied-
I tripped over the handle
And landed on my bride-

Everyone laughed except me
They felt sorry for my wife-
Said she deserved a better sweeper
For the rest of her life-

Things got better as time went on
I became a smoother sweeper-
And when the rabbit died
I knew my wife was a keeper-

Our family now grew with a child
The one thing that made us whole-
Now when people see us
I make sure the truth is told-

When we first jumped the broom
My laces were untied-
I untied them on purpose
To land on my bride-

46.

"KEEPING A HOLD ON MY SOUL"

I don't believe in love at 1st sight
Or even at 2nd sight, for that matter
I can feel love when it's right
When it's not, I select another batter.

I keep a tight rein on my soul
And rarely allow it to run free
I find I have to keep it under control
If not, I'd unleash the real me.

The world is not ready for that day
When I finally open Pandora's Box
When I truly give my heart away
I'm going to be crazy like a fox.

On the outside, I appear to be cool
But inside, my soul is running wild
Aching to release my inner fool
Yet the world will have to wait awhile.

47.

"SUNS SET"

Suns come and suns go.
The one that rises is not the same one that falls.
When the sun rises, it thoughtfully
Shines its light throughout. It lights
Up the day with its power and spreads
A special feeling of warmth.
When the sun sets, it nonchalantly casts
A shadow of darkness and leaves an air of gloom.
Some say not to worry, for the sun will surely rise again.
Yes, the sun will rise again, but it will be a different day
Since days cannot be recaptured.
Where do suns go beyond the horizon?
Why do they have to set?
How can we capture their power
And use it to make us rise again when we are low?
Suns come and suns go.

48.

"Siamese Twins"

The Success of Failure:

"Continuous failure is sometimes very valuable when viewed as a great reinforcer of purpose toward one's final point of satisfaction."

The Failure of Success:

"The headache of success is not being able to take one's hat off to those who helped paved the way, and not being able to put it back on for being too BIGHEADED."

III

ESSAYS

Essay – An essay is a piece of writing that is written to convince someone of something or to simply inform the reader about a particular topic.

My essays are generally about topics that I care enough about to share my knowledge or viewpoint in a thoughtful fashion. Rather than persuasively convince a reader to see it my way, I try to at least make a reader think about the subject at hand in an introspective way.

My hope is that these essays will cause you to think about aspects of the subjects you never thought about and apply what you learn to your general "toolbox" knowledge base. I enjoy writing essays that expound upon ordinary things we may take for granted.

CHAPTER TWENTY-ONE

"BUY ANY MEANS NECESSARY"

WE <u>LOVE</u> GUNS in America!

I recently read a news article proclaiming there are more guns than people or books in the United States. Our current population of 332 million people has been dwarfed by the number of guns we possess.

The number of guns we possess speaks directly to the meteoric rise in the number of shootings, mass killings, suicides, and easy access by minors. Add to the equation the lax gun laws or no gun laws in many states, and one can easily connect the dots.

The names of mass shootings in places like Columbine (1999), Sandy Hook (2012), Las Vegas (2017), Parkland (2018), Uvalde (2022), and the Allen, Texas, Mall shooting (2023) will forever be with us as the list grows longer each day. Still, no stringent gun laws have been passed in the U.S. Why so many guns? Why so many shootings? Who's buying all the guns?

The Second Amendment asserts that as an American citizen, you have the individual right to arm yourself. It further states that the government cannot infringe upon that right.

The Second Amendment was ratified on December 15, 1791, which was two centuries, three decades, and two years ago (232 years). It was one of the first ten amendments to the U.S. Constitution that came to be known as the Bill of Rights. This amendment, more than any other, has been broadly interpreted as the bedrock foundation for American freedom. But at what cost?

The authors of the Constitution could not have possibly imagined the arrival of AR-15s for personal use. Had they been able to foresee that these weapons of mass destruction belong with and only with the military, they would have reacted differently to this individual right to bear arms.

Thank God the public was not able to see photos of the bodily remains of the young students in the aforementioned school shootings; in some cases, there was not much left of the body after the AR-15 rounds ripped through their flesh and blew their tiny bodies apart. This is a parent's worst nightmare.

As a former federal law enforcement officer, I am amazed at how easy it is for some to obtain these destructive weapons. I doubt that I, with my retired federal law enforcement credentials, could go out and buy multiple weapons, thousands of rounds of ammunition, and bullet-proof armor without someone questioning me or being suspicious about my motives.

In June of 1964, when Malcolm X called for freedom, justice, and equality "by any means necessary," his famous comments were broadly interpreted as a call for using violence as a tactic to accomplish these ends. Although there was much violence associated with the 1960s and Malcolm himself fell to a violent end by being shot to death, Blacks as a whole have not resorted to amassing weapons and ammunition in anticipation of an all-out race war other than to use them in Black self-genocide.

Yet, for some time now, many other people have been amassing weapons and ammunition at an alarming rate; the famous slogan has now changed to "Buy Any Means Necessary," referring to the purchase of any and all types of weapons for an eventual Armageddon.

I pray that we in America come to our senses before it's too late and before many more innocent victims fall to violent shootings from weapons not anticipated to be used for an individual's right to bear arms.

By any means necessary, I hope that we can enact common sense laws to stop the mass gun sales and cease the senseless killings of our own American citizens, who all deserve the right to have life, liberty, and the pursuit of happiness – *by any means necessary.*

CHAPTER TWENTY-TWO

"PEANUTS, TWILIGHT ZONE, AND SEXUAL HEALING"

My Personal Tributes to
Dr. Carver, Rod Serling, and Marvin Gaye

When asked the names of the three people who inspired my life to be what it is today, I often say my parents, my teachers, and my friends. In large part, this is certainly true; however, if I am specifically asked which people have energized my adult life more than anyone else or the names of the three people I would most like to have met, I would without hesitation say Dr. George Washington Carver, Rod Serling, and Marvin Gaye – a scientist, a writer, and a singer.

As a reference to Mitch Albom's novel *The Five People You Meet in Heaven*, I would like three of those people to be Carver, Serling, and Gaye. These three men could not have been more different from each other, and apparently, they had nothing in common. Yet, I found them each to have influenced me exponentially.

By the time Dr. Carver died in January 1943, Rod Serling was eighteen years old, and Marvin Gaye was only three years old, which makes these men unwitting contemporaries – although I doubt they ever met in the flesh.

Dr. Carver actually visited my hometown of Dothan, Alabama, in 1938; Rod Serling visited the residents of Dothan weekly from 1959 to 1964 via his *The Twilight Zone* television series; and in the early 1960s until his death in 1984, Marvin Gaye lived in Dothan daily through his records and songs being played on all our radios, record players, and jukeboxes.

Although I obviously never met any of these men or have any direct connection to them other than my fascination with their lives, I feel a strong spiritual connection to each of them, and they often serve as muses for many of the things I've accomplished in my life. I credit Dr. Carver with giving me my philosophy of life in the way I see things and treat people. I imagine Dr. Carver as one of my ancestors, maybe even my great-grandfather, as part of my bloodline and family tree.

Rod Serling is responsible for my literary creativity, and this evidence is best manifested in the way I weave and blend fantasy and reality throughout my writings. I see Serling as more a teacher or writing coach, since his writings have influenced my way of crafting stories with a twist or an odd touch.

Marvin Gaye's music provided a special soundtrack for my life, and every day, I feel his music in what I am doing or where I am going. Whenever I drive long distances, I always take Marvin Gaye's music with me. Marvin Gaye is like a long-lost uncle or older brother that I barely knew. Much of his life seemed to parallel mine in certain ways, as I feel I have experienced some of the same inner personal demons he faced. If only I could have spent time with him to help him find another way before it was too late.

For many people, Dr. Carver epitomized the ultimate Renaissance man in that, in addition to having been a slave, he was a renowned scientist, a poet, a painter, a musician, a teacher, an inventor, a doctor, and a farmer. For all the marvelous things that he did, Dr. Carver will forever be associated with the peanut – something that he believed contains the unlimited secrets of God's great universe.

Dr. Carver spent his whole life studying the prolific peanut, and he discovered that more than three hundred products could be made from the tiny pod. He also discovered that over two hundred products could be made from the sweet potato and soybeans. Dr. Carver never allowed any textbooks into his laboratory, known as God's Little Workshop, for he always claimed to have no need for them; he said that God was speaking to him and advising him how to make his discoveries on a daily basis. I believe Dr. Carver was one of the greatest heroes produced in the twentieth century, and by now, Hollywood should have made a movie in his honor; however, who could actually play this gentle, scientific giant?

Rod Serling, a writer who specialized in television science fiction, also wrote for the big screen as well; he also taught at Ithaca College. Though brought up in a Jewish family, Serling became a Unitarian Universalist. Unitarian Universalism is a liberal religion with Jewish-Christian roots. It affirms the worth of human beings, advocates freedom of belief and the search for advancing truth, and tries to provide a warm, open, and supportive community for people who believe that ethical living is the supreme witness of religion.

My favorite television program of all time is *The Twilight Zone*, which was the brainchild of Rod Serling. Many of Serling's episodes bear witness to his religious beliefs and can be seen in the way he devised his plots, dialogue, and in his characters. Each black-and-white episode expertly captured my imagination and still intrigues me to this day.

The life of Marvin Gaye and his music had the same effect on me as did Carver and Serling. I was deeply saddened by his death, mainly because I held him in such esteem, especially after he issued *What's Going On?*, my favorite Marvin Gaye album. His music had a healing effect on me and others even though it masterfully combined the vices of sex and the virtues of religion, as evidenced by his divided soul. When it's all said and done, my mind, body, and soul have been forever stimulated and influenced by Carver's peanuts, Serling's *Twilight Zone*, and Gaye's musical and sexual healing; thus, my essay with tributes to them.

Dr. George Washington Carver
(c. 1864-January 4, 1943)
American Agricultural Scientist (age 78-79)

History books tell us that George Washington Carver is said to have been born into slavery in Newton County, Marion Township, near Diamond Place, now known as Diamond, Missouri, on or around July 12, 1864. His exact birth date and year are not known, but speculation has it that it was before slavery was legally abolished in Missouri in January 1865. Carver never knew his father, and history has yet to identify him; however, Carver was said to have ten sisters and one brother, all of whom preceded him in death. Moses Carver, George's owner, purchased George's mother, Mary, on October 9, 1885, for seven hundred dollars. After Carver was kidnapped as a baby, his owner traded a horse for him to be returned. Of course, the rest of Carver's life made for a remarkable history lesson, as he lived to be close to eighty years old, but his contributions—scientific, cultural, philanthropic, and historical—would last forever.

My first introduction to Dr. George Washington Carver cannot be found in history books, but it is deeply etched in my mind. It was in 1977 in Dothan that I and several other young people my age first became familiar with Dr. Carver. In April 1977, a small group of young citizens met to discuss the teenage apathy situation that existed in Dothan. Dedicated to the belief that the young can play active and constructive roles in society, we formed a non-profit youth group and proclaimed ourselves the Participants in the Public's Interest (PPI) to help support various causes and shortfalls in the city of Dothan, like bridging generation gaps, sponsoring sexual awareness and personal hygiene seminars, and feeding people who had a food deficit.

At the height of membership, the Participants in the Public's Interest had over forty members from Dothan, Ashford, Slocomb, Headland, Webb, Gordon, Shorterville, Cottonwood, Eufaula, and Ozark. Some of the active members were Mit Kirkland, Greg Kimble, Larry Graham, Verdell Barrington, Charles Bowman, James Thompson,

Deborah Robinson, Jerry Long, Tommy Turner, Jacquie Stringer, Elias Dabit, Kathy Salter, Kathy Neal, Kenneth Collins, Lois Russell, Allen Johnson, Janice Cook, Deborah Smith, Mary Anderson, James King, Naomi Neal, David Russ, Ricky Graham, Kenneth Rumph, Eliga Reynolds, Dennis McLoyd, David Bennett, Lovie Langston, Joyce Bell, Harry Blythers, David Hayes, Chris Register, Olivia Thornton, Danita Shipman, Mark Kite, and Tom E. Smith. Mr. Bonnie Dickens served as an adviser to the group, and Commissioner John Glanton was a major supporter of PPI.

Consisting primarily of young adults between the ages of eighteen and thirty-five, PPI's first objective was to require each of its members to become registered voters. Believing that voting is essential in making better-informed citizens, we conducted voter registration drives to register citizens who had never before voted and give them an incentive to be better participants in the public's interest.

After doing all these things, we wondered if we could do more for the city in a different way. Since Dothan was known as "The Peanut Capital of the World," every year, it has a National Peanut Festival celebration with parades, programs, and contests that all focus on peanuts. Celebrating the peanut is the central focus of this multi-day event, and the whole community is invited to take part. I love peanuts, and I have eaten them in every way imaginable, including green boiled peanuts – a local delicacy in Dothan.

In the parades, there were decorative floats depicting the peanut and celebrating its worth. It dawned on us that although the peanut was being celebrated, there was no lasting monument to Dr. Carver, the man who studied the peanut and made so many derivative products from it. Although the National Peanut Festival has been celebrated in Dothan since 1938, there has not been one monument or statue dedicated to Dr. Carver within the city.

Believe it or not, our small nonprofit youth group learned that Dr. Carver was invited to be the main speaker for the first Peanut Festival in Dothan. Local Dothan authors Wendell H. and Pamela Ann Stepp's book, *Dothan: A Pictorial History*, reports the following passage: "The date was Friday, November 11, 1938, and nearly freezing on opening night, but a crowd of almost 6,000 gathered to hear Dr. Carver speak."

Mrs. Claudia Williams, one of Dothan's Black educators, reported that she and her family were one of the few Black families present to see Dr. Carver then. She said she remembers being about four years old and her brother was six when their father took them to see Dr. Carver. She said she had a vivid memory of her family sitting underneath a nearby canopy when a White man told them they had to move to another location suitable for them. She said her father quietly relocated them to a section with other Blacks.

During his talk, Dr. Carver urged crop diversification. He pivoted his lanky body on the stage, turning so that everyone could feel he was addressing them in the segregated crowd. He suggested to the Dothan farmers to replenish their soil by rotating their crops and planting peanuts instead of so much cotton. The farmers ultimately did what Carver advised, and they soon learned that his information was accurate. Soon, the farmers had vitamin-enriched soil to grow more crops.

In 1938, Dothan began calling itself The Peanut Capital of the World. But as time went on, Dothan was remiss in acknowledging Dr. Carver with a permanent monument to show its gratitude. In nearby Enterprise, Alabama, about thirty-five miles away from Dothan, they erected a permanent monument dedicated to the boll weevil; the boll weevil was the mighty and destructive beetle that plagued southern cotton crops and caused farmers to modify its one-crop system. Rather than honor Dr. Carver, they honored an insect.

After learning this, PPI set out to right this wrong by getting Dr. Carver his monument. We didn't know exactly how we were going to do it or what we were going to do, but we knew we had to do something. One of the group members suggested we visit Tuskegee, Alabama, to see the Carver Museum and learn all that we could about him before we started our efforts in Dothan.

I was one of the two members who made the two-hour drive to Tuskegee to see Dr. Carver's work along with member Greg Kimble. When we first arrived, I was struck by the statues dedicated to Booker

T. Washington, Dr. Carver, and other important Blacks who had helped put Tuskegee on the map. Once inside the museum, I was astonished to see Dr. Carver's laboratory and all the artifacts left over from his work. We saw some of his inventions and some of his tools still intact, as if he had just used them and walked out of the laboratory.

Dr. Carver's abundant work and life made such an impression on me that upon leaving the museum that day in 1977, I wrote the following poem dedicated to him.

"Perception"

Who would perceive life inside a peanut,
Or look to find freedom inside a shell?
Probably one who believes that honey is in a coconut,
Or the color of a rose does not determine its smell.
And what in him sparked HIS interest to make him see?
Possibly his belief and his humbleness,
Or maybe just his sincerity.
Whatever HE had perceived, he went on to confess.
The life of the peanut was soon illuminated,
But freedom was still far behind.
Yet, HIS spark of interest was communicated,
As it forever remained in his mind.
For just as the sheep of the shepherd are spread in herds,
He used the peanut (among other things) to spread HIS words.

The trip to Tuskegee galvanized us and our mission. It was now clear to us what we needed to do for Dr. Carver in Dothan, although we still were unclear how to go about it. On my own, I continued to conduct more research on the life of Dr. Carver. I went to the library and read everything I could find about him. In a book I read, he had a famous credo that he lived by: "Start where you are with what you have. Make something of it, and never be satisfied." That was it. Now, PPI had its new credo and a roadmap as to how we would get to where we needed to be.

We reported our experience back to the whole group and suggested we commission a bronze bust of Dr. Carver and dedicate it to the city of Dothan. Everyone agreed that it was a fantastic idea; however, we had two major problems to consider: no money and no one to make the bust.

A few of us went back to Tuskegee to ask for ideas and suggestions on how to go about our task. Mrs. Stefania Jarkowski, one of the art professors at Tuskegee, suggested we drive to Montgomery, Alabama, and meet with an artist named Col. C.B. Whitehead. In addition to being a noted sculptor, Col. Whitehead was also a highly decorated retired military officer. Professor Jarkowski said she had worked with him before and that he might be interested in our project. Thinking we had nothing to lose, we made the short drive from Tuskegee to Montgomery and later knocked on the door of Col. Whitehead's genteel home. The professor had alerted the Colonel that we were on our way to see him.

Although it seemed odd that two young Black men with afros were meeting with a White southern gentleman in 1977 in Montgomery, Alabama, to discuss Dr. Carver, we continued our mission. Colonel Whitehead and his wife were extremely polite and invited us in and offered us refreshments. They both sat and listened intently as we told them our hopes and plans to commission a bronze bust of Dr. Carver and donate it to the city of Dothan. He didn't show it on his face, but Colonel Whitehead must have been a little amused at me because I was very animated and passionate in describing how we wanted to right some of the wrongs by giving Dr. Carver his due.

After about an hour-long conversation with Col. Whitehead, he agreed to make the bust of Dr. Carver for us. Astounded, we looked at each other in surprise at how easy it was to convince the sculptor. Col. Whitehead told us that he, too, was a great admirer of Dr. Carver and was often struck by the flowers he always wore in his lapel.

Then came the awkward part about money and how much it would cost. Col. Whitehead estimated that the total cost for the bronze bust would be about $2,500, including the cost to ship it to New York to have it bronzed. In 1977, $2,500 was like two million dollars to us because we didn't have any money. Just when we were sure he was going to ask us for a deposit, Col. Whitehead reached out his hand to shake ours and said, "I'll go ahead and get started on it, and you can pay me after you raise the money." With that, we shook hands, which was the only contract we ever had when we commissioned the bust from Col. Whitehead. We thanked him, and we left to get back to tell everyone we needed to raise $2,500.

The members of PPI readily embraced our mission, and for the next ten months or so, we had car washes, raffles, sold fish sandwiches, chicken dinners, aluminum cans and glass bottles, solicited donations, and anything we could do legally to raise money for the bronze bust.

Surprisingly, the citizens of Dothan, both Black and White, responded favorably, and within a year, we had raised the money necessary to pay for the bust. In the meantime, we made frequent trips back to Montgomery to check on the progress of the bust. By then, we had become fast friends with Col. Whitehead, and he did not mind us dropping in on him without calling first. In fact, he called us in mid-September 1978 and told us that the bust was finished and ready to be viewed.

We eagerly drove to Montgomery and let Col. Whitehead give us a private unveiling of the bust before it became public. When he took the cover off Dr. Carver's bust, we almost cried at its beauty and reverence. We finally realized a dream by giving Dr. Carver his due: a bronze likeness to be housed in the Civic Center of Dothan, Alabama.

A few weeks later, on Sunday, October 8, 1978, the bronze bust was officially dedicated to the city with a huge ceremony. Dothan Mayor Jimmy Grant accepted the bust from the members of PPI, and Col. Whitehead was there to take a bow as the sculptor and creator of the bust. We all smiled as the bust of Dr. Carver sat proudly on display for everyone to see. Approximately forty years after his visit to Dothan, Dr. Carver was widely recognized for all his contributions to the robust economy of Dothan and elsewhere due to the cultivation of the peanut.

Years went by, and the bust of Dr. Carver sat largely unnoticed near the entrance of the Dothan Civic Center. Although it sat there on display in plain view, no one really paid homage to it, like we had hoped. There was never any news media follow-up after it was placed -- even on Black History Month. It now seemed that although Dothan had its monument to Dr. Carver, it was not being showcased enough. The members of PPI aged, and about five years later, in 1983, we disbanded and moved on. PPI was an interracial non-profit community organization in Dothan from 1977 to 1983.

Around 2000, Dothan got its own permanent museum called the G.W. Carver Interpretive Museum. The primary founder and curator of the museum was Dr. Francina Williams, a Dothan native, family friend, and tireless worker in the city who helped bring about social and racial change for the good of all citizens – just like Dr. Carver.

In early March 2006, some of the former members of PPI presented an idea to Dr. Williams that since Dothan now had a permanent Carver Museum, we should consider relocating and rededicating the Carver bust to the new museum. I was living in Philadelphia at the time, and the other members of PPI were scattered all over; however, many were still living in Dothan, too.

PPI wrote a letter to the mayor of Dothan, Pat Thomas, and asked if it would be possible to rededicate the bust and relocate it to the new museum. Mayor Thomas responded affirmatively, and a plan was put in motion to rededicate the bust with an official public ceremony.

When we decided whom we should invite to the ceremony, I immediately thought of Col. Whitehead but assumed he may be deceased by now. Col. Whitehead was probably in his 60s when we first met him, and this was now almost thirty years later. If he were still alive, he would be almost ninety and probably in poor health, or at least I presumed.

One day in Philadelphia, while on my computer, I googled Col. Whitehead's name and found an address and phone number for him; he was still at the same Montgomery, Alabama, residence where we first met him. I called his number and actually got him on the phone. When he answered, I told him that I was a voice from the past and wanted to say hello. I asked him if he remembered me and the PPI when we came to his home and commissioned the bust. He immediately said yes and called me by my name. I told him of our new plans to rededicate the bust in Dothan to the new museum, and he said to count him in. He also added that he had recently turned ninety years old but that he was still in pretty good shape.

As destiny would have it, my connection to Dr. Carver had now come full circle and was about to be complete. On Saturday, March 26, 2006, the former members of PPI, Col. Whitehead, former Mayor Jimmy Grant, then-Mayor Pat Thomas, and others met in Dothan at the G.W. Carver Interpretive Museum and rededicated the bronze bust of Dr. Carver to Dr. Williams and her new museum. Both Col. Whitehead and I served as keynote speakers as we reminisced about our earlier meeting and connection to Dr. Carver.

Today, the bronze bust of Dr. Carver is forty-four years old. The sculptor, Col. Whitehead, passed away on February 25, 2010. The members of PPI made history forty-four years ago when it commissioned the bronze bust of Dr. Carver by first adopting his simple credo: "Start where you are with what you have. Make something of it and never be satisfied."

Rod Serling (December 25, 1924-June 28, 1975) American Screenwriter (age 50)

Rodman Edward "Rod" Serling was born on Christmas Day in 1924 in Syracuse, New York, to Samuel and Esther Serling, but raised in Binghamton, New York. He later earned his B.A. in 1950 from Antioch College in Yellow Springs, Ohio. After that, he served as an Army paratrooper and Demolition Specialist. Although Serling was only 5'4" and slight, he was a noted boxer during his military days. Serling was seriously wounded in the wrist and knee during combat and was awarded the Purple Heart and Bronze Star.

During his lifetime, Rod Serling received six Emmys for his writing. One of his biggest successes was cowriting *Planet of the Apes* in 1967, which is still considered the beginning of one of the most popular movie franchises in history. *Ahead of the release of "Planet of the Apes," Serling told the L.A. Times in 1967, "The singular greatest evil of our time is prejudice."* Many of the ninety-two episodes he wrote for *The Twilight Zone* series focused on prejudices in one form or another.

Serling was also ranked #1 in TV Guide's list of the "25 Greatest Sci-Fi Legends" in the August 2004 issue. Due to his wartime experiences, Serling suffered from nightmares and flashbacks, which may account for some of his science fiction creations dealing with similar things.

The Twilight Zone television series, which ran from 1959-64, was my first real introduction to Rod Serling. Each week, he would appear onscreen to introduce episodes of his celebrated new sci-fi show. *The Twilight Zone* caused me to have many nightmares and flashbacks when I was a child. Even the theme music used to introduce the series sounded very scary and menacing.

I can vividly remember hiding my face while watching some of the creepier episodes, but like a glutton for punishment, I wanted more. I was awestruck at the beauty of the black-and-white episodes and how light and shadows were dramatically used to spell danger. The soundtrack also signaled that something bad was going to happen.

As a high school English teacher in the early 1980s in Atlanta, I often turned to Serling's *Twilight Zone* series when we discussed science fiction. Most of the fourteen-year-olds in my class had never watched the earlier black-and-white episodes, so I would bring my VHS tapes in and play them in class. Amazingly, the students were enthralled and wanted to watch more, even as the bell was ringing for them to go to their next classes. I soon became known as an expert on the TZ series, as I collected all of the 156 original episodes on VHS. Today, I own the complete, remastered collection of the TZ series on DVD. Serling wrote ninety-two of the 156 episodes.

What I really enjoy about TZ is how Serling was able to tell one story and layer it with another story or many stories. There is always a subplot or parallel subject present in Serling's work. The episodes were great examples of tongue-in-cheek writing, as Serling's stories made me feel he was winking at me. Of course, Serling knew he was only teasing as he entertained us, but he was also educating us about the extraordinary things in life at the same time.

Like Dr. Carver, Serling was a special man with a special talent. God blessed him with an innate ability to touch people deeply through his writings and his television plays. It is no wonder that today, we are celebrating the sixty-fifth anniversary of his ground-breaking television series. TZ is still televised all over the world, and there are millions of fan clubs devoted to the preservation and memory of Rod Serling and his work.

While all of the fans have their own favorite episodes, I also have mine. I enjoyed the fact that many of Serling's stories had to do with time travel – both backward and forward. He also entertained us with theories that profess there is a parallel world or matrix around us that contains our twins or our doubles, and they live along with us in that parallel world that we can't see. This thought makes us question who we really are and what is real in life. Essentially, Serling was good at creating magical worlds within worlds and being able to stop those worlds at any time to let anyone who wanted to get off or escape.

One of my favorite episodes is "A Stop at Willoughby." In this episode, a tired ad agency executive longs to leave his stressful, dog-eat-dog job and find a simpler, more pleasant life. His boss is a tyrant, and when he turns to his wife for help, she ridicules and belittles him. During this wintry train ride home from work, he falls asleep and dreams the train has made a stop at a quaint, sleepy town called Willoughby – *where a man can slow down and live his life full measure.* It is summer in Willoughby, and boys are seen fishing while band concerts are playing in the park. Before the man can get off, the train starts up again, and when he awakes, he's back in the present day. Things get so bad at work and home for the man that he vows to get off at Willoughby the next chance he gets. When he falls asleep again on another train ride home and wakes up at the Willoughby stop, he decides to get off and remains there forever. I won't ruin the twist at the end by telling you the rest, but I will recommend this as one episode worth seeing and not to miss.

Another favorite episode is "Kick-the-Can." This episode features a convalescent home with several "old" people milling around and longing to escape their lives and be young again. When one of the residents sees a group of kids outside playing kick-the-can, he suggests to his elder companions that they should sneak out one night to play kick-the-can to restore their youth. He tells them that the magic of replenishing one's youth is in playing the game. The others are too frail and too afraid they will get hurt or get into trouble; they also don't believe that the game could help bring back their youth. The man manages to convince all of them to at least try, except one, who remains behind and contacts the authorities when the others sneak out at night to play. When the authorities and the tattletale rush outside to capture the oldsters, all they see are a bunch of kids playing kick-the-can. When the authorities leave, the man left behind realizes that those kids are his friends who have somehow become young again. He then cries and begs them to take him with them, but it's too late.

"Kick the Can" was updated in color on a new *Twilight Zone* series years later, and it featured the famous Black actor Scatman Crothers as the old man who incites the others to play the game. Both versions are recommended.

One of the most famous TZ episodes of all time is "The Eye of the Beholder." In this episode, Serling masterfully uses light and shadows to tease and manipulate us. In the opening, we see a young woman with her face bandaged as she pleads with her doctor to remove her bandages so she can see if her final attempt at facial surgery has made her normal. When the bandages are finally removed, we see a young lady with a beautiful face. We then see the doctor drop his scissors and proclaim the operation was a failure in that she is still ugly. Then we see the features of the doctors and the nurses, who all have grotesque faces that are quite the norm. This story was made in the 1960s but is more relevant today as plastic surgery has become the norm for many. The moral of the story, of course, is that beauty is skin-deep and in the eye of the beholder.

The final episode I will relate is another one that gave me nightmares. It is titled "Five Characters in Search of an Exit," and it involves five characters – a soldier, a clown, a ballerina, a hobo, and a bagpiper – who all find themselves in a strange abyss or hole and can't figure out how they got there or who they are. They try and try to get out, but they can't. The soldier finally realizes they must be in hell. They make one last attempt to get out by standing on each other's shoulders and letting the soldier climb to the top. When the soldier gets to the top of the rim, he falls off with a loud yell. The others now realize they will never get out. Then, we see the figure of a doll soldier lying in the snow on the ground next to a Salvation Army collection barrel for toys. A little girl picks up the doll and puts it back in the barrel with the other four dolls. It seems the soldier may have been correct in that the dolls were in a sort of hell. I was scared to death to think what hell is really like – an inescapable, dark abyss.

I will forever remember Rod Serling and the things he made me feel, believe, and write. His stories continue to fuel my imagination, and there is no doubt that I am a proud citizen of the *Twilight Zone*. I believe we all are, and I think Rod Serling was way ahead of his time in predicting that we live in a wonderful world full of hope, wonder, magic, and love.

Marvin Gaye (April 2, 1939-April 1, 1984) American Singer (age 44)

I vividly remember when music first became both relevant and irresistible in my life. It was 1968, and I was in the eighth grade. A song called "Cowboys to Girls" by The Intruders from Philadelphia debuted, and it perfectly coincided with my adolescent awakening. Then, a year or so later, Stevie Wonder released "My Cherie Amour" around the same time I met a pretty ninth-grade girl named Sherry. I was doubly enchanted by her and by the song; it seemed it was written just for us. My heart then opened wide and let all the music in as I became ruled by every lyric and every rhythm. But it was around 1971 when everything changed for me; things got more serious.

Marvin Gaye's "What's Going On?" was released, and it was a musical masterpiece in every way. Although only thirty-eight minutes long, the album spoke volumes to the world as it opened our eyes to some of the atrocities of the Vietnam War, drugs, love, God, and love for mankind. Marvin hit a home run with every song on the album, and it quickly became a million-selling Motown classic. It was considered the first and ultimate concept album in that each song was related to the other and there was a central theme.

Of course, Marvin had many other chart-topping albums and songs before this one, but *What's Going On?* broke the mold for me. He did win a Grammy for the single "Sexual Healing," but that was long after his 1971 classic album. For me, the album is both spiritual and sexual; it is also soothing to me. When I drive long distances by car, I always have a copy of the CD with me to play. I find that I can drive for three hundred miles or more by repeating the album and enjoying it just as much every time I hit repeat. I get lost in every song, and it makes my drive seem shorter and more pleasant.

Marvin once said he was being used as an instrument, as God was actually writing the songs on the album. Like Dr. Carver, Marvin also claimed to be in tune with God in this creative musical endeavor. Even though that may sound a little too Twilight Zone-ish for some, I really can identify with his assessment.

When one closely listens to how Marvin's many voices are multilayered over each song and how each voice is a different Marvin, you'll quickly understand how what he achieved is nothing less than divine or otherworldly. Both "Save the Children" and "God is Love" are my favorites next to the title song. I also love "Mercy Mercy Me" and "Inner City Blues." Over the years, many different artists have covered these songs by paying tribute to Gaye, but no one has come close to *Marvinizing* his songs the way he did. When Marvin said, "Let's Get it On" and "Got to Give it Up," we all followed his advice.

Although I was initially connected to Marvin by my love for his masterpiece album, my real connection to him came in another, more tragic way. On March 18, 1984, I started at the Federal Bureau of Investigation training academy in Quantico, Virginia, as a trainee to be a Special Agent. I was twenty-nine years old and uncomfortable with the idea that I could become an FBI agent after having been an English teacher for four years. In short, I was afraid that I was not good enough to make it.

At night, my roommate, Joe Tipton, and I would listen to music to help soothe us as we studied our homework for the next day. We soon learned that Motown was our favorite music. Joe was from Speedway, Indiana, and I, of course, was from Alabama – what an unlikely pair – but we got along very well. Joe and I became inseparable best friends.

I shall never forget the night that Joe and I sat there studying and listening to the radio in our room when the disc jockey interrupted the music to say, "Marvin Gaye is dead." It was April 1, 1984. Gaye was forty-four years old and died the day before his forty-fifth birthday. For the rest of the night, the disc jockey played Marvin Gaye songs as a tribute to him. Joe and I, two men training to become FBI agents, cried as we listened to the songs on the radio.

It was then that I resolved I would survive my training as a tribute to the late Marvin Gaye, a friend I just never met in person. I was no longer afraid, and my spirit had found a new purpose. When we graduated from the FBI Academy in June of 1984, Joe and I parted and promised to remain close. Throughout the years, we have, and the tears that we shed together remain something that bonded us for life.

In 1986, I couldn't wait to call Joe and tell him that I had just bought a brand-new Chevrolet Blazer and named it Marvin. Joe laughed and said he understood. I kept Marvin for over ten years, and when I sold it, I wept again. I wasn't ready to give it up. I felt the car protected me and kept me close to Marvin Gaye at the same time.

Two of the books that I am most familiar with about Marvin Gaye are *Divided Soul: The Life of Marvin Gaye* by David Ritz and *Marvin Gaye, My Brother* by Frankie Gaye, Marvin's younger brother. Despite some of the proven truths that both books report about his demons and how he lived, I prefer to remember a different Marvin. I see him as kinder, gentler, and a musical genius who caused a generation of people to love, think, act, and help save the children and our world. Tragically, he was shot to death by his own father, Marvin Gaye, Sr.

Marvin Gaye's music has left an indelible impression on my soul, and there's not a year that goes by that I don't miss his music and pray for his soul. He left a huge musical void in my life and the life of so many others, as there has been no one else who could take his special place. I miss Marvin Gaye, and I will always love his music.

The world that Dr. Carver lived in and struggled through could accurately be described as something like Serling's Twilight Zone, yet it was far too real to be television; however, he left a better world than the one he found.

One can assume that Marvin Gaye's life would have made a perfect episode for Serling's Twilight Zone since it had many of the same elements: fate, despair, magic, irony, and redemption.

Even the life that Serling created for himself embodied his Twilight Zone to a "T." For all his creativity and literary contributions, his life took an unexpected twist when he tragically died of a heart attack at age fifty.

While I have no doubt that by now these men have met through God's own heavenly introduction, I would still enjoy meeting them and discussing our special bond. Yet, somehow, I feel they are already aware because I sense them looking over my shoulder while I pen these tributes. Long live Dr. George Washington Carver, Rod Serling, and Marvin Gaye.

CHAPTER TWENTY-THREE

"THE GHETTOSBURG ADDRESS"

The whole often misinformed history surrounding slavery and the Gettysburg Address by our sixteenth president, Abraham Lincoln, has been interesting to me as a student of both American history and Black history.

Called "The Great Emancipator," President Lincoln is credited with bringing about the emancipation of enslaved people in the United States, many of whom were my ancestors. Lincoln signed the proclamation, known then as Proclamation 95, on September 22, 1862, but when it was published on January 1, 1863, it became known as The Emancipation Proclamation. It only took President Lincoln two minutes to deliver the 272-word address on November 19, 1863.

History reports, *"The battle of Gettysburg was fought July 1-3, 1863, in and around the town of Gettysburg, Pennsylvania, by Union and Confederate forces during the American Civil War. The battle involved the largest number of casualties of the entire war and is often described as the war's turning point. Between 46,000 and 51,000 Union and Confederate soldiers combined died in the three-day battle."* (Wikipedia)

And I say, "Wow!" What a short war, an even shorter address, and a massive loss of lives to have such a lasting effect on our country and its people to this day.

But history has not been as readily reliable about the total number of Black lives lost before, during, and after the Civil War, which was likely an astronomical number. One would think the accounting process for all lost lives would be the same.

However, let us not forget that there was the Three-Fifths Compromise that was *"an agreement reached during the 1787 United States Constitutional Convention over the inclusion of slaves in a state's total population. Article 1, Section 2 of the Constitution of the United States declared that any person who was not free would be counted as three-fifths of a free individual for the purposes of determining congressional representation. The 13th Amendment of 1865 effectively gutted the three-fifths compromise by outlawing the enslavement of Black people. But when the 14th Amendment was ratified in 1868, it officially repealed the three-fifths compromise."* (Wikipedia)

So, is it safe to assume that one of the reasons there is not an accurate account of how many Black lives were lost is because individual slaves only amounted to being three-fifths of a person rather than one whole person? The only other logical rationale not to report an accurate number is because the number is so staggeringly large.

My family and I moved from Texas to Pennsylvania in August of 1995. Our home in the borough of Collegeville is only a two-hour drive (125 miles) from Gettysburg. I told my wife I wanted to visit Gettysburg to see for myself this famous town and its national landmark – an infamous killing ground; however, I also wanted to learn more about the role of Blacks in the area during the Civil War. So, on Tuesday, April 25, 2023, we took a day trip to visit the historic area. We both were excited and surprised that we never considered going there before.

However, a month before our visit, I read a fascinating 2005 book on Gettysburg by author James M. Paradis titled *African Americans and the Gettysburg Campaign*. Paradis is described as a former licensed battlefield guide at Gettysburg National Military Park. On the dedication page of his book, Paradis wrote: "To the late Dr. Russell F. Weigley, who encouraged me to write it, and to the long-forgotten African Americans whose stories inspired it." Neither man appears to be of African American descent, yet they believe that history belongs to all of us; a history book is only as good as its historian.

Paradis' book primarily dispels *"the myth that no Black men fought or were killed defending Gettysburg from the Confederate invasion, and*

*confirms that there were Black citizens living in prewar Gettysburg who had
an influence on the military outcome and the impact of the Civil War on their
lives."* (James M. Paradis)

My purpose in visiting Gettysburg was to gain whatever
knowledge I could about Gettysburg and to specifically learn more
about the role my ancestors played. By trying to experience Gettysburg,
I was aware of the many ghost stories that persist to this day, affirming
that sightings of ghosts of both Union and Confederate soldiers have
been reported by many; however, I was not expecting to see any ghosts
in the daytime during my visit.

Gettysburg is a very quaint little town, and it reminded me of
where we live in Collegeville. The population for both is around 7,000
or 8,000. Collegeville has Ursinus College (1869) with approximately
1,500 students, and Gettysburg has Gettysburg College (1921) with
approximately 2,400 students. The townspeople in both are very
cordial and friendly. The downtown hotels and eateries appear to be
small and locally owned.

I brought my copy of Paradis' book to have it handy in case
I needed it. The book is only 110 pages. I also carried a poem I had
written that centered around Gettysburg that I had hoped to read while
I was there. When we arrived at the national park, I spoke to one of the
younger park representatives at the customer service booth and asked
her if there were any particular landmarks regarding Blacks.

She looked at me and said, "I'm not familiar with any Blacks that
fought in the Civil War in Gettysburg, and we really don't have any
prominent markers along the battlefield to identify Blacks."

I was stunned by her comment, so I flashed my book to say,
"Well, that's not what I read in this book written by a former licensed
battlefield guide who worked here. Have you ever heard of the book
African Americans and the Gettysburg Campaign by James Paradis?"

The lady answered, "No, I haven't," and proceeded to thumb
through the book I showed her. She appeared to be amazed to see her
contradictions in print.

After looking at some of the information in the book, she looked
up and said, "Well, like I said, we know there were a few Blacks who

227

were around here during the war, but there were no uniformed Black soldiers at that time."

I said, "According to Mr. Paradis, there were actually Black uniformed soldiers and Black militias formed during that time that did fight against the Confederate soldiers and are documented in his book."

I couldn't help but think how odd it was that this representative was not updated about the book and was unaware of the things I was telling her about the place where she worked. I wanted to suggest that she should read Paradis's book to learn some of the "facts" about Blacks at Gettysburg, but I thought better of making that comment based on where I was at the time.

At any rate, I thanked her for her time, took my book back, and we continued on our self-guided tour. My wife and I did note that during the time we were visiting the national park, we were the only Blacks we saw out of maybe 100 tourists on that day at that time.

My wife and I completed the tour and then purchased tickets at the Gettysburg Visitor Center Cyclorama to watch a beautifully produced twenty-minute film called "A New Birth of Freedom," narrated by actor Morgan Freeman. Freeman told the whole story of the Battle of Gettysburg, and the film included some impressive images and sound effects illustrating the massive fight.

Although the panoramic sound and impressive reenactment in the film were astounding, I noted that Morgan Freeman's voice was the only obvious significant Black presence, notwithstanding the mention of slavery that precipitated much of the war. If there were any mention of other significant Black participation during the Battle of Gettysburg, it was minimal and I missed it.

Then, I wondered why we didn't see more Blacks visiting the national park on the day we were there. I surmised that visiting Gettysburg for some Blacks may have been similar to the large number of Blacks who refused to watch *Alex Haley's Roots* on TV. Many said they understood the importance of the film, but they simply did not want to relive the horror. How could anyone argue with that?

I recalled when my son was about eight or nine, I bought the complete DVD set of *Roots* and planned to show him the entire series and discuss it with him. At first, he was eager to learn and watch the movies together. When the scene came on that showed LeVar Burton's character Toby being chained and beaten, my son started crying and begged me to turn it off. It didn't dawn on me that he was very sensitive to violence and could not stand to see people being treated that way. I put the *Roots* DVDs away, and we never watched them together again. I took a different approach to teaching him about our Black heritage from that point on.

Not to dismiss the importance of President Lincoln's Emancipation Proclamation, the significant lives lost during the Civil War, the essential work being done by the tour guides at the national park, or the important facts unearthed in Paradis's book, I would encourage people to read and educate themselves on the battle of Gettysburg and its inclusion of facts regarding the contributions of all people involved.

Toward that end, I took out the poem I had written and stood on the grounds of the same battlefield where Lincoln visited. I was unsure exactly where he stood, so I picked a random spot. Then, I read my 350-word address modeled after The Gettysburg Address called "The Ghettosburg Address" to my Black and White ancestors in hopes that they and their ghosts would hear me. Upon finishing reading my poem, I experienced a cool April wind blowing through me and in the trees above me to affirm a reception of my words.

"The Ghettosburg Address"

Four hundred and some odd years ago,
our foreparents were brought forth on this continent,
conceived in slavery and dedicated to the proposition
that they were not created equal in the eyes of others.
Then, they were engaged in that
peculiar institution that
forced them onto plantations and in
ghettos all over the world,
testing whether they could long endure all the pain
and suffering of a people with a dark hue.

Today, we are engaged in a great
battle with the remnants
of the same peculiar institution that
we seem doomed to repeat
if we do not take heed of our long
history of oppression.
The battlefield is all around us, and
even in us, as the battle
is not only for our lives and our children's
lives but also for our souls.
We dedicate a portion of that battlefield
bearing the colors red, black,
and green to represent the blood, the
people and the land sacrificed for us
as a final resting place so that each of
us may continue to drink water
from wells we did not dig. It is
altogether fitting and proper
that we should do this.
But, in a larger sense, we cannot mitigate their pain,
we cannot denigrate their contributions,
and we cannot commemorate them without
honoring ourselves by standing our ground.
The same ground that has been
consecrated with their blood
far above anything we could ever give
to repay them for our lives.
From this point on in our history,
it is for us to be dedicated to
God's proposition that we should
not be judged by the color
of our skin but by the content of our character.
We should also respect ourselves
by not perpetuating any of
the myths about our great heritage.

It is rather for us not to forget that this address
represents all people of color, as today we all are
blended together under God's rainbow,
and that the LOVE of the people,
by the people, for the people shall not perish
from this Earth without each of us perishing
along with it. Amen.

CHAPTER TWENTY-FOUR

"OUR 50TH HIGH SCHOOL CLASS REUNION" (1972-2022)

Fifty years ago, at Dothan High School, it literally felt like "Together we fall, divided we stand!"

We all realized there were walls between us. The walls were specific, numerous, and included such things as race, gender, religion, politics, and ideologies.

Fifty years is a long time to maintain so many walls. The planning committee's idea for the Dothan High School 1972 Class Reunion was to build small bridges instead of more walls. For eighteen months, the planning committee hoped that what was said in the movie *Field of Dreams* was actually true: "If you build it, they will come!"

And come they did.

On Friday, June 10, 2022, we had over 190 nervously excited classmates sharing the beautifully decorated ballroom at Bella's in downtown Dothan for a long-awaited meet-and-greet that was historic in many ways and for many reasons. We desperately needed this time together as a class to let go of the past and grab onto the future together.

On Saturday, June 11, 2022, we had over 200 classmates at the welcoming ballroom of the Highland Oaks Golf Club. Classmates we had not seen in decades happily stood before us in the same space as we all marveled at how much we had in common rather than focusing on our differences.

We were now close enough to see the eyes of all the Dothan High Tigers that filled the room. We smiled, laughed, and hugged each other tight and let our body language serve as unspoken words of longing. For many of us, these hugs allowed us to cross bridges we had not crossed before and release our unbridled passion for freedom.

We were all very proud of our history of being the first class to graduate after three full years of integration. It felt good to finally get to know each other on our own terms. There were no dark clouds hanging over our heads and no longer any walls to separate us. The affection we felt and generated was both healing and authentic.

The committee's one criterion for attending our fiftieth class reunion was very simple: "If you started high school with us somewhere along the way, you were invited to come and celebrate with us. Period!" We consciously strived to be *"inclusive"* rather than *"exclusive."*

Our committee envisioned and created a unifying logo for our fiftieth class reunion that said, "All for one together." Our logo equally displayed the colors and welcomed students from Dothan High, Carver High, and Houston Academy – all Houston County schools. Next, we felt that monthly letters from a cross-section of classmates would help galvanize our efforts and get buy-in from our student body. Different classmates volunteered to submit letters regarding their memories and experiences of our high school years together. Both the new class logo and the monthly letters were big hits and proved vital in bringing our class together in record numbers. We felt that constant outreach and communication through social media platforms, email, phone calls, texts, snail mail, and face-to-face interactions were key to creating a successful reunion.

The planning committee worked hard for those eighteen months to generate and maintain a "Lost Classmates" list that we sent out monthly so that others could help us locate and invite everyone associated with our class. We were able to locate many lost classmates but not all, due to changed names and changed addresses.

We also maintained a list of "Deceased Classmates" so that we could honor and remember them in our Special Memorial for our program. We developed a moving slideshow of classmate photos combined with thoughtful music to allow us to reflect on the faces we saw on the screen.

When it came time to dance, the planning committee opted for an energetic live band rather than a DJ to help us relive the diversity in the soundtracks of our lives. For us, music has always been the one thing that could bring us together quickly. We danced and partied together like there was no tomorrow and no yesterday.

We added such FUN things as award certificates, a free raffle, gag gifts, food, and a cash bar to help overdeliver on our promise to bring people together for a historic weekend. It all worked, and we set a new standard for class reunions in Dothan and elsewhere.

The end seemed to justify the means as we all sang the words to our alma mater "Hail to Thee, Old Dothan High School" together, in unison, as if to make up for the times we were not in unison. This was one class reunion that defied the odds and set a new standard going forward for class reunions everywhere that is going to be hard to beat.

CHAPTER TWENTY-FIVE

"THE SUPREME COURT JESTER"

Most people LOVE a clown, but not quite everyone.

In the 14th century, a clown or court jester was described as *a fool or joker who was a member of the household of a nobleman or a monarch employed to entertain guests during the medieval and Renaissance eras.*

The name of the fool in King Arthur's fictional court was Sir Dagonet; he was portrayed as *a foolish and cowardly knight and a violently deranged madman who also sat at the Round Table.* Sir Dagonet, secretly called *Dagger* behind his back by some, was knighted as an award for his errant loyalty and comedic talents but not for his decision-making – no matter how important a decision was. In order to get a good laugh, he often masqueraded in Black face.

History notes that *"[i]n France, the tradition of the court jester ended with the French Revolution. In the 21st century, the jester has been revived and can still be seen at medieval-style fairs, pageants,"* and in the U.S., on the highest court in the land. Most court jesters were male; however, they were rarely portrayed as masculine.

A fear of clowns is described as *coulrophobia,* and it is caused by *"negative experiences that relate to a particular experience."* The Supreme Court Jester's willing participation in the abolishment of Roe v. Wade and affirmative action qualify as negative experiences. Believe it or not, there are many people in our general population who have this phobia of clowns. These people believe that clowns are evil, dangerous, and frightening. For some, the only cure is the clown's retirement.

The modern-day abbreviation for Court is CT, which is identical to the initials of one of the current Supreme Court Jesters in the fictional Supreme Court of King Donald. He was knighted as a jester over three decades ago and has remained loyal and dependable ever since then.

Anyone who has been paying attention to the conservative direction the U.S. is headed in should not be surprised at some of the "supreme" decisions that have been rendered lately. Many of these decisions have not been based on law, although all of the decision-makers are lawyers. Judges are not supposed to be political and put politics over laws, but many believe that is what we are seeing in this country. Some are surprised and some are not; some are angry and some are not.

I am one of those who believes that history does repeat itself and that we are doomed by our history if we do not heed the writings on the wall. One of these ancient writings can be found in the words of Ecclesiastes 1, verses 8-9, which reads: *"All things are wearisome, more than one can say. The eye never has enough of seeing, nor the ear its fill of hearing. What has been will be again, what has been done will be done again; there is nothing new under the sun."* (New International Version [NIV] translation)

These words serve as an eerie warning and reminder that if we are not headed in a direction that has been heavenly ordained for us to go, then where we will end up is not going to be heavenly. For me, I would rather be a 14th-century clown than a 21st-century fool. So, please do not be *fooled* by the latest Supreme Court rulings because there will be nothing new under the sun as long as we have our Supreme Court Jester.

Most people LOVE a clown, but not quite everyone.

A well-known American Black history scholar once said:

> *"This Supreme Court Jester went from being a self-proclaimed victim of a failed 'high-tech lynching' on A. Hill to being the happy hangman who is systematically responsible for lynching generations of Blacks and other minorities ever since the death of the Supreme Court's first Black American justice, Thoroughgood "Thurgood" Marshall."*

CHAPTER TWENTY-SIX

"CLASSY-FIED"

From 1984 to 2007, I worked for two different federal law enforcement agencies, where I took an oath to protect my country from enemies, both foreign and domestic. This oath included protection against terrorists and insurgents from outside and inside our country. I, among many other federal agents, took this oath out of a profound love for our country and we understood the seriousness of what we were hired to do.

During my tenure, I worked under four different presidents, including Presidents Ronald Reagan, George H. W. Bush, William Clinton, and George W. Bush. I also worked under two different FBI directors, William S. Sessions and William H. Webster.

In my position as a sworn federal agent, I held a Top Secret security clearance that allowed me to read and handle classified documents. I knew and understood the consequences of mishandling or leaking information from these classified documents. We all had learned the lessons and results of mishandling classified documents from a previous administration that included Watergate. During my twenty-three years of service, I never heard of a single case of outrageous mishandling of classified information. Then, Edward Snowden leaked highly classified information from the National Security Agency in 2013.

Within my professional circle of federal agents, we had secure protocols and procedures on how to handle classified documents to protect American interests, and these protocols were never trivialized. We did our sworn patriotic duty to protect the information within these documents with our lives.

But that was a different time when we were apolitical and believed that we should never let politics or race interfere with our charged duties and responsibilities when it came to protecting America. Since that time, a new culture has arisen within this country that has attempted to redefine and limit inherent American ideals like patriotism, freedom, citizenship, and life. We all know that there has never been a time in America when it was described as being great for everyone, yet some have reimagined a time when it was.

One can only imagine the voluminous amount of classified material circulated and protected among the presidents, from George Washington to the current president, Joseph Biden. Why is there now such a ferocious debate on what classified documents are, how they should be handled, and how they must be declassified? With over 200 years of democracy behind us, why are we now trying to undermine the very things that gave us strength and unity before?

Plain and simple is the clear definition for classified information: *"Classified information is material that a government body deems to be sensitive information that must be protected. Access is restricted by law or regulation to particular groups of people with the necessary security clearance and need to know, and mishandling of the material can incur criminal penalties."* (Wikipedia)

In a divided America, laws are being promulgated to protect people in certain classes versus others who require that same protection. The class system is alive and well in the U.S. This class system is tearing us apart and has changed the definition of classified documents to "classyfied" documents that indicate that certain people appear to be above the law. That does not seem very classy to me.

CHAPTER TWENTY-SEVEN

"REAL MEN DO CRY... UNLESS!"

When I was in second grade, I hit my thumb with a hammer while trying to hammer a nail into a board. It hurt so bad that my thumb began to swell, and I began to cry. I ran to my mother and asked for help. She put antiseptic on it, a bandage, and she added a kiss. I looked at her with tears in my eyes and asked her if I was a crybaby. She smiled at me and said, "No, you are not a crybaby, but even if you were, you'd still be my baby."

I said, "But boys aren't supposed to cry!" My mother then said, "That's nonsense. Everybody cries sometimes!"

I'm not sure where I ever heard that males don't cry, but I know now that it's part of the Big Lie. Males and females have an equal number of chromosomes and an equal number of tear ducts. There's nothing manly about not having the ability to cry, especially when one is in pain. Silent tears on the inside are still considered to be crying.

I cried when my puppy got run over by a car. I cried when my grandmother died. I cried when my best friend got married because he was happy. I cried when I turned age thirty. I cried when I got transferred from Houston to New York City. I cried when my mother turned 101 years young. I cried when I watched the video footage of George Floyd being killed on camera. I cried when I realized all the lives lost in the war in Ukraine and the ones whose names the world will never know. I cried when I visited the Legacy Museum in Montgomery, Alabama, and witnessed information regarding all the millions of Blacks who have been enslaved, murdered, lynched, and tortured over the 400 years of slavery. Today, the plantations have been replaced by the penitentiary for many Black and Brown people who are still crying behind bars.

I cry every time I receive an Amber alert. I cry every time a child is killed with a loaded gun. I cry when I see people going hungry when this country has an abundance of food. I cry when people put money before human lives and think that they are just. I cry when I realize how far our country has strayed from the American Dream and the Golden Rule.

I have heard of many famous people who shed tears, including Jesus, Gandhi, and Nelson Mandela, among others. They cried because of their love for mankind and not out of concern for themselves. Each had a selfless love for the world and its promise to be a better place to live for all people.

Greed and hatred most often inhibit our ability to cry for others, but then we are being selfish and not selfless. Every time it rains, I imagine the raindrops are imaginary tears from heaven and God's way of reminding us that it is okay for humans to cry.

In a world consumed with robots, clones, and artificial intelligence, real men do cry...unless they are not real men.

CHAPTER TWENTY-EIGHT

"THOUGHTLESS KILLERS"

As a child, I stomped on ants, roaches, and bugs with regularity. Unashamed, I killed many mosquitos, flies, and wasps as a matter of instinct.

As I grew older, I sling-shotted birds, squirrels, and snakes, many times unprovoked.

I was at war with nature without even realizing it.

It was my unexplained nature to kill without thinking about the consequences.

No matter how you look at it, I was a killer, and I never gave it a second thought

As a young man, I hunted deer, foxes, and raccoons for sport.

Later, while on a safari, I took aim at lions, tigers, and elephants in the Congo.

My thirst for killing reached an all-time high as I hunted monkeys, apes, and baboons, creatures who resembled me.

Overseas at war, I hunted those who had been identified by my country as my enemies, yet I had never met a single one.

I took aim without thinking and felled my enemies as fast as I could pull the trigger.

With shouts of victory, I took pride in my deadly deeds and proudly wore my medals.

As a police officer, I stood my ground and shot the perpetrators by claiming I was doing my duty.

With the dead bodies lying in the street, I reported that it was a righteous kill because I was in fear for my life – although the perpetrators were unarmed.

When guns were found near the bodies of the bad guys, I identified them as the ones they had used against me.

At night, I pray that if I should die before I wake, I pray the Lord my soul to take.

Do unto others as you would have them do unto you.

Thou shalt not kill and thou shall not murder. Amen.

BONUS WRITINGS

A bonus is getting something of value beyond the normal expectation of a recipient.

In the old days, a bonus was like getting a few extra songs on your favorite album or compact disc. The same feeling applies today for those who stream their music.

I like getting bonuses!

As a reward to everyone who purchased my last book, *Just My Imagination Running Away with Me*, and were kind enough to leave a book review on Amazon, I offer these extra writings as a bonus for your loyalty and as my appreciation.

As a reward to any new readers, I offer these free writings out of love because love should be free.

All of these extra assortments of writings many not directly follow the same central theme of love as the rest of this book, but they do offer an indirect path to love.

My love of writing allows me to go beyond the norm and reward my readers with something of value that comes truly from my heart.

Love is not only like glass slippers, but it is also like the person who gives you their love for free.

Omnia vinct amor (Love conquers all)

CHAPTER TWENTY-NINE

"SWEET POTATO COFFEE"

In the early to mid-1920s, John William Starr and Jernigan Buck Jameson were two of the most notorious moonshiners the state of Mississippi had ever seen but were never caught moonshining. They were first cousins and struggling potato farmers who dreamed of being outlaws. There were no outlaws in Mississippi and barely any in-laws in the 1920s.

They grew up in a rural, unincorporated community that was actually named Whynot, Mississippi, located about sixteen miles from Meridian, Mississippi. Meridian is considered part of the East Central Hills region of Mississippi, known for its low rolling hills. The most famous Black person ever born in Whynot was soul singer David Ruffin, lead singer of The Temptations. Ruffin was born there in Lauderdale County on January 18, 1941, on the poor side of town – which was all of Whynot.

Whynot was not famous for anything else except its exceptional potatoes. The white-fleshed Irish potatoes were grown there, but they were not as plentiful or as popular as the Mississippi sweet potatoes.

Beauregard and Evangeline were the two most famous varieties of sweet potatoes because of their deep orange flesh and their smooth, rosy outer skin. Folks who knew potatoes said that Mississippi sweet potatoes were to die for because they were the sweetest.

During the Depression Years from 1929-1939, most people were glad to eat anything they could find, especially potatoes. During this same timeframe, Prohibition in the United States was a big concern because some people used white potatoes for more than eating – they made moonshine from them.

John and Jernigan claimed they turned to making moonshine in order to make enough money to buy food to feed their families. They were said to take potatoes that looked like they were going bad and cook them in their stills to make moonshine or *white lightning*. Depressed and starving people would often turn to cheap, homemade alcohol to try and forget how hungry they were; many became alcoholics and died in poverty.

The two men hid their stills amidst the low rolling hills in the Mississippi mountains that were home to only coyotes, otters, raccoons, skunks, opossums, deer, beaver, and muskrats. Back then, there were no hiking trails or campgrounds in these areas; people were too poor to take vacations or care about looking at nature.

The fifty-five-gallon, eighteen-gauge steel drum had been around since 1905 and was perfect for brewing and transporting moonshine. It was easy to add wheels to the drum bottoms and roll them through the rolling hills from spot to spot.

In other parts of the country like Ohio, Kentucky, and Tennessee, Prohibition agent Eliot Ness was making a name for himself along with his *Untouchables* as they raided all the Moonshine Mountains that cropped up all over the place.

The two outlaw cousins were well aware that what they were doing was illegal. Along the way with their moonshine distilleries, they became brazen and cocky; some folks called them *The Uncatchables*, a name that mocked Eliot Ness's crime fighters. They knew that Ness and his gang were never coming to Deep South Mississippi to find them in their maze of mountains, trees, potatoes, and skunks. Yet they hired a few armed lookout men to be sure.

For two years straight, the two moonshiners brewed more moonshine from potatoes than anyone could ever imagine. They managed to refine their process by making the resulting spirits into a clear, white liquid that looked almost like water. Today, what they made would resemble vodka or gin, but it tasted like a forest fire in a bottle;

the moonshine was probably around 150 proof. Their moonshine business was booming.

Also, around this same time in the 1920s, Dr. George Washington Carver announced that he had discovered more than 100 products and uses made from the sweet potato, including a kind of coffee.

John and Jernigan were amazed at that news and had never thought of using sweet potatoes in their business. They began to experiment with boiling sweet potatoes and running their pulpy orange flesh through their distillery. It wasn't long before they stopped because the sweet potatoes' thick meat was clogging up their tubing. They were unable to figure out how to readily use sweet potatoes as a byproduct or alternate income stream.

Almost a year went by since they experimented with the sweet potatoes. Then one day, Buck got an idea to use dried sweet potatoes by setting them out in the sun to make them easier to pulverize into a powder.

The pulverized, orange-colored powder had a strong, flavorful aroma. They then ran the powder through the distillery and added water to make it flow smoothly through the tubes. Out the other end came a boiling, bubbly mixture that looked like a kind of coffee but had the aroma of burnt sweet potatoes.

The men kept on refining their new mixture and began using themselves as guinea pigs or taste-testers by drinking the dark liquid. John tried drinking it cold, then hot. There was no need to add any sugar because the potatoes were sweet enough. Jernigan decided to drink it out of a mug and added a little cream to it. The taste was smooth and flavorful.

Within three months, the men had discovered that Dr. Carver was on to something when he claimed he had made coffee from sweet potatoes. The men went on to revolutionize what they created and founded the first-ever Sweet Potato Coffee Company, though they didn't attribute any of their success to what they had gleaned from Dr. Carver.

Sweet potato coffee became a bigger success than their moonshining business. They gave away some of their *coffee* to a few friends who were struggling to put food on the table. Their friends couldn't afford to buy real coffee, so they were glad to be able to drink a coffee substitute. There were no expensive coffee beans involved but a lot of beautiful sweet potatoes were used.

Word-of-mouth got around, and everyone who could afford it wanted to try this new coffee. Since Whynot was known for its sweet potatoes, it soon became known for its sweet potato coffee. John and Jernigan had made enough money from their white lightning that they quit taking chances on skirting the law; they now sought to obtain a patent on their sweet potato coffee and become legitimate coffee businessmen.

It was not illegal to make, sell, and drink coffee. Eliot Ness and his band of Untouchables would have no need to raid the hills of Mississippi to bust up the coffee stills of John and Jernigan's enterprising business.

The Sweet Potato Coffee Company was the initial name of the business, but it was not a catchy name. However, for the next five years, that's what the company was called. In the year 1930, an advertising company was hired to create a new name for the successful sweet potato coffee business. It seemed Mississippians everywhere fell in love with their own unique brand of coffee. Other states tried to create sweet potato coffee, but most failed due to not having access to the famed Mississippi sweet potatoes.

After a month of presenting different names for the coffee company, one name stuck out as the winningest and catchiest company name: Starr-Bucks Coffee Company. The name was eventually shortened to just Starbucks.

Facts: In the 1920s, Dr. George Washington Carver discovered more than 100 products and uses made from the sweet potato, including a kind of coffee. David Ruffin was born in Whynot, Mississippi, on January 18, 1941. Sweet potato coffee is a real thing.

Fiction: Much of the other preceding story _facts_ were created out of thin, imaginary air and sweet potato folklore.

CHAPTER THIRTY

"BILL OF FIGHTS"

The following is a list of ten actual town and city names found in America. I'm sure that each of these states has its own strange origin explaining how and why these places were named as such. I'm also sure there are many more of these unusual municipal names out there, but whatever the reasons, here they are:

1. Two Egg, Florida
2. Cut and Shoot, Texas
3. Intercourse, Pennsylvania
4. Booger Hole, West Virginia
5. Hot Coffee, Mississippi
6. Accident, Maryland
7. Boring, Oregon
8. Peculiar, Missouri
9. Blue Ball, Arkansas
10. Mosquitoville, Vermont

Based on the logic of some of these actual names, I have constructed this next story about a small town named Fights, Pennsylvania. If you can believe some of the real names above, then you will have no problem believing this story.

Bill Justice, a concerned local real estate agent in Fights, PA, was fed up with all the crime, drugs, and decadence that were victimizing his town—the place where he was born. Everywhere he looked, he saw things he didn't like, such as graffiti, trash, bottles, cans, and sometimes condoms; he'd often stop to pick up all the debris he saw, except the condoms. He took pride in living a clean life.

As a youth, Bill played football for Fights Central High School; he was the quarterback for the not-so-famous Fighters that won the local championship against their rivals, The Miners, from nearby Sycamore County.

Fights, PA, is located in South Central Pennsylvania, although, with just 2,500 residents, it can barely be found on a map. It was incorporated in 1899 when it broke away from another town called Pennsylvania Junction and formed its own government. Reportedly, several individual fights broke out in the middle of town over political annexation matters whereby territory was illegally claimed and appropriated. The matters could not be resolved amicably, so the town split. Its only claim to fame besides the Fighters High School football team is that it is also the home of local boxing celebrity Joseph "Hard Head" Sims, a welterweight fighter from the 1960s who won over fifty fights in his heyday. But those days are long gone as Fights struggles to suppress all the progress that many small towns face.

Bill was well aware that as crime increased, the value of real estate properties decreased. As he drove his 2017 Jeep Grand Cherokee through the streets of his town, he saw boarded-up homes and businesses from several foreclosures. When the elder residents died off, their entitled children were not interested in maintaining the properties. Many of the houses were lost due to unpaid taxes because the remaining family members would not pay them; thus, the town would foreclose on the homes and try to sell the contents through estate sales. Due to inflation and a poor housing market, many houses became eyesores.

The Mayor of Fights, Anthony "Tony" Weissmann, had been in office for twenty years and was set to retire. He said he would have retired sooner, but the town was unable to find a suitable replacement. Although elections for mayor were regularly held, no one else was willing to step up and provide fresh leadership.

Fights had one high school, one junior high school, one elementary school, and one kindergarten; they were all part of the South Central PA School District. There were three churches, a Walmart, a Dollar

General, a 7-Eleven with a gas station, a small library, a bank with an ATM machine, a mom-and-pop grocery store, and the Fights Police Department with three officers and a police chief. Police Chief Jerry Pazda supervised officers William "Bill" Stewart, Emily Jackson, and Ismael Lopez. The opioid crisis was alive and well in Fights, as evidenced by the frequent drug arrests that had been skyrocketing.

The Fights Volunteer Fire Department was all-volunteer for real. Although the firemen were not paid, they often received free meals at the local Fights Diner that specialized in serving their famous Fight-Time Pizzas and Fight-Time Cheeseburgers. There had only been one fire in the last twenty years in Fights, and that was due to an old kerosene heater that exploded in the basement of Mr. Moody's house. Mr. Moody was seventy-five years old then, and they say the heater was older. Luckily, the house only sustained minor damage due to the fire department being located right next door.

Bill's wife, Margaret, was part of the Fights Women Bridge Club along with Tony Weissmann's wife, Jennifer. Jennifer told Margaret that Tony was getting ready to retire and she thought her husband Bill should run for mayor.

"Margaret, I think Bill would make a great mayor. He would be a shoo-in since everyone knows him," whispered Jennifer.

"Hmmm, I don't know, Jen. Bill has never really shown much of an interest in politics before, but I'll see. And I agree that he would be a good mayor if he were elected to the job."

A few weeks later, The Fights Time Chronicle, the local newspaper, announced that Mayor Weissmann would be retiring in thirty days. Margaret showed the article to Bill and suggested he throw his hat in the ring.

"Bill, it couldn't hurt, dear. I think you would make a fine mayor."

"Yeah, but there are so many things I see wrong with Fights. I wouldn't even know where to start," replied Bill.

"Well, you can start by going to the Town Council and registering your name for the ballot... if you're serious about applying."

Within a month, Bill had decided to run for mayor and use Margaret as his campaign manager. When he went to the Town

Council, he noticed that two other names had been registered to run for mayor. He saw the names of police officer William "Bill" Stewart and grocery store owner Billy "Bill" McGhee. Three Bills running for mayor would be a once-in-a-lifetime thing for Fights.

Officer Bill Stewart, a very physically fit man, was sort of a newcomer and not a native of Fights. He transferred over from Sycamore County to be closer to the girl he was dating, Molly Sullivan. Molly was a schoolteacher and one of the best-looking women in Fights; she was smart, feisty, and brave to teach the lower grades at the elementary school. Most of the younger kids were real pistols and very mouthy, but Molly stood up to them and was always in control of her classroom. Bill and Molly were engaged to be married soon, and he sought a calmer lifestyle.

Billy McGhee, whom everyone also called Bill, was the Pops of the Moms-and-Pops grocery store in town. He was a short, round, bald man in his fifties but looked older. Although he and his wife Edna had lived in Fights for about ten years, he was originally born in New Jersey; he moved away due to the high Jersey property taxes and saw Fights as a good place to raise a family.

The race for mayor was now on, and each candidate was charged with coming up with their campaign slogans geared toward being the catchiest. Although a catchy campaign slogan was not a guarantee to win, it went a long way in establishing the veracity and acceptance of the candidate. It could also backfire if the wrong slogan was used. Mayor Weissmann won his campaign with "Wise Men Always Vote for Weissmann." The real reason he won was that he ran against Bob Burke, the town alcoholic, and the fact that the Fights women did not boycott the election due to feeling left out of his campaign slogan.

Bill Stewart's campaign slogan was "A Vote for Bill is a Vote for Real." It was obvious the police officer did not have a campaign manager and that he had created this slogan on his own. Most people assumed he used his fiancée's elementary school students to create his campaign slogan.

Storeowner Bill McGhee appeared to be a little more creative with his slogan: "Vote for Me and I will Bill You Later." The slogan made people laugh but also nervous at the same time, as they didn't know if it was a slick way to announce he would be raising their taxes if he won.

Margaret and Bill worked hard trying to decide upon a good slogan. She thought he should incorporate justice into his slogan since that was his real last name: Justice. But Bill wasn't so sold on that because he thought it sounded corny. He was more concerned with trying to distinguish himself from the other two Bills so as not to confuse the voters. He also did not want a long campaign slogan; he wanted something that everyone could easily remember.

They both went to sleep that night without coming up with anything solid. Bill and Margaret figured they could get a fresh start the next day since their slogans were due at the Town Council by noon.

Then, in the middle of the night, Bill woke up and shook Margaret, saying, "I got it! I've got the perfect campaign slogan."

Barely opening her eyes, Margaret said, "What is it, dear?"

Bill jumped out of bed and stood in an animated stance like George Washington crossing the Delaware River in a boat and proclaimed, "VOTE FOR THE BILL OF FIGHTS!"

Margaret laughed and said, "That is so precious! Yes, let's go with that. I love it!"

Over the next several weeks, there were hundreds of printed lawn signs and flyers all over town and many planned campaign speeches in the town square. Bill Justice cruised around town in his Jeep Grand Cherokee with a magnetic campaign sign on his car door. Everyone clapped when he drove by to show approval of his witty campaign slogan.

There were not really any planned debates because the three friendly men did not want to appear adversarial with each other. They each felt equally qualified to be mayor but would respectfully accept defeat if they lost for the betterment of the town. They agreed that Fights did not deserve another reason to reinforce the origin of its town name.

On election day, almost all of the two thousand-plus citizens stood in lines to cast their votes at one of the three polling locations: the high school, the library, or the Volunteer Fire Department. Fights still used paper ballots that had to be hand-tabulated by the volunteer poll workers; the town was too small for computerized voting machines. The final election results were expected to be in by 6 p.m. that evening but would not be announced until the following day.

Traditionally, the outgoing mayor would read off the election results in the middle of the town square, and then the results would be documented at the town municipal building. Police Chief Jerry Pazda was more anxious than most because if Officer Bill Stewart became the new mayor, the police chief would be working for him in a twist of fate.

At 10 a.m. sharp the next morning, the clock in the town square gonged and former mayor Weissmann started to read off the election results in the loudspeaker: "Officer Bill Stewart received 638 votes. Bill McGhee received 531 votes. And Bill Justice received 992 votes. The new mayor of Fights, PA, is Bill Justice!"

Thunderous cheers could be heard from the crowd gathered around. Margaret kissed Bill on the mouth in front of everyone, and the crowd went wild. The other two Bills walked over and congratulated the new mayor with firm handshakes and pats on the back as if they were relieved the race was over.

Chief Pazda smiled as he congratulated Bill Justice. He then verbally flexed his authoritative muscles by suggesting to Officer Bill Stewart that he should go out and patrol the highways to look for speeders.

Store owner Bill McGhee took this opportunity to tell everyone in the crowd that his store was having a two-for-one victory sale on hotdog buns.

Honiss Clark, one of the volunteer firefighters, joked, "Hey Bill, why don't you ever put the hotdog weenies on sale? Better yet, why not give us the buns for free and bill us later for the weenies?"

The day after the election, Mayor Bill Justice sat at his mayoral desk inside the municipal building and wondered what he should tackle first. The former mayor was kind enough to leave a detailed list of things left undone during his administration.

The list included getting a new clock tower for the town square, repaving the street in front of the library, ordering new bodycams for the police department, repairing one of the two ten-year-old fire trucks, painting over some of the graffiti-laden buildings, and beefing up the Opioid Crisis Hotline with more volunteers.

The phone rang and he answered with, "Mayor Justice speaking... how may I help you?"

"Hello dear, it's just me checking to see how your first day is going and if you want me to bring you any lunch," said a cheerful Margaret.

"Hey, honey... no, I promised Honiss I would meet him for lunch at the diner. He's buying me a Fights-Time Cheeseburger," he said, laughing.

She teased, "Oh, I guess you no longer need a campaign manager anymore. Can I still be your wife?"

"Honey, you'll always be both to me. I love you and will see you this evening."

Bill frowned as he reviewed the list again left behind by Mayor Weissmann. He really didn't see anything on it that exalted him into urgent action. He surmised that the clock tower was almost 100 years old already; the street in front of the library was just paved ten years ago; the three police officers did not really need new bodycams; the one fire truck was okay for the size of the town; painting over the graffiti could probably be done over time as an ongoing project for the Boy Scouts; and boosting the hotline by just one more volunteer would be optimal for the town based on the frequency of the calls received.

Bill wanted to start a new town initiative, something that had never been done before but was needed at the same time. He continued to rack his brains until it was time to go meet the volunteer fireman for lunch.

Once he met up with Honiss at the diner, he took the opportunity to ask him what he thought the town needed most. He expected his response would easily be something that related to the needs of the fire department, but that was not how Honiss responded.

Honiss hesitated before biting his cheeseburger and said, "Well, Bill, honestly, I think we should allow cannabis shops to open up here since medical marijuana has been legalized almost everywhere else. That would go a long way in de-criminalizing it and relieving our drug crisis. Furthermore, I think we need to consider bringing the lottery in so we can use that money to improve our town. Sycamore County got the lottery, and look how fast they're growing."

"Wow," said Bill. "I didn't see that answer coming from you. Are you serious about what you said? You don't think those things would further complicate our lives here?"

"How so? If it's managed properly, we can come out looking like a big winner, and Fights can then be put on the map. Let's face it, our town is slowly dying and we don't have any big industries in town to save us," replied Honiss.

"I must say that you have given me something to think about, and I appreciate your honesty, Honiss," said Bill with a straight face.

"Anytime. You asked and I thought I would give you my best thoughts on the subject. Not that I'm looking to use any cannabis or lose all my money buying lotto tickets," joked Honiss as he bit into his burger.

The two men continued to converse and eat their lunch. Bill watched Honiss devour two Fights-Time Cheeseburgers with a large order of fries and a chocolate milkshake. Instead of fries, Bill ordered a green salad and only had water to drink. Afterward, he thanked Honiss for the lunch and said that the burger was tops. Honiss belched a loud "you're welcome" and proceeded to pay the bill.

When Bill got home that evening, he told Margaret about his conversation with Honiss. He knew that his wife was level-headed and would be able to balance out the conversation to make it fit within the confines of the town.

"Well, dear," said Margaret. "I'm not saying that his idea is completely off the rails, but it would take some getting used to around here. I like his point about the infusion of money into our town, but I'm not so sure about the benefits when it comes to crime reduction."

"Yes, that's my same concern, too. I'll do some research and work out a cost-benefit analysis in relation to other towns our size. If things pan out, I will present those suggestions to the town," said an unconvinced Bill.

Over the next month, the new mayor met with other local and state representatives about the merits of adopting the lottery and certified medical marijuana shops in his town; he preferred the word "marijuana" over "cannabis."

* * * *

Mayor Justice had finally decided, after many weeks of ideas, meetings, and deliberations, to present a plan of bringing in the lottery and then phasing in the marijuana shops slowly and strategically. He liked the idea of using the lottery to help fund the local economy and also use the legal marijuana shops to ease the drug crisis. He thought the townspeople would be able to see all the immediate advantages they could bring without any major compromises.

The day before the mayor was going to meet with the town council to present his plan, a huge fire broke out at one of the three churches in town. It was the smaller of the three churches in town, but it was also the only Black church – Saint Richard African Methodist Episcopal (AME) Church. The wooden church tower had caught fire as a result of a lightning strike. The church was built in 1901 and named after Richard Allen, a Black minister, educator, and founder of the AME church in 1794 in Philadelphia.

The small Black congregation was devastated to learn that their church had been destroyed along with its history and heritage. They knew they would not be able to readily rebuild, and it would take some time to raise the money to begin construction. The Black population in Fights had decreased over the years to only about 200 residents; the crime and drugs had taken a bigger toll on their community than any other.

When Mayor Justice found out about the fire, he jumped into his 2017 Jeep Grand Cherokee and raced over to the scene. Upon his arrival, he could tell that much of the building had been destroyed, and there was little hope of the one fire truck being able to distinguish the huge fire.

He met outside with the church pastor, the Reverend Eddye W. Thompson, a well-respected man of the Fights community. The Rev. Thompson also liked and respected Mayor Justice, someone he knew long before he was the mayor.

Looking up at the burning building and then facing Rev. Thomas, the mayor said,

"Pastor Thompson, I am sorry and as devastated as you are about this tragic fire. I promise to do everything in my power to help make this building whole again."

"Thank you, Bill. God works in mysterious ways, and I have never once questioned His acts of showing us the light, the truth, and the way. Our building was old and decaying, anyway. Maybe it's time for a new beginning in His holy name."

Mayor Justice walked away heavy-hearted at the loss of the church, but he was also struck by something that the pastor had said: *Maybe it's time for a new beginning in His holy name.* He went home and told his wife about the fire and his conversation with the pastor. He also told Margaret that he had changed his mind about presenting the plan to bring in the lottery and marijuana shops in Fights.

"Honey, I think I'm going to do something more radical and see if the town will back me."

"What do you mean, Bill? What are you going to do?"

"Well, first I'm going to propose that we invite the congregation at Saint Richard AME Church to worship with our church, St. James Episcopal Church, each Sunday, until they can find a replacement building. Our church is big enough to hold both congregations. And then, I'm going to suggest that the town raise funds to help them rebuild their church," Bill said excitedly.

Margaret stood silent for a minute as her mind raced through all the potential issues with Bill's idea. She knew this was a radical idea since there were no mixed churches in Fights.

Before she could respond, Bill added,

"And just think...maybe this move could help bring us closer together as a community and curtail some of the crime and violence if we all learned to live together. It sure couldn't hurt. Then we wouldn't need to bring in such apparent vices like the lottery and marijuana shops."

"Wow, Bill, that's a huge gamble, but I love where your heart is. As your wife, I'd be willing to stand behind you on this, but will the townspeople?"

"I think they might. We've got some good people around here. They just need to be presented with an opportunity to learn from each other. After all, Honiss Clark is a member of Saint Richard, and he didn't think twice about buying me a burger when I won the mayor's race."

"Okay. I'm convinced...now let's see how many others you can convince," Margaret said and kissed Bill on the lips. "Just don't give them a kiss when they agree with you."

* * * *

The mayor invited Honiss to lunch at Fights Diner and told him how sorry he was that his church caught on fire. Then, he shared his plan to bring the two congregations together until a new church could be found.

Honiss was proud and very appreciative of the mayor's intervention and the offer to bring the two churches together. Honiss recognized that both churches were part of the same Episcopal doctrine and were almost the same except for the African Methodist part and the members. Of course, the other obvious difference was that Saint Richard was Black, and all the pictures shown of Saint James had always depicted him as White.

"Honiss, I need your help in convincing members of your congregation to at least give this idea a chance. I know the Rev. Thompson will like this idea, and I hope it will give him a chance to share his message with a bigger congregation."

Honiss smiled and said, "I know the Reverend will love that. He likes to hear himself preach!"

The two men enjoyed their lunch. This time, Bill tried a Fights-Time Cheeseburger, a large order of fries, and a chocolate milkshake. Surprisingly, Honiss ordered a green salad and a glass of water, saying that he needed to lose some weight. Both men laughed out loud as they continued eating.

That was the start of a new beginning in Fights, PA. The two congregations worshipped together for two years without any incidents until the new Saint Richard church was completed. Even after it was completed, the two congregations still agreed to worship together and visit each other's churches regularly. Racial harmony had given all the citizens the glue they needed to create a new beginning, and it was all because of lightning striking an old church; many people said the burning church incident was symbolic of the Burning Bush parable related in the Bible.

Mayor Bill Justice served as mayor for three terms because everyone approved of his actions. Soon, the crime rate went down and arrests from drug users decreased as well; they never did get the lottery or marijuana shops. The TV show 60 Minutes featured a segment on Mayor Justice and how he helped to heal a dying town called Fights, PA.

Mayor Justice again asked to meet with Honiss Clark at the Fights Diner. This time, he had another radical idea to share. He told Honiss that he was retiring and suggested that he throw his hat in the ring to become the first Black mayor of Fights. Bill said that Honiss would be a shoo-in since he had become such an important and trusted man in town.

Honiss subsequently agreed, and he came up with a winning campaign slogan on the spot: "Honiss for Honesty."

CHAPTER THIRTY-ONE

"ON BEING BAPTIZED"

Our pastor, The Reverend J.S. Sugar, was a real sweet man; however, he was a fire-breathing minister who preached hellfire and damnation every Sunday to all sinners. We were members of the Creekside Holy Ghost Church, a church with a very long history. It'd had only had five pastors in its 100-year existence.

The Rev. Sugar was a serious man of the cloth who did not play with God and was never seen without his thin white clergy collar. He was medium built with a long forehead and wore tiny wire-framed eyeglasses. The gray hair on his head matched his gray beard to openly advertise his many years behind the pulpit.

His reputation as a long-winded, evangelical preacher was legendary as he came from a big family of ordained clergy. His father and grandfather were preachers, and so were his two brothers. Although his parents named him John Samuel, he thought that using the initials J.S. made him sound more dignified and respectable. The only thing he loved more than preaching was baptizing.

Being baptized was not originally my idea. My parents insisted on it, especially if I was going to live under their roof. Since my father was a church elder and my mother sang in the choir, they were embarrassed that all but one of their children had not been baptized already. But when I turned twelve, my parents mandated it. In order to save face, I agreed, but mainly because my parents threatened to disown me if I didn't. Since I was the last born, my folks named me Jefferson Omega Smith.

Normally, I wouldn't mind a long sermon. However, I was being baptized the coming Sunday and hoping my baptism would be short and sweet. I equated long sermons with long baptisms and feared I would be forgotten underwater.

When the Reverend Sugar and Deacon Ward told me they were going to baptize me in the nearby creek, I was afraid. They didn't ask me if I could swim or even hold my breath underwater. I was too embarrassed to tell them not only could I not swim, but I was deathly afraid of going under the water.

When Sunday came, I stood there trembling knee-deep in the creek, with the preacher placing one of his hands on my forehead while he held his Bible in the other hand. Deacon Ward stood behind me with his hands on my shoulders. Wearing a loose white tee shirt and white cut-off pants, I looked up at the sky and felt the sun beaming down on my face. I took that to mean God was watching me and waiting impatiently as a gentle breeze blew on my backside.

Although the weather was warm in June, the fear was making my knees shake below the water; it was a good thing nobody else could see them. All the while I was being reassured by The Reverend that they wouldn't let me drown and that everything would be okay. When I appeared apprehensive about the baptism, Reverend Sugar joked, "Child, would you rather be baptized in water or by fire?" He and the deacon got a big chuckle out of that, but it wasn't funny to me.

It soon became obvious I was the last one in my family to get baptized. My parents and siblings watched anxiously, as they knew I was afraid of water and would be dunked at any minute. They had warned me not to scream and shout and make them all look bad; they were afraid of looking bad, while I was afraid of drowning and dying.

I heard the reverend whisper, "It's time," and that was my signal to start holding my breath. He said the whole thing was only supposed to last about ten seconds, but sometimes, the reverend used too many words when he asked God to bless the candidates and wash them clean in the blood of Jesus. I reasoned that it should take him less time to baptize me since I had already taken a bath earlier that morning.

Trying to assure me that I was in good hands, Deacon Ward said, "Son, we've been baptizing folks in this creek for 100 years, and we haven't drowned anyone yet."

Then, in my mind, I saw The Reverend Sugar in the pulpit one Sunday when he took off his wristwatch and placed it on the podium to keep track of his preaching time. Although he told the congregation that he was only going to speak for about ten minutes, he went on for forty. Cephus, my older brother, started a joke about preachers after that. He said, "What does it mean when a preacher takes off his watch and sets it on the podium?" Before anyone could respond, he would quickly say, "Absolutely nothing!"

"You ready, child?" the reverend asked. I was about to say "yessir" when my whole body was pushed backward and dunked under for what seemed like an eternity. I could hear the reverend's muffled words coming through the water when he said, "Lord, place your loving hands around this child and let your blood run through his veins like the water is running through this creek. We know that you are the only one who can save us, and we ask you to save this poor child in your holy name." My feet started kicking when my brain realized it had been underwater longer than ten seconds, and the Reverend had not yet ended his prayer with an "Amen."

Deacon Ward could see my hands waving and feel me kicking, so he must have motioned to the reverend to bring me up. Suddenly, I was back up with a loud "Aaaa-men!"

People in the crowd standing nearby clapped and said, "Amen and thank the Lord!" as I was led up and out of the creek. My parents looked pleased and my siblings couldn't stop snickering, especially Cephus.

"Reminds me of the time the reverend baptized me," Cephus chuckled. "I was beginning to turn blue-black, I was down there so long."

"Aw, hush up, Cephus," Momma said. "Leave that boy alone. He's been saved by the blood of Jesus now. Come on, Jeff, let me dry you off."

Papa looked big and proud as he stood with the other elders and shook hands with them. Papa then started passing out cigars on the church grounds as if to signal a new baby had been born.

My mother wrapped a huge beach towel around me and told me to go inside and change clothes in the church bathroom. After a few minutes, I exited the bathroom with my street clothes on, and I was past ready to go home.

On the drive home, my mother asked me if I felt any different after being baptized and saved.

"Huh?" I said. "Different...what do you mean, Mom?"

"I mean, now that you've been saved, you should feel different," Momma insisted.

"Uh, my ears are kind of stopped up with water, and I feel cleaner... is that what you mean?"

Papa laughed. "No, son. Your momma wants to know if your heart has changed and if you can feel the love of God inside you with his presence."

"Oh, I guess so...I just thought my stomach was growling because I was hungry," I said.

Cephus laughed out loud in the back seat of the car and said, "Now that's funny...we've got the Father, the Son, and now the Holy Ghost inside Jeff's stomach."

My sister Ruthie high-fived Cephus with, "That's a good one, brother!"

Momma and Papa seemed to give up and stopped asking me if I felt different after being dunked and almost drowned at church. If God had been present at my baptism, He sure did not try to *save* me from drowning.

CHAPTER THIRTY-TWO

"THE MISSING CORPSE"

Here is a short scene depicting two funeral home employees who were on their way to the cemetery with a body when the driver stopped to get a lottery ticket and the other employee went to the bathroom. When they came back, the body was gone.

--Man #1—(Sam)

"Man, what do you mean you don't know what happened to the body? How could you lose a body coming straight from the church to the cemetery? How are we going to explain this to the family? It's a crying shame. Hey, I'm telling you this, John... I'm not in this. I don't want any part of this. I can't lose my job because I've got mouths to feed. Who loses a dead body on the way to the graveyard? Don't just stand there looking stupid. Don't you have something to say?"

--Man #2—(John)

"Sam, what can I tell you? You saw the pallbearers put the body in the back. I can't help it if I stopped to get a lottery ticket and the body got up and walked away. Maybe he wasn't dead after all. Do you know if he was ever actually embalmed? This could just be a prank. Why are you getting so hysterical? I'm sure the body will show up sooner or later."

--Man #1—(Sam)

"Sooner or later? John, are you crazy? The gravediggers are standing by to plant this guy in the ground. They are not going to wait for sooner or later...and I'm not either. I'm going home to be with my old lady and leave you here to deal with this. I'm not joking."

--Man #2—(John)

"Go ahead, man. You're acting like a punk. I thought you were my man, Sam. It's just a dead body. No big deal. It's not a live person, so we are not going to get in any trouble for killing somebody who is already dead, man. I don't see the problem. How far can a dead body get in this neighborhood with makeup on his face?"

--Man #1—(Sam)

"I give up! I'm going home, man. I can't believe you. You're acting way too cool for someone who has no idea where the corpse is that just got funeralized. We are supposed to be a respectable funeral home to take care of the dead and give them a proper burial with perpetual care. How are we going to do that now with no body?"

--Man #2—(John)

"That's it! Let's just tell the gravediggers that the body is inside, and we drop it and go. They are not going to look inside. Who's ever going to know?"

CHAPTER THIRTY-THREE

"KARMA"

My name is Calvin Johnson. In the summer of 1965, while working at my job at the Philadelphia 30th Street Post Office, I got word that my beloved grandfather had passed away down South. Taking a plane was not really an option for many reasons, so I took a Greyhound bus to go home for the funeral. My grandfather was the one who taught me how to live by the Golden Rule when I was a teenager.

It was a long, hot bus ride all the way from Philadelphia to Alabama. When we changed buses in Atlanta, I was asked to move to the back of the bus. Two days earlier in Philadelphia, it was 1965, but when I got to the Deep South, it seemed like it was 1865.

As I stepped off the bus in Alabama, a large *black and white* sign laughingly reminded me that I was no longer in the North and back home in the South; we didn't have constant reminders like that in Philadelphia, and things seemed a lot better there. If discrimination was more covert in the North, it was more overt in the South.

The segregated signs at the bus station directed me to the Colored Waiting Room to fetch my baggage and wait for my ride. There was a water fountain inside next to a bathroom that bore the same cruel signs for Colored.

I sat there and watched White people take all the taxis parked out in front with White drivers. I was told by the bus station manager I had to wait for the Colored taxi driver to come before I could get a ride from the bus station. So, I waited...and waited...and waited.

After about ninety minutes of waiting, I decided to use the bathroom. The bathroom was separate but definitely not equal; other than the stinking smell and dirty floor, there was no toilet paper in the stalls. I knew better than to ask the bus station manager for some, so I used some extra napkins I had gotten in Atlanta with my greasy fried chicken sandwich and cold French fries.

I walked out of the bathroom to sit and wait some more in our waiting room. After another fifteen minutes, I asked the manager how much longer I had to wait before my taxi arrived.

"I don't know. How long ago did you call for your taxi?" he asked.

"Well, I didn't call for a taxi. I just assumed one would come by on a regular basis like they do up North. Don't they?"

"Not the Colored taxi drivers. We don't allow them to come unless you call for one. You can use that special phone over there to call Roscoe, and he'll come pick you up. His number is on the wall."

"Thank you," I said and used the pay phone to call the hand-scribbled phone number on the wall for Roscoe. Then I sat down to wait some more.

It seems the weight of discrimination makes the waiting a lot longer and a lot heavier at times. I was glad to be able to attend my grandfather's funeral, but I could not wait to get back to Philadelphia. The love of family can sometimes be uncomfortable.

While waiting, I noticed a young Negro mother and her child sitting in the same waiting room with me. She was beautiful and looked to be about my age, twenty-something. With a puffy afro, she reminded me of Angela Davis.

I smiled and tipped my hat like I was always taught to do. She smiled back and nodded her head without speaking; her eyes dared not to look at mine.

Soon after, the young child, about four years old, quickly broke away from her and darted toward the water fountain marked for Whites Only.

Before the station manager or anyone else could complain, I reached for the little boy and walked him back toward his mother.

The mother thanked me by saying, "Thank you, sir. I appreciate that. He's thirsty, but obviously he can't read."

We both laughed and made light of the uncomfortable situation. I introduced myself to her as Calvin Johnson and told her that I had come in for a funeral.

She provided her name as Karma Belle and said that she was in town for a funeral, too. She said she came in from New Jersey.

"That's a strange coincidence," I said. "What is the name of your lost loved one?"

"Mrs. Hattie Mae Langston," she said. "She was my grandmother."

"I'm here for my grandfather's funeral. His name was Nathan George Sistrunk," I replied.

We both smiled and continued to have a friendly conversation. I asked if I could take the little boy over to the Colored water fountain to let him drink. When she gave me her approval, I picked up the chubby little boy and held him up while he drank water from the white porcelain fountain. His loud slurps caused some to look around at us.

A few minutes later, I heard an amplified voice call out saying, "I'm here to pick up Calvin Johnson...this is Roscoe."

I waved my hands to show that I was the one who had called for the taxi. I returned the child to his mother and picked up my bag. I asked Karma if she had a ride from the station. When she said that she wasn't sure how much longer her ride would be, I asked if she wanted to share my taxi with me.

She smiled and said, "If you don't mind. I really don't want to wait here any longer, especially alone like this." There were no other Negroes in the station at that time.

There seemed to be enough room for all three of us in Roscoe's taxi, which was a light green 1960 Chevrolet Corvair. We all piled in and gave Roscoe our intended addresses. He tipped his hat and said, "Hi, yawl. I'm Roscoe Cooke. I'm a distant relative to Sam Cooke, the singer."

Karma and I both looked at each other and smiled. Her little boy overheard what Roscoe said and yelled out, "I know how to cook, too!" We all laughed.

While in the back seat with Karma, I told her that I was sorry about her grandmother and that I hoped she has a nice visit with her family.

Karma thanked me for the condolences and said likewise about my grandfather. Her plan was to stay for a few days and then go back to New Jersey on the bus. She had a job there as a secretary for an insurance company.

I shared with her that I worked at a post office in Philadelphia and that New Jersey was not that far away.

She said, "I've never been to Philadelphia, but I hear they make delicious cheesesteaks."

I laughed and said, "Yes, we do, and we have a whole lot of history there, too."

"Like what?" she asked.

I said, "Like Philadelphia is home to the very first hospital and the very first zoo in America. And we also have Mother Bethel African Methodist Episcopal Church there. It's where the A.M.E. Church was started by Richard Allen with free Negroes, not slaves."

"Wow, I never knew that," she said.

"Hmmm, maybe I will have to come visit Philadelphia one day," she added with a big smile.

"And I'll take you to church and then buy you a cheesesteak." I laughed.

At that moment, Roscoe stopped his taxi and said, "We're here at the first address already. Who's getting out first?"

Karma reached in her purse to pay Roscoe for the ride, but I stopped her.

"This one is on me since I was coming this way anyway. I hope you and your son have a nice visit."

"Thank you, Calvin," she said and leaned over to kiss me on the jaw.

"I'll take one of those too in place of a tip," Roscoe laughed.

"And Snookie is my little brother, not my son. I don't have any children," Karma said as she exited the taxi.

Karma and Snookie waved bye as Roscoe prepared to transport me to my destination. I turned around to get one last look at her. She was looking in the direction of Roscoe's taxi at the same time.

Ten minutes later, Roscoe and I arrived at 412 Houston Street, the address for my grandmother. I paid the fare for both my ride and Karma's, and I added a big tip for Roscoe.

"Thank you, Roscoe, for the ride. I wish I had known to call you sooner."

He smiled and said, "If you had, then you might not have met that pretty lady."

Roscoe had a good point. He was comical but not without smarts. I wasn't sure if he was really related to Sam Cooke, but I was sure that two of Sam Cooke's biggest hits, "Cupid" and "You Send Me," were playing in my head every time I thought about Karma.

On the day of my grandfather's funeral, we all piled into the church at Parks Chapel A.M.E. Church on Montana Street. The Rev. W.F. Thompson was the presiding minister and church pastor.

I sat on the front pew near the casket with my grandmother and other relatives. It was a somber day, but all funerals are that way.

After a few songs and a brief eulogy, the funeral home director closed the lid on the casket, and the benediction followed. We all then started to proceed out the door for the burial in the cemetery behind the small church.

My grandmother was the only one crying since they had been married for fifty years. I hadn't seen my grandfather since I was a kid, so I felt kind of numb, but I did love him.

I wondered when and where Karma would be having her grandmother's funeral. On the way to the car, I asked my grandmother if she knew a Mrs. Hattie Mae Langston.

"Mrs. Hattie Mae Langston recently passed away, and they are having her funeral tomorrow at North Highland Baptist Church on Houston Street," my grandmother replied. "Why do you ask?"

"Oh, I met her granddaughter down at the bus station, and I gave her a ride in my taxi. I just wanted to know if you knew the family."

"Yes, Hattie and I both worked in the lunchroom together at Lake Street Junior High School years ago. She was a fine woman."

"I see," I said. "Where is her house located?"

"Er, her house is on Walnut Street, right across from the old Carver Theater."

The next day, I borrowed my grandmother's car and drove past North Highland Baptist Church around the time the funeral was to start for Karma's grandmother.

Once I saw a stream of people parking their cars near the church, I parked my car and went inside the church to attend the funeral, but mainly to see Karma again.

I was dressed in the same suit I had on the day before since I'd only brought one suit and had not planned to attend two funerals. Karma and her family were seated on the front pew, so I sat in the back of the church, out of sight, and watched.

When the funeral was over and people started filing out to attend the burial, Karma looked over and saw me standing in the back pew. Despite the sad mood on the faces of all the people there, her face looked surprised when she saw me. Without using her lips to say hello, her eyes brightened.

I waited to be the last one to leave the church since everyone else was family or friends. I stayed behind and decided not to attend the burial because I felt that was more private and didn't want to intrude.

Afterward, Karma walked over to me and said, "Calvin, what are you doing here? You didn't know my grandmother, did you?"

"Ah, no, but my grandmother used to work with your grandmother in the lunchroom, and I wanted to come pay my respects to her. She's still mourning my grandfather and couldn't come. His funeral was yesterday."

"Oh," said Karma. "Two funerals in two days? You must be tired and hungry. Want to join me at the repast for my grandmother?"

"Uh, yes, if you don't mind," I managed to say. "And how's Snookie doing?"

"Snookie is fine, but we left him at home with some of the other young people. He is too young to understand funerals," she said with a smile.

We went back inside and headed for the church basement, where the food was being served for the repast. It looked to be a typical southern church meal with fried chicken, green beans, cornbread, and potato salad.

It had been a long time since I ate that kind of food; Philadelphia food was different and best known for cheesesteaks, pizza, and hoagies.

Once she introduced me around to all her relatives, I felt more comfortable. It made it easier when they all realized who my grandmother was and that I actually grew up in the same town but had moved away.

After the repast, Karma thanked me for coming to the funeral and walked me to my car. I had a burning question to ask her, and I felt the time was now since we were alone.

"Karma, why did you kiss me on the jaw in the taxi?" I asked.

She looked embarrassed but managed to say, "Well, I was grateful for the ride, and I thought what you did was sweet. I'm sorry if I offended you."

"No, no," I said. "I was not offended. My point was that I really like you and I was hoping that kiss was the start of something between us. I mean, I think you are beautiful and..."

"Calvin, I like you too," she interrupted. "I guess my kiss did mean more than my gratitude. I thought about you all last night and wondered if I'd see you again before you left. You saw the look on my face when I saw you today. I don't have anyone that I'm seeing in New Jersey."

I smiled and said, "Wow, I can't believe it. Looks like I'll be buying you that cheesesteak and taking you to church after all in Philadelphia when you visit."

We both laughed and looked at each other with a longing gaze. I wanted to kiss her, but I wouldn't dare in front of the church. I squeezed her hands real tight to send her a nonverbal signal. She squeezed mine back to indicate she got the message.

We saw each other every day that we were back down South. I brought Karma by and introduced her to my grandmother. My grandmother smiled and said, "I see that Hattie has a beautiful granddaughter."

I even arranged for us to take the same bus back North together since our states were so close together. The next day, it was time for Karma, Snookie, and me to go back to the bus station. As luck would have it, we called for a taxi and Roscoe came to pick us up.

When he arrived, we were all standing together with our luggage packed and ready to go. My grandmother waved and said, "Hi Roscoe!" Then she looked at us and said, "Did you know he is related to Sam Cooke, the singer?"

We both laughed, and I said, "Yes, he told us that when he picked us up before. Is it really true that he's related to Sam Cooke?"

"I don't know, but why would anyone lie about something like that," she replied.

"She's got a good point," said Karma.

Snookie said, "I know how to cook, too."

Roscoe drove us back to the same bus station where we had waited for so long, but this time, things were different. Since the three of us were traveling together, the station manager assumed we were a family: husband, wife, and child.

He actually treated us with respect and told us that the bus back North would be departing in about fifteen minutes. Surprisingly, he even took the luggage from Karma and carried it to our waiting room section.

I turned around to pay Roscoe for the ride, but he had already pulled off. I grabbed Karma and Snookie by the hands, and we walked inside to wait for our bus.

Once inside, Snookie ran for the water fountain again, but this time he found the right one marked Colored. I picked him up so he could take a drink and then Karma and I took our seats.

I thought about how I dreaded being at the bus station down South with all its signage and separate but equal things going on. But then I realized that had I not come, I would have never met Karma.

I remembered something my grandfather told me years ago. He said, "When life closes a door for us, God opens a window." I loosely translated that to mean that although I came for my grandfather's passing, I was given the opportunity to meet Karma. If my grandfather symbolized the door, then Karma was the window.

Glancing around the old, segregated bus station, I rationalized to myself that there was a major difference between bad karma and good Karma. I looked over at her, and she kissed me on the jaw. Watching us closely, Snookie climbed on the bench near me and kissed me on my other jaw.

CHAPTER THIRTY-FOUR

"SELF PORTRAIT"

I am a man who loves without *Boundaries* and whose love is *Boundless*.
Love for me is a *When* and not a *What*.
My love is also a How and not a Where.
I believe in the love of *We* and not just of *Me*.
My love has a *Start* without a *Stop*.
I believe in an unselfish *Ours* and not a stingy *Mine*.
My love is *Irreplaceable* and *Unforgettable*.
My love is *Gender-free* and *Color-blind*.
My love is *Rare* but *Real*.
My love is *Fragile* but *Resilient*.
My love is sometimes *Misty* but always *Crystal Clear*.

CHAPTER THIRTY-FIVE

"VULNERABLE"

Today's men are more vulnerable than once believed.
Just trying to live up to the hype of
masculinity is a chore for some.
It's especially hard for those who haven't achieved,
And for those who don't understand what they have become.

Some men suffer stress from lack of self-esteem,
And they cry out for understanding when taken for granted.
Many men have fallen short of what they dream,
And in many ways sometimes feel that they are stranded.

A gentleman can be a gentle man and still exist,
In a world with other men who are Type A.
They often just need a little assist,
From others to help show them the way.

It's a great thing to see men supporting each other,
And ignoring the survival of the fittest.
All men are fortunate to have a brother,
To get them from the smallest to the biggest.

Women appreciate real men who are real,
And they are not looking for a carbon copy.
Women want men with the ability to feel,
And not those who act like it's just a hobby.

In the end, a man is his own net worth,
But must understand where he stands.
A man is designed to be a man at birth,
For his destiny is in his own hands.

CHAPTER THIRTY-SIX

"INVULNERABLE"

Women have emerged as the stronger sex.
It took centuries for the truth to be revealed.
No more dealing from the bottom of the deck,
They have bested men in every modern field.

> Once thought to be the weaker sex but not anymore,
> Women outnumber men and are more than equal.
> They are invulnerable and stronger than before,
> And naturally gifted as God's favorite people.

Eve and Mary from biblical times,
Proved essential in showing men the way.
Men have often committed most of the crimes,
But women are the ones who have saved the day.

> Being invulnerable is not the same as impregnable,
> A woman needs a man to be a helpful, equal, mate.
> Women made falling in love highly possible,
> For men are the ones that they were meant to date.

Women view competition as a beautiful thing,
While some men view it as an inevitable threat.
Women are uninterested in becoming the King,
Essentially, they just want to win the bet.

    Overall, invulnerability is just an imaginative word,
    Because we are all subject to some kind of harm.
    Men should accept that women need to be heard,
    And offer them a place that's kind, gentle, and warm.

CHAPTER THIRTY-SEVEN

"THE eNIGma"

Whoever said, "Sticks and stones may break my bones, but words can never hurt me," was badly misinformed or had never been a victim of name-calling. In this new world we live in, name-calling has become the major weapon used by many cowardly people who hide on social media and everywhere else; however, there are some very famous people who excel in name-calling out in the open for all the world to see. Those with limited vocabularies tend to name-call the most.

When I was a young man, I heard someone call me an "eNIGma," and I thought it was a bad word. That simple, six-letter word had my mind bouncing like an NBA basketball as it conjured up all kinds of demeaning images and Black racial slurs. I got angrier and angrier because I didn't know the proper meaning of the word. I found a dictionary and realized that the word was intended to be more of a compliment about me and my behavior rather than a detriment. It was the way I heard it that set me on edge.

I recall a time when a good friend of mine was acting all nervous and suspicious about something around me. I didn't quite understand what was going on with him, so I said, "Why are you being so HINKY?" My friend immediately got offended and thought I had called him a White racial slur instead. After I explained to him that the word "hinky" meant suspicious or nervous, he calmed down, but not before I showed him the meaning of the word in the dictionary.

Years later, I overheard a conversation between two young girls at a food court. One of the girls called the other girl OBTUSE. The second girl took it as a compliment as they both laughed together. I'm not sure if the girl who originally used the word thought it was a compliment, but it wasn't. Obtuse actually means insensitive, stupid, and slow to understand.

Learning new words to add to our daily vocabulary is a good thing. In order never to be caught with my word guard down again, I went out and purchased a weapon that I secretly call my trusty DERRINGER, a slang term I now use for my miniature dictionary that I keep up my sleeve in order to be ready for my next wordy assault.

If some of you think that this is strange behavior for someone like me to perform, then I guess it's alright to call me an ENIGMA rather than an eNIGma. FYI. The dictionary definition for the word "enigma" is "a person or thing that is mysterious or puzzling."

CHAPTER THIRTY-EIGHT

"THREE KILOS"

This is an impossibly true story.

Well...almost.

While in my hometown of Dothan, Alabama, visiting my mother recently, I stopped by the local Piggly Wiggly grocery store just to browse and reminisce for old times' sake. I grew up with my family shopping at Piggly Wiggly like everyone else in my hometown.

And apparently, so did Miss Daisy in the 1989 movie based in the American South, *Driving Miss Daisy* starring Jessica Tandy and Morgan Freeman. In this true-life story, Tandy played Miss Daisy Werthan, *an elderly Jewish woman committed to maintaining her independence*, and Freeman portrayed Hoke Colburn, her Black chauffeur *hired to drive her around*; they were two unlikely elderly friends.

There was a scene in the movie that prominently mentioned the Piggly Wiggly store when Hoke is trying to drive the independent and defiant Miss Daisy to the store as she is seen walking alone along the street, unwilling to be driven by her hired chauffeur.

Hoke yells, "Get in the car, Miss Daisy! I'm trying to drive you to the Piggly Wiggly."

As I walked up and down each aisle of the store, reminiscing about the good old days when prices were lower, I spotted a sale on Jim Dandy grits, the brand name of grits of my childhood and upbringing. I didn't know they still made them; apparently, they can only be bought in the South and not in Philadelphia, where I live.

The sale price was $1.69 for a two-pound bag. Since I don't visit home that much anymore, I decided to stock up and buy three bags to take to Philadelphia with me inside my carry-on luggage aboard Southwest Airlines.

Grits are a southern favorite tradition that I love and have eaten since I was a child. Almost everyone in my hometown ate the old-fashioned grits and cooked them the same way by boiling them for about twenty minutes and then adding salt, butter, and pepper to taste afterward. We would never, ever eat instant grits.

A typical southern breakfast would include piping hot grits, scrambled eggs, bacon, toast, juice, and coffee. The local Waffle House serves this delicious combination all day, every day, for about $6.99.

Early the next morning, I left Dothan to drive back to the Atlanta airport in my rental car to catch my flight home to Philadelphia. Since I have TSA Pre, I usually zip through the TSA line in no time and rarely have any delays or searches. At the airport, I put my carry-on bag with the grits on the conveyor belt like normal and watched it move through while I walked through the metal detectors without any alarms going off.

On the other end, I noticed that my black leather bag was rerouted so that it could be hand-searched by TSA personnel. I couldn't understand why they would want to search my bag because I didn't have any weapons or sharp objects in it.

The large TSA man looked at me as he grabbed my bag and asked, "This your bag?"

I said, "Yep," and I followed him over to a counter, where he unzipped it and conducted a physical search wearing his rubber gloves.

I witnessed him take out the plastic Piggly Wiggly shopping bag and take a closer look at its contents. I could clearly read the store's slogan on the outside of the bag as the oversized Georgia TSA man opened the bag to see the grits.

The slogan read, "Save Big with the Pig" as he asked me, "These your grits?"

I said, "Yessir. Those are the best grits I ever tasted."

The TSA man grinned and said, "You're right, I love me some Jim Dandy grits, too."

He put the grits back in the plastic bag, zipped up my carry-on, and handed it back to me, saying, "Have a safe flight, sir."

My flight to Philadelphia was scheduled to depart at 11:55 a.m. I couldn't wait to get home because my wife and I were planning to leave the next day for vacation in Australia.

When I arrived at my gate, a female Southwest Airlines staff member alerted me that my flight would be delayed for about four hours. Of course, I wasn't happy about the delay, but I decided to sit down, relax, and just wait along with everyone else.

While sitting there, I reflected on how the TSA man had searched my luggage and found the bags of grits. It was funny how I never realized before that a bag of grits does sort of resemble a bag of drugs at first glance. With its flat, rectangular shape, I could certainly see how the X-ray scanner was convinced.

I laughed to myself and thought, "That incident might make a good, comical short story about a man smuggling drugs hidden inside a bag of grits. I could title it *Cocaine Grits.*

With four hours to kill, I started jotting down some ideas using a Word document app on my smartphone. After a while, I got sleepy and closed my eyes for only a few minutes to take a quick nap while clutching my bag that had the grits.

When I awoke, my wife and I were standing in line waiting to go through Customs in Australia. The Australian Customs agents searched our bags to make sure we were not carrying any contraband or illegal substances.

My wife's bags went through without any problems. When one of the agents searched my bag, he pulled out my three bags of grits; I must have inadvertently left them in my bag by mistake.

The agent looked at me and asked, "Sir, is this your bag?"

I replied, "Yes, it is."

He then blew a whistle to signal other Customs agents to surround me to prevent me from going through with my wife.

The agent asked, "What are these, sir?' as he pointed to the three bags of grits.

I said, "Those are grits."

With his Down Under accent, he asked, "What are GRYTTS?"

"Grits are grains of white hominy corn used primarily as a breakfast food," I answered. "Kind of like cream of wheat or oatmeal, but different."

"Are you sure GRYTTS is not a street name for an American drug?"

"No, sir," I said. "Grits are...just grits."

He just looked at me with a blank expression, as if he was waiting for me to confess.

Then he called for a drug-sniffing police dog to be sent over to sniff the bags of grits.

The pointy-tailed dog trotted over and sniffed all three bags of grits. Afterward, he came over to me and started sniffing my fingers, one-by-one.

Surprisingly, the dog then stood upright on his hind legs to smell my breath. He sniffed my face for a few seconds and then started barking uncontrollably. I remembered that I did stop by Waffle House early that morning and had grits for breakfast.

The Customs agents seized my bag and told me to follow them. My wife yelled, "Where are you taking my husband?"

One of the agents answered her with, "Madam, this should only take a minute to clear up. Just wait over there in the waiting area."

I watched my wife sit down with a worried look on her face. I yelled, "Don't worry, honey, it'll be alright."

The agents transported me to a small room and asked me to take a seat. The one agent said someone would be with me in a minute.

After a few minutes, an authoritative-looking man in a uniform came in and introduced himself as a supervisor or something like that; I was too nervous to listen to what he said.

He held my passport in his hand and said, "How are you today, Mr. Thompson?"

I said, "I'm fine, sir, but what is this all about? I'm just here in Australia on vacation with my wife."

He said, "Do you usually travel with three kilos of white powder in your bag?"

"Three kilos of white powder," I echoed. "What are you talking about?"

He said, "We found these three kilos of what you say are Grytts, but we don't believe you since we never heard of Grytts before down here."

"You've got to be joking, sir," I said. "Those are two-pound bags of grits, not kilos of any kind of drugs. Grits are edible...they are Jim Dandy grits!"

"Jim Dandy's Grytts," he asked. "I thought you said they were your Grytts. Who is this Jim Dandy person? Were you smuggling these Grytts for your boss, Mr. Jim Dandy?"

"No, Jim Dandy is the brand name of the grits like it says on the package. Jim Dandy is not a real person...I don't think, but I'm not sure," I exclaimed.

"We have a strong view against drug traffickers in Australia, and we will prosecute to the fullest extent of the law...if convicted."

"Sir, I promise you that I am not a drug trafficker. In fact, I am a retired American federal agent with twenty-five years on the job."

"We'll see about that after we run your record and your fingerprints," the supervisor promised.

He looked at my passport again and asked if James Thompson was my real name or an alias.

"Yessir," I said. "My full name is James L. Thompson, Jr."

"Where do you currently reside now?"

"Uh, I live at 555 Shackster Avenue in Philadelphia, Pennsylvania."

"Oh, the City of Brotherly Love," he joked. "Well, I hope you are telling the truth for your sake."

After about fifteen minutes, another uniformed man walked in and whispered something to the supervisor.

The supervisor looked at me and said, "You're in luck, Mr. Thompson. We have an on-duty judge who is willing to give you a speedy trial. We were also able to put together a jury of your peers quickly, and the trial will begin in five minutes."

"What...a trial? Why do I need a trial? I haven't been convicted of a crime. These are just grits!"

"Yes, and that's the problem. In Australia, we have never heard of Grytts, and we are skeptical about your story."

"So, you're going to put me on trial?"

"Yes, that's the way we solve crimes quickly down here. You will go free if you are telling the truth. If not..."

"If not, what?"

Just then, they moved me to a larger room next door that they used like a courtroom. A man in a judge's robe walked in and sat at the head of a long desk.

Next, a group of twelve people walked in, dressed in everyday clothes and took their seats near the long desk. I was told they were the jurors. One of the jurors bore a striking resemblance to a kangaroo.

The judge banged his gavel and said, "Let the trial begin."

The supervisor assigned me a man he said was my public defender attorney since I did not have one present.

"Mr. Thompson, this is your attorney, Mr. Bailey. He has been apprised of the relevant facts of the case already."

I said, "I'm confused, Your Honor. What am I on trial for? And do I really need an attorney for having three bags of grits?"

The judge looked at me with a straight, solemn face and said, "Sir, in my courtroom, we take these matters very seriously. We don't take too kindly to drug trafficking in our country, unlike they do in the United States."

"But—" I started to say.

"Be quiet, Mr. Thompson, so we can get on with this hearing. Mr. Bailey, please control your client," the judge said as he loudly banged his gavel three times.

Without thinking, I jumped up and said, "But this is a travesty of justice and nothing but a kangaroo court. What about my due process rights?"

At that moment, the one juror I thought looked like a kangaroo stood up and protested, "Your Honor, I object!"

The judge said, "Sustained."

As it turned out, the juror was a real live kangaroo.

Apparently, jurors can object in Australia, and they can also be kangaroos. It must have been a female kangaroo because I could see her pouch when she stood up, and she was carrying a baby kangaroo who tried to mimic her mother's objection with a squeaky-voiced "Your Honor, I am an object!"

Everybody in the courtroom laughed out loud except me.

The judge continued with, "Mr. Thompson, I see here where you said that these kilos of white powder are really edible breakfast foods."

I said, "That is correct, Your Honor. I've been eating grits all my life. I was born and raised in the South."

"I see," said the judge. "Then you wouldn't mind opening one of these bags and eating from them in front of the jury right now, would you?"

"Well, sir, the grits can't be eaten right out of the bag like that... uh, they have to be cooked first," I replied.

"Really! Okay, we'll make preparations for you to cook some of these Grytts while we watch. And then we expect you to eat them in front of us. Is that understood?" the judge asked with a stern look.

The judge hit his gavel and said we'd take a thirty-minute recess. He then instructed my attorney to provide me with everything I needed to cook the grits in the courtroom.

Mr. Bailey was able to quickly locate a portable gas top grill from the court cafeteria and a metal pot for the grits. I also asked him for some salt, pepper, butter, a spoon, a large bowl, and a jug of water.

Soon after we had all we needed, the judge called the court back to order and the jury was reseated. He looked at me and said, "Okay, Mr. Thompson, let's get to cooking those Grytts."

It was clear that he did not believe me.

Without wasting any time, I lit up the gas grill and put the pot on top. Next, I poured in some water so that it could start heating.

I opened one of the bags of grits and poured in about half the bag. I stirred the grits several times before I added a pinch of salt.

I could feel the jurors' eyes on me as I continued stirring the grits. The judge was leaning over his desk to get a good look. I set the timer on my watch for twenty minutes and kept watching the pot to make sure it didn't boil over.

Next, I took my spoon and stirred the grits for about a minute to get them good and thick, and so they wouldn't stick to the pot.

Just when it looked like the judge was about to lose his patience with me and use his gavel, I quickly announced to the court that the grits were done. I scooped some out of the pot and put the grits in the bowl. I added a little pepper, more salt, and butter on top to let it melt into the grits.

I held up the bowl to the judge and jury for all to see.

The judge said, "Go ahead and eat some."

So, I did.

The female kangaroo could be heard saying, "Why, that looks like porridge! I know how to make porridge."

The rest of the jurors agreed as they marveled at what they were seeing and smelling.

I asked the judge if it was okay to pass the bowl around to the jurors for them to taste the grits if they wanted to.

The judge agreed and asked Mr. Bailey to get some plastic spoons and forks for the jurors.

I said, "Your Honor, if I had some bacon, scrambled eggs, toast, and coffee, I could make a complete breakfast so you could get a better idea."

Disappointed that I had succeeded in court, the judge waved his hand and said, "We don't have time for that. I'll wait for the jurors to render their verdict."

After each one of the jurors had a chance to taste the grits, they went into an adjacent room to deliberate.

They returned in five minutes. The judge asked them what their verdict was.

The jury foreman, who was the female kangaroo, stood up with her pouch showing and said, "Your Honor, we believe the defendant and think he should be set free...although I still object to his earlier insulting comment regarding this being a kangaroo court."

I stood up and deeply apologized to the jury foreman for my remark and added that I was stupid for saying that.

That seemed to satisfy the jury foreman, and she sat down with a smile. However, her young baby squeaked from the pouch, "Your Honor, I'm still an object!"

The judge banged his gavel one last time and said, "This court is adjourned, and the jury is dismissed. Mr. Thompson, you are free to go...however, the court is seizing these kilos of Grytts in order to keep you from being arrested again while you're here."

The jurors all said, "YES!" at the same time, indicating that they would be eating my grits for breakfast.

My attorney apologized for the inconvenience and took me to the room where my wife was waiting impatiently.

When she saw me, she jumped up, hugged my neck, and asked where I had been and what took me so long. I explained everything to her in detail and told her that the court seized my bags of grits because they thought they were drugs.

Rather than being angry, she laughed hysterically. At one point, she playfully slapped my face and said, "Well, kiss my grits...come on, honey, let's go."

The echo of "Come on honey, let's go" rang in my ears over and over again.

I opened my eyes to see the female Southwest Airlines staff member saying, "Come on honey, let's go. Your flight to Philadelphia is boarding now. You're the last one left to board."

I said, "What?"

She said, "I didn't mean to slap you, but I couldn't get you to wake up."

"Thank you," I said as I grabbed my bag and ran to board the plane.

When I got seated, I felt like I had been dreaming but couldn't remember all the details. I knew it had something to do with my grits, though.

I reached for my bag to see if my grits were still there. I unzipped it, and there they were. I pulled out the plastic bag just enough to read the slogan again on the bag.

It read, "Save Big with the Pig."

I said to myself, "I love me some Jim Dandy GRYTTS."

ACKNOWLEDGMENTS

My mother nursed sick bodies to help heal them.

Hopefully, my books will nurse wounded hearts to help repair them.

My father was a constructor who built buildings.

I am an instructor who builds books.

The buildings my father built yesterday are still standing today.

Hopefully, the books I build today will last for tomorrow.

Both the Egyptian pyramids and the ancient scrolls of yesterday still co-exist in a weird competition for everlasting legacy.

The steps to building a building and/or building a book are all the same -- one brick at a time and one word at a time.

This book is eternally dedicated to the lives and souls of four of the people responsible for who I am today: Ada Mary Louise, my mother; James 'Shacklebones' Sr., my father; 'Granny' Emma Jane, my grandmother; and Anita Louise, my sister."

My mother, Mrs. Ada Mary Louise Daniels-Thompson
(born 1922, circa mid-1940s)

My father, Mr. James L. Thompson Sr. (1921-2012)
aka "Shacklebones" and "Mr. Shack" (circa mid-1940s, WWII)

My mother's mother, Mrs. Emma Jane Daniels (1882-1974)
("Granny" circa late 1960s to early 1970s)

My sister, Miss Anita Louise Thompson (1950-1987)

ABOUT THE AUTHOR

American author James L. Thompson, Jr. describes himself as an "extroverted introvert." He enjoys writing and playing with words; wordsmithing is part of his unique writing style. Although he has distinguished himself in many separate careers, he was born to be a writer because that is his passion.

His writing style is unique in that he is equally adept at writing poems, short stories, and essays that combine wit, humor, history, wisdom, and imagination. His playfulness with words makes his writing seem easy to read, but a deeper look shows his skill and mastery of always using the exact words to paint colorful pictures for his readers. Long years of practice have given him the confidence to pen stories that have a universal appeal regardless of race or gender. Thompson likes perfection, and he works tirelessly to make sure his writing is tight and error-free.

In college, he was one of a few Black men who majored in English at his alma mater, Troy State University, in Troy, Alabama. He later became one of the first Black men to earn a master's degree in English at the same college. When he got his first teaching job after college, he was the only Black male English teacher at Henderson High School in DeKalb County, Georgia, where he taught for four years.

When he joined the Federal Bureau of Investigation as a Special Agent in 1984, he was only one of three Black men in his class of forty recruits. He is believed to be the first Black man from Dothan, Alabama, to be recruited by the FBI.

At the Environmental Protection Agency, he is credited with being the first Black to be promoted from the working agent ranks to Assistant Special Agent-in-Charge and then to Special Agent-in-Charge of its Criminal Investigation Division.

Thompson has managed to distinguish himself in whatever he does by being dignifiedly qualified to do whatever job he undertakes. He is also an actor, director, and producer of short films. Thompson is cited by many admirers as a Renaissance Man. He recently started working on his first full novel, which is currently untitled.

Thompson's unique voice is a welcomed addition among the many voices that tell stories about Black History being rightfully blended with American History as an overlay to our collective human experiences. We hope to read many more of his and others' imaginative works to come as he debuts his new book publishing company, *Peanut City Press, LLC,* and continues *Telling Our Stories.*

www.ingramcontent.com/pod-product-compliance
Lightning Source LLC
Chambersburg PA
CBHW031206020726
47499CB00002B/505